THE WHOLE TRUTH

THE WHOLE TRUTH

KIT PEARSON

Emalyn

HarperTrophyCanada™

The Whole Truth
Copyright © 2011 by Kathleen Pearson.
All rights reserved.

Published by Harper*Trophy*Canada™,
an imprint of HarperCollins Publishers Ltd

First published by HarperCollins Publishers Ltd in a hardcover edition: 2011
This Harper*Trophy*Canada™ digest paperback edition: 2012

Harper*Trophy*Canada™ is a registered trademark
of HarperCollins Publishers Ltd.

HarperCollins books may be purchased for educational, business,
or sales promotional use through our Special Markets Department.

HarperCollins Publishers Ltd
2 Bloor Street East, 20th Floor
Toronto, Ontario, Canada
M4W 1A8

www.harpercollins.ca

Library and Archives Canada Cataloguing in Publication
Pearson, Kit, 1947–
The whole truth / Kit Pearson.

ISBN 978-1-55468-853-1

I. Title.
PS8581.E386W56 2012   jC813'.54   C2012-903386-3

Printed and bound in the United States
RRD 9 8 7 6 5 4 3 2

FOR KATHERINE

What are heavy? Sea-sand and sorrow;
What are brief? Today and tomorrow;
What are frail? Spring blossoms and youth;
What are deep? The ocean and truth.
—Christina Rossetti

PART ONE

AFTER
IT HAPPENED

CHAPTER ONE

THE TRAIN

After it happened, they were sent away.

In the train compartment they sat opposite Mrs. Tuttle, who was taking them as far as Vancouver. Maud called her the Turtle.

Polly stared out the window at golden fields full of stooks and grain elevators. It looked as if the outside was moving and the train was standing still. A man on a tractor waved, but Polly didn't wave back.

"You aren't listening to me, child," complained the Turtle. "I asked if you needed to go to the bathroom."

Polly shook her head.

"She hasn't gone once since we left Winnipeg," said Mrs. Tuttle to Maud, as if Polly were three, not nine.

"Leave her alone!" snapped Maud. "Polly's not a baby."

Mrs. Tuttle's fat cheeks shook. "Don't you speak to me in that tone of voice, Missy! I've never met such a rude child! If you're going to be like this for the whole trip, you'll make it very unpleasant for all of us. You should be grateful I agreed to look after you. If I wasn't such a good friend of your grandmother's—"

Maud threw Mrs. Tuttle one of the fierce glares that usually quelled grown-ups. "Polly and I don't *need* to be looked after. I'm fifteen! I could easily have taken care of Polly on my own."

"Don't be absurd, Maud—you're far too young to travel by yourselves." Mrs. Tuttle pressed her lips into a smile. "Let's try to get along, shall we? Would you like a game of cards?"

"No, thank you," said Maud icily. She bent her head over her brochure. Mrs. Tuttle sighed and got out her knitting.

Polly studied her sister. Maud's beaked nose and sharp chin stood out confidently from her long face, as if they could cut through any difficulties. Her brown eyes glittered with determination. Thick braids pulled her hair back so tightly that it looked like a warrior's helmet. Maud would have been perfectly capable of taking Polly to the west coast by herself; after all, she'd looked after Polly almost on her own for the past two years.

Most of Polly's hair had escaped from its barrettes and hung in strands down her cheeks. She nibbled the end of one and wondered how she would ever manage without her protective older sister. After they arrived at their grandmother's on Kingfisher Island, Polly was only going to see Maud on weekends.

The feeling of her insides being scraped out with a sharp spoon came again, as it had several times a day ever since—ever since it had happened. The train whistled as it went around a curve, a thin, lonely sound. It was going to be a miserable journey.

———

They ate lunch and dinner in the dining car, at a table set with a white cloth and heavy silver. The train's motion made the water in the glasses slop from side to side.

Mrs. Tuttle and Maud wolfed down the hearty food. "What generous helpings!" said the Turtle. "You'd never know there was a depression. Eat up, Polly—you're much too skinny."

Maud frowned. "Don't nag her! She's always been a fussy eater."

Mrs. Tuttle glowered back, but then she gave up and concentrated on her mashed potatoes.

After dinner the train stopped in Regina. Polly watched a girl her age emerge onto the platform out of a cloud of steam, run to a laughing man, and leap into his arms.

The man must be her father. The pain hurt so much then that Polly bent over with it.

An hour later the train arrived in Moose Jaw. Then a porter came and magically turned their seats into a single bed and two bunks.

Mrs. Tuttle found their pyjamas and told them to change. She went into the toilet and emerged looking even more like a turtle, in a voluminous green flowered night-gown with a matching nightcap. Her face was smeared with mint-coloured cream.

"Isn't this a treat, girls?" she said, burrowing under the covers. "Your grandmother was so generous to pay for a drawing room. It's much more comfortable than the sleeper car I usually go on."

"I want Maud to sleep with me," whispered Polly from the lower bunk. It was the first time she had spoken all day.

"Nonsense, Polly, there's no room. Maud and I are right beside you. Go to sleep like a good girl."

Mrs. Tuttle blew them a kiss and turned out the lights. When they heard her snoring, Maud climbed down and joined Polly. The bunk was so narrow they were squished together, but Maud's firm, warm body was so comforting, and the rocking train so soothing, that Polly finally slept.

Polly woke up to find herself alone in the berth. She panicked for a second, but then Maud came out of the toilet. Mrs. Tuttle was already dressed.

"Up you get, child!" she said to Polly. "We're already in Calgary. Isn't that amazing?"

Maud had brushed out her hair, which reached below her waist. She stood in front of a tiny mirror and tried to rebraid it. "Poll, will you help me?" she asked.

The Turtle got to her first and Polly was relieved. Several times since Daddy had gone, she'd tried to braid Maud's hair, but it slipped in her fingers and the braids came out messy and uneven. Finally Maud had struggled with it herself.

"You girls look so old-fashioned," said the Turtle. "I'm sure all that hair cascading from Polly's little face is sapping her strength. This is the Thirties! No one has long hair any more. Why don't you get it bobbed?"

"We *like* it long," muttered Maud.

Polly winced. Daddy had loved their long hair. Each time he'd brushed out Polly's tangles he'd told her she was a princess with golden tresses.

The Turtle was good at braiding. Maud examined the neat ropes in the mirror and thanked her stiffly.

"That's better, Maud," said Mrs. Tuttle. "You see? You can be pleasant if you try."

When they returned from breakfast, their beds had been turned back into seats. The Turtle collected their things and led them to the observation car at the back of the train. As in the dining room, there weren't many other passengers.

"Before the crash, this car was packed!" the Turtle told them. "We're lucky. Lots of people can't afford to travel during these hard times."

Polly sat next to the window and gaped at the jagged grey shapes that loomed against the bright blue sky. Mrs. Tuttle said they were the Rockies. They passed a mountain that had a line of bighorn sheep perched along its pleated cliffs. How could they be so high up and not fall off?

At Banff they got out of the train and breathed in crisp air that smelled like pine. Mrs. Tuttle bought some postcards. When they boarded again, she offered some to Maud and Polly, but Maud said haughtily, "No, thank you. We have no one we want to send postcards to."

"Poor little orphans," clucked the Turtle. Polly's stomach leapt and she fled into the toilet.

The rest of the day was a dreamy bubble out of time. Polly tried not to think of her life before or after. She kept staring out the window as the majestic mountains, rushing rivers, and green valleys slipped by. When the train chugged around a curve, she could see the front of it, like a steaming snake. The scenery looked like pictures of Canada in Polly's geography book, except it was in colour. Even so, it didn't seem real. She spotted more sheep, several moose, and a bear scrambling up a bank, but they looked like something in a movie. Polly pinched her hand—*she* didn't seem real either.

The Turtle's relentless chatter was like a shower of sharp little stones raining down on them. Yet again she went over details she'd already told them several times.

"I don't suppose you remember your mother much. You were only two when she died, Polly, and Maud was seven. I knew her well, of course. Una was good friends with my daughter, Blanche, and she sometimes came to stay with us when we lived in Winnipeg. Your grandmother and I go way back. My parents knew her parents in Scotland, and they all came to Canada about the same time. You girls are going to enjoy Kingfisher Island. I've been there often. When my husband was alive, we'd stay at your grandparents' hotel for two weeks each summer. The island is a pretty place, although much too quiet for my liking. Are you excited about living there?"

When they failed to respond, the Turtle looked offended. "You girls haven't heard a word I've said! You could at least answer my question. I don't see why I should be expected to spend this whole journey talking to myself."

Maud eyed her coldly. "No, we are *not* excited about living on the island. How could we be?"

Mrs. Tuttle flushed. "I'm sorry, Maud. I shouldn't have asked that. But I would appreciate it if you paid at least a *little* attention to me. Do you want me to tell your grandmother how rude you're being?"

Maud sighed. "I didn't know our grandparents ran a hotel. What happened to it?"

"It's still there, but after your grandfather died, your grandmother sold it. By then she didn't need to work, of course, since she'd inherited a trust fund from her husband. Everyone was so surprised at that—no one knew that Gilbert had a private income of his own."

Polly didn't pay much attention to any of this, but she began to listen more closely when the Turtle told them a story about Una and Blanche when they were children. They had found a gold watch on the beach. "I was so proud of them—they put up posters all over the island and a summer visitor claimed it."

The Turtle paused. "I hope *you* will always be that honest, girls, not like—"

"Mrs. Tuttle!" Maud glanced at Polly.

The Turtle covered her mouth. "Sorry, Maud. I forgot." She looked as if she longed to say more, but she bent her head over her knitting.

Polly clenched her fists. Mrs. Tuttle and Maud knew something she didn't! She leaned her head against the cool glass of the window and let the steady puffing of the train calm her down.

"Why don't you play with something, Polly?" Mrs. Tuttle asked her. She poked in Polly's bag. "Here are your dolls! And some crayons and paper! Shall I take them out?"

"No, thank you," mumbled Polly. Dolls and crayons were part of another life. Now her only life was being on the train.

After lunch they returned to the observation car. For the trillionth time Maud opened the brochure that was labelled "St. Winifred's School for Girls, Fall 1932." It had been fingered so much that its pages were coming loose. She read Polly items from the clothing list: "'Two pairs of black sateen bloomers to wear under tunics'—what do you think bloomers are, Poll?"

Polly wouldn't answer. She hated talking about this school that was taking Maud away from her.

"Bloomers!" Mrs. Tuttle laughed. "Blanche wore those at *her* girls school. They're loose drawers that you wear over your regular drawers."

Polly couldn't imagine wearing a school uniform at all—it looked so ugly in the pictures. But Maud kept going over every item with relish.

"I need to get black *and* white running shoes for sports. Look at this, Polly—they have grass hockey and basketball and lacrosse. I bet I'll be good at all of those."

Polly glanced at the photos of hearty girls in tunics prancing around with various balls. They all looked like Maud, confident and competent. Her sister would fit in perfectly. Maybe she would like St. Winifred's so much that she wouldn't think of Polly at all.

"Where will you buy your uniform?" asked Mrs. Tuttle. "At the school?"

"No, at a special store in Victoria." Maud looked worried. "School starts on Wednesday—that's only five days away! What if the store has run out of uniforms? I don't want to be different from everyone else."

"If they've run out, they can order what you're missing," said Mrs. Tuttle. "And I'm sure no one will mind if you don't have everything, especially since—"

"Look!" cried Polly. She pointed out the window. "A—a moose!"

"Where?" the other two asked.

"It ran into the trees. I think it was a moose . . . maybe not," finished Polly lamely. At least it had made the Turtle change the subject.

"Shall I read to you?" Mrs. Tuttle picked up *Jalna*.

Maud shrugged. "If you want to."

Polly closed her eyes and leaned her head against Maud, pretending to listen.

———

Polly woke up when the Turtle stood and yawned. "I'm going back to our room to have a little nap, girls," she told them. "Will you be all right by yourselves?"

"Of course we will," said Maud.

"Don't talk to strangers," warned Mrs. Tuttle, "and don't go out on the open deck—you might get a cinder in your eye."

"We won't," promised Maud.

After the Turtle had disappeared, Maud said, "Come on!"

"Where?"

"Outside, of course."

They pushed through a heavy door and stepped onto the open platform at the end of the train. Their hair whipped back in the wind and they could smell smoke from the engine. Mrs. Tuttle was right about the cinders—Polly had to brush one away from her face.

CHUchuchuchuCHUchuchuchu roared the engine. "Isn't this swell?" shouted Maud.

But then the whistle sounded and Polly screamed as the train approached a tunnel. Maud grabbed her hand and they dashed inside just in time.

"I don't want to go out there again!" said Polly, brushing bits of grit out of her hair. She wiped her grimy hands on her dress—luckily it was black.

"Okay, but at least we did it, and the Turtle will never know!" Maud patted the seat beside her. "Come and sit down. This may be our only chance to talk and we have lots to discuss."

Polly quaked. Ever since it had happened, all of Maud's discussions were scary.

"Listen to me, Doodle," said Maud. She opened up her notebook. "I've written down some rules for us."

"Rules?"

"Yes, rules. Once we arrive in Vancouver we'll be surrounded by relatives. They may be really snoopy. The rules are to help us remember how to act. Especially you. I don't want you to give in while I'm gone."

"Gone?"

"Polly, stop repeating everything I say! Yes, gone! You know that next week I'll go away to school. I'll come home on the weekends and of course for the holidays, but during the week you'll be on your own. I've told you that a thousand times!"

"Sorry, Maud. What are the rules?"

"Number one: Don't tell *anyone* what happened."

"Of course I won't!"

"It won't be as easy as you think," said Maud. "All sorts of people are going to ask about Daddy. Relatives, teachers, kids at your new school . . . Can I absolutely trust you?"

"Of course you can! I already promised you I wouldn't tell and I won't." Polly looked at the finger that her sister had pricked with a needle two weeks before. Maud had pierced her own finger as well and they had rubbed the blood together in a pact.

"Maybe no one will *want* to talk about Daddy," said Polly.

"They might. Lots of people are going to tell you how sorry they are and expect you to answer. Just keep saying, 'I don't want to talk about it.'"

She looked at her notebook. "Rule number two: Don't *think* about it. Don't think about what happened and don't even think about Daddy. I want you to forget about our life with him in Winnipeg. We're starting a new life now."

"I can't *help* thinking about it! It's always *there* in my mind. And I can't not think about *Daddy!*"

Maud looked afraid, something she very seldom did. "I know . . . it's always in my mind too. But we *have* to forget." She took Polly's hands in hers and stared into her eyes as if she were hypnotizing her. "Daddy is *dead*. You have to believe that. I know it's hard, but he's gone, and we have to get on with our lives."

"But Maud, I *can't* forget Daddy! I miss him so much! And I don't understand why—"

Maud squeezed Polly's hands so tightly that Polly winced. "Doodle, that's enough! You have to *forget!* Do you understand?"

Polly started to cry. "No, I don't! And let go, Maud. You're hurting me! I don't understand, and I think you're hiding something!"

Maud released Polly's hands and handed her a handkerchief. "I'm sorry, Poll, but there's nothing more to say. I'm not hiding anything. Really, I'm not!"

Polly knew that Maud was lying. She was lying to protect Polly. Her secret was locked up inside her as tightly as her hair was braided. Pleading wouldn't unlock it; when Maud was this determined, there was nothing Polly could do.

She wiped her eyes and whispered, "Okay. I'll try to forget. Are there any more rules?"

"Yes. Number three: Don't trust *anyone* but me."

"That's easy," said Polly. "I already follow that rule."

"Good. Number four: Be brave. I'm really sorry I'm going to boarding school and leaving you alone, but it's important for me to get a good education. This is all horrible, but at least it gives me a chance at that. You're going to miss me at first. I'll miss you, too, Doodle. But we both have to be as brave as lions!"

"I could *never* be as brave as you are," said Polly.

"You have to be," said Maud. "You have no choice. Rule number five: Be polite and helpful and well-behaved. It's important that Grandmother likes us. We want her to keep us, because we have nowhere else to go."

"But what if we don't like *her*? What if she's mean?"

"Then it's even more important that we make a good impression. But I don't think she'll be mean. She offered to take us, after all. And she's always sounded nice in her letters."

Grandmother had written to them several times a year. They had sent short notes back, to thank her for birthday and Christmas presents. She had seemed so far away, in another life. But now they were going to be part of that life!

"Maud, why haven't we ever met our grandmother?"

"We *have* met her. She came to Mother's funeral—I can just barely remember her. I don't know why she hasn't come to see us since then. I asked Daddy once, but all he said was that she and our mother had a terrible argument and stopped speaking to each other."

Polly leaned against Maud. She started to weep again. "I don't *want* to go to the island and live with Grandmother! I just want to stay on the train with you forever! I'm scared!"

Maud squeezed Polly's shoulder. Her own eyes were moist, but she sniffed and said firmly, "You're already forgetting rule number four: Be brave. I should add one more: No crying!" She gave Polly a forced smile. "Let's try to look on the bright side, Doodle. I bet our relatives will be fine. Maybe they'll even have a dog!"

Polly swallowed her tears. They gathered inside and filled her until she felt like choking. "That would be nice," she whispered.

Maud took her hand. "It must be almost time for dinner. Let's go back to our room before the Turtle comes to find us."

CHAPTER TWO

THE ISLAND

Early the next morning the train pulled into Vancouver. Polly followed Mrs. Tuttle into the crowded station, clutching her small suitcase in one hand and Maud's hand in the other. Behind them, a porter wheeled the rest of their luggage.

"Maud! Polly!" Four adults rushed up to them. Everyone was talking and hugging and kissing and the Turtle was fussing about their bags and Maud kept saying, "I'm so happy to meet you!" in a high, false voice.

But Polly couldn't speak. If she did, the tempest inside her would erupt. All she could do was stare. Sorting out four new people was hard work.

The tall young man was Gregor. "I'm your first cousin once removed!" he informed her. Polly didn't know what that

-18-

meant, but her frozen tongue wouldn't let her ask. Gregor lifted her right off the ground and gave her forehead a smacking kiss. He had woolly curls and a round, grinning face.

His parents were Great-Aunt Jean and Great-Uncle Rand. Uncle Rand was as moon-faced as his son, but he had hardly any hair. He pecked Polly's cheek. "Welcome, young lady," he said quietly. "We're blessed to have you with us at last."

The next kiss was from Aunt Jean, a spry little woman, holding a cigarette, with short springy hair that curled around her purple hat. "Oh, chickie, you're the image of your dear mother! She was my niece, you know."

Polly couldn't take this in. Maud had told her about all of these relatives, but the only one Polly had thought about was Grandmother.

And here she was. A stooped woman in a tweed suit, her hair pinned up neatly. She took Polly's hands and stood in front of her for a long moment.

Grandmother's face was angular and her mouth was set in a straight line. Her sad grey eyes behind her glasses were full of such fierce compassion that Polly almost let her tears loose—but then she would drown in them.

"Oh, hen, it's been so, so long since I've seen you—not since your mother's funeral. You were only two . . . and look at you now!" Her voice was gruff and bubbly, as if her words were water flowing over pebbles. Aunt Jean had the same strange accent, but hers was milder.

Grandmother didn't kiss her, but she kept one hand in Polly's. Her firm grip felt safe, as Aunt Jean and Gregor threw eager questions at Polly and Maud: "Did you enjoy the train?" "Was the food good?" "Were the Rockies splendid?"

Maud answered politely, but Polly couldn't speak. She pressed into her grandmother's side.

"Stop pestering them, you two. We'll hear about their journey soon enough," said Grandmother.

Uncle Rand looked worried. "We should get a move on," he told them.

They manoeuvred their way through the noisy crowd. In the parking lot they said goodbye to Mrs. Tuttle, who lived in Vancouver. "Thank you *so* much for taking care of Maud and Polly, Lydia," said Grandmother. "Come and visit us sometime!"

The Turtle kissed each of the girls. "We ended up having a good time, didn't we?" she said, smiling at Maud. But Maud had turned away to help Gregor tie their suitcases on top of the car.

"Where are we going now?" Maud asked, as they left the station.

"Straight to Steveston to catch the car ferry," said Aunt Jean. "We should be able to make it if you drive fast, Rand."

"I won't drive any faster than I should, my dear," said Uncle Rand calmly.

"How did I end up with such a cautious man?" asked Aunt

Jean merrily, turning around to them from the front seat. "He thinks because he's a rector he has to obey every rule!"

"A rector?" repeated Maud.

"Yes, Rand is the rector at our little church on the island. Didn't you know that, chickie?"

Maud nodded. "I remember now. Grandmother told us in her letters."

It took a long time to reach the ferry terminal. First they were in the city, then they passed fields of cows and horses. Uncle Rand was quiet, but the other adults talked all the way.

"Clara, I can't believe you asked Lydia to come and visit!" said Aunt Jean. "I can't bear that woman!"

Who was Clara? wondered Polly. Then she realized that Clara was Grandmother.

"Don't worry about Lydia, Jean," said Grandmother. "She'll never visit. She only came to the island because her husband liked it—she always said it was much too quiet for her taste."

"Well, I certainly hope you're right. Gregor, I want you to remove a wasps' nest from the church porch roof before the service tomorrow. And we need more wood, and the lawn needs cutting."

"Yes, Ma." Gregor grinned at Polly and Maud. "Isn't my mother a taskmaster? You'd better be careful, or she'll have you working as well!"

"Maud and Polly are not to do anything strenuous this weekend," said Grandmother. "They've had a long journey and I want them to have a good rest."

"But don't forget I have to be at the school by Tuesday evening!" said Maud.

"Don't worry, Maud. We'll get you to school. We have lots of arrangements to discuss, but let's leave that until we reach the island."

"What arrangements?" Maud asked, but Grandmother just said, "Wait and see, hen."

Her quiet words had so much force that Maud turned to Gregor. "What do you do?" she asked, in the chirpy, being-polite-to-grown-ups voice she'd been using ever since they'd arrived.

"I'm studying theology in Vancouver," Gregor told her. "I'm going to be a preacher, just like me old dad!"

"I can't see you in holy vestments—you were such a holy terror of a child," said Aunt Jean. Her face, however, beamed with pride.

"That will make him all the more understanding of other holy terrors," said Grandmother.

"Thanks, Aunt Clara!" Gregor winked at Polly. "Don't you believe a word of what my mother says! I was an angelic child! I had blond curls and I sang in the choir!"

"And stuck chewing gum under the pews!" said his mother.

Why are they all arguing so much? thought Polly. She leaned against her grandmother and was almost asleep when they arrived at the ferry terminal.

The car drove right into the belly of a huge boat. They trooped upstairs and had lunch in the dining room. All Polly could see out the windows was an expanse of green-grey waves merging into a blurry sky. She'd never seen the ocean before—it looked so vast and deep and cold. Her stomach moved up and down with the boat's motion, and the air smelled fumy. She couldn't eat her lunch, but no one commented. Uncle Rand hid behind his newspaper and the others continued to chatter.

"You're going to adore Kingfisher Island, chickies," Aunt Jean told them. "It's a little paradise—so peaceful and safe. You'll be much freer than you were in Winnipeg. When Gregor was a wee laddie, he'd be gone from dawn to dusk and I never worried about him."

"You *should* have worried, Ma," said Gregor. "There's no point in telling you now, though," he added hastily.

"The island *is* a lovely place, hens," said Grandmother, "but I hope you won't find it dull after the city. We lead a very simple life. We grow our own vegetables and pick berries, and the men hunt."

"They also fish," said Aunt Jean. "And we have lots of clams and oysters . . . As they say, 'When the tide goes out the table is set!'"

"Yes, we eat very well—we're not going hungry, as so many are these days. But I'm afraid we have no electricity and no indoor plumbing," said Grandmother. "We did at the hotel your grandfather and I used to run—we had a generator. How I miss that!"

"No indoor plumbing!" said Maud. "But what—" She stopped, her cheeks pink.

Gregor laughed. "What do we do when nature calls? Use the privy! Or you might call it an outhouse or a biffy or the throne room. It's fine, if you hold your nose."

"Gregor!" scolded Aunt Jean. "Don't listen to him, chickies. Our privies are perfectly clean!"

"Stop teasing your mother, Gregor," said Grandmother. "Let's go outside."

———

They stood on the high windy deck. Now the boat made its way through a choppy passage between several large and small wooded islands. The ferry drew up to a long wharf on one of them—Uncle Rand told them it was called Walker Island. They watched cars drive off below them.

Then the ferry backed up, turned around, and approached

Kingfisher Island on the other side of the passage. The grown-ups pointed out a lighthouse that looked like a white candle. Mist rose from the steep sides of the island, revealing a blanket of dark firs. A few houses were perched here and there, some along the shore and some higher up. The ferry slowed down as it came towards another long, wide wharf. The sun flashed from behind the clouds and the waves turned from grey to silver.

"What a peach of a day!" said Aunt Jean. "Look, chickies! Those long buildings near the wharf are the store and the hotel. The white house farther along the road is your grandmother's, and the brown one next door is the rectory, where Rand and I live. And there's the church—isn't it lovely?"

Polly only had eyes for the white house. She held on to her hat as she stared and stared at it. It stood out like a beacon, with its blue roof and wide verandah. It was much larger than her house in Winnipeg.

Several people were waving from the wharf. "Time to go downstairs," said Uncle Rand.

They drove off the ferry and along a fern-lined dirt road past the store. Now the sea glittered so brightly that Polly had to squint. In a few minutes they pulled up at the white house. In front of it three deer were nibbling the grass.

"Poll, look!" cried Maud. The deer flicked their black tails and bounced into the woods.

Aunt Jean laughed. "There are lots of deer on King-fisher Island. More deer than people!"

"Welcome to your new home, hens," said Grandmother as they got out of the car. "If you can manage your small suitcases, Gregor will take your large ones up to your room."

Aunt Jean held open a screen door. Polly hesitated behind the others, the sharp spoon scraping her insides. Was this *really* their new home? Did that mean they would never go back to their old one? *Oh, Daddy!* she moaned inside.

"In you come, chickie," said Aunt Jean. Polly entered a dark hall that smelled like damp wood. She followed Gregor and Maud up slippery stairs to a long, narrow room on the second floor.

Gregor set their bags on the floor. "Come down for tea when you're ready," he told them. "I'm starving, aren't you?" His big feet thundered down the stairs.

The bedroom had a slanting ceiling and faded pink wallpaper. Two white iron beds were covered with puffy blue satin eiderdowns. Sheepskin rugs dotted the floor. A tree with strange orange bark pressed against the window, its leaves like green curtains. Beyond the tree was a glimpse of sparkling waves.

On a round table were some boxes of jigsaw puzzles, a few worn-out stuffed animals, and a set of Lincoln Logs. A jug and a basin stood in one corner. "Come and wash," said

Maud. She helped Polly pour the water into the basin and they tried to get rid of the train grit on their hands and faces.

"You can have the bed by the window," offered Maud, "since I'll only be here on the weekends."

"Oh, Maud, please don't say that!" said Polly.

"I'm sorry, but it's true . . . so you may as well have the best bed. Don't cry!" Maud warned as Polly's eyes filled. "At least you're talking to *me!* Why are you being so silent with everyone else? You have to talk to them or they'll think you're rude!"

"I can't," whispered Polly.

"Why not?"

"I don't know—I just can't!"

"All right, then," sighed Maud. "But you'll have to after I'm at school. They're your family now, Poll. You should be friendly."

Daddy is my family! Polly wanted to say. Instead she swallowed hard and asked, "What do you think of them?"

"They seem fine. I'm not worried at all about leaving you here."

"But Grandmother said they hunt. That means they shoot animals!"

"They live in the country, Poll—that's a natural thing to do."

Polly shuddered. "I don't like it! And why do they call us those chicken names?"

Maud shrugged. "Maybe that's how they talk to children in Scotland. Grandmother and Aunt Jean are from there—that's why they still have Scottish accents. Come on, Doodle. We're supposed to go down for tea."

———

Polly followed Maud downstairs into a large, sunny living room at the front of the house. Off the living room was a verandah and beyond that was the road and the sea. The gentle swoosh of waves mingled with the tick of a grandfather clock.

Polly examined every corner—there was no sign of a dog. The room was dominated by a huge fireplace, its stones blackened with soot. Framed photographs crowded its mantel. The furniture was worn and comfortable-looking. Books stuffed a tall shelf and more books and many magazines were piled on the floor and tables.

The grown-ups were gathered around a low table. A tall, strong-looking woman with a thatch of white hair burst into the room and crashed down a tray full of cups and saucers and a teapot. Then she gazed at Maud and Polly hungrily.

"This is my housekeeper, Mrs. Hooper," Grandmother told them. "She's been with me ever since I got married."

Mrs. Hooper rushed up to Maud and Polly and gripped their hands. "Una's girls!" she cried. "You're here at last!"

She was wiping her eyes with the corner of her apron as she left the room.

The table was already covered with plates of food. Polly had barely eaten all day; for the first time since she had left home she felt hungry. The plates were full of small sandwiches and many kinds of cookies. A bowl of whipped cream stood beside a dark cake coated with yellow icing.

Polly climbed into a slippery, overstuffed chair. Her feet couldn't reach the floor. Normally she would have drawn her legs under her, but that seemed rude, so she stuck them out awkwardly. A milky cup of tea was handed to her.

"Which would you like first, Polly?" asked Grandmother. "A sandwich, a cookie, or a piece of cake?"

Polly couldn't answer.

"Try the cake," said Aunt Jean. "I made it myself. It's an old family recipe—whiskey cake with lemon frosting."

"Is that good for Polly?" asked Maud.

"It won't hurt her one bit—there's scarcely any whiskey in it," said Grandmother, topping a piece of the cake with a dollop of cream.

Polly didn't know where to put her cup and saucer while she ate the cake. Grandmother took them from her and put them on a small table beside the chair. "Pull your feet up, hen," she told her. "We're not fussy here."

Maud gulped down three cookies and a huge piece

of cake. Polly knelt on the chair and nibbled at the moist, chewy cake, in between reaching over for sips of sweet tea.

"Now, girls, we have a few things to talk about," said Grandmother. "First of all, we must agree on what you will call me. You're my only grandchildren, so you can choose."

"'Grandmother,'" said Maud. "That's what we called you when we wrote to you."

"I know, hen, but 'Grandmother' sounds rather formal. What did you call your other grandmother?"

"'Grannie,'" said Maud.

Polly was beginning to forget about Grannie. So much had happened since she had died two years ago.

But how terrible to forget her! Grannie had looked after them since Polly was a toddler. She had been small and timid, so different from this flinty grandmother who was asking them to name her.

"How about 'Nanny'?" suggested Aunt Jean.

Gregor laughed. "That sounds like a goat!"

"'Noni,' then," said Uncle Rand. "That's what I called *my* grandmother."

"I like that," said their grandmother gravely. "What do you think, Maud and Polly? Would you like to call me 'Noni'?"

Maud shrugged. "All right."

"What about you, Polly? Do you like that name?"

Polly nodded.

"'Noni' it is, then," said Noni. She put down her cup. "I want to tell you how very sorry I am about your father's death. I know you'll feel sad about it for a long time, but I hope that being a part of this family will help you recover from your grief. I'm also sorry we couldn't make it to the funeral. We would have come and then brought you back here with us, but then we heard Lydia Tuttle was in Winnipeg visiting friends. It made more sense for her to do it."

Noni didn't sound sorry. Her words sounded forced and she seemed relieved to have them over and done with.

Then she looked embarrassed. "You're living in a small community now, girls, where people are far too interested in one another's business. I'm afraid someone might ask you how Daniel died. You won't want to tell them the truth, of course. I suggest that you simply say your father drowned. Don't you think that's best?"

"That's what we already say," said Maud. She looked straight at Polly as her voice rang out. "We tell people that our father drowned by accident, not that he drowned himself."

Aunt Jean gave a little gasp and Uncle Rand and Gregor looked down at their plates.

Polly's head whirled. That wasn't the truth either!

"Very good, Maud," said Noni. "I'm glad we understand each other."

"I liked your dad," said Gregor. He smiled at Polly and Maud. "I only met him once, but I remember him. It was at your parents' wedding on the island. I climbed up his legs and he flipped me over. He was a nice guy."

Polly's eyes stung. Daddy used to do that with her too! At least Gregor looked sad. The other adults didn't at all. She wanted to ask if *they* liked Daddy, but the words wouldn't form.

Noni was giving Maud a strange look—a warning look.

Polly wanted to explode. Before they'd left Winnipeg, Grandmother had telephoned Maud at the foster home, and Maud had ordered Polly to wait in the other room. Whatever secret Maud was keeping from Polly, whatever Maud and Mrs. Tuttle knew, Noni knew also. Perhaps the others did as well.

They were all treating her like a baby! It was so unfair, and there was nothing Polly could do about it. Her stomach twinged and she wished she hadn't had any cake.

Noni's thin mouth smiled at both of them. "All these years we've missed out on you, but now we can get to know you at last. I'm sorry you have to go away to school, Maud, but the island school only goes up to grade seven."

"I'm really looking forward to it," said Maud. "St. Winifred's sounds swell—I've been reading about it ever since you sent me the brochure."

"I'm glad you're so eager, Maud. It *is* an excellent school, and I firmly believe in girls receiving a good education. Your mother refused to go away to school. She had a governess, as Jean and I did when we moved here from Scotland. We scarcely learned a thing!"

"That's because we spent all our time playing tricks on her!" giggled Jean, exactly as if she were still a schoolgirl.

"We'll have you home every weekend, Maud," continued Noni, "but would you mind waiting another week before you start? I'd like you to get used to us and the island first before you have another huge change."

"Another week! Please, Grandmother—I mean, Noni— I really want to start on time. I don't want to miss anything!"

"Are you sure? You want to go away again so soon?"

"Yes!"

"Very well. Jean and I—and Polly, of course—will take you to Victoria on Tuesday. We'll get your uniform in the afternoon and you'll be at St. Winifred's by the evening."

"Oh, thank you!" Maud looked ecstatic, but Polly gulped. *Tuesday?* That was two days after tomorrow! And how could Maud be so enthusiastic, when she'd be leaving Polly behind?

"Polly will attend school on the island, of course, but I think *she* could wait another week, right, hen?"

Polly nodded with relief.

"I don't think she should," said Maud. "She'll get behind if she starts school late."

"A week off won't hurt Polly. She's only in grade five, after all. And she's been through so much she needs a breather." Noni met Maud's fierce stare just as fiercely, until Maud lowered her eyes. Polly was awed—Maud had met her match!

"Noni, do you think the store in Victoria will have everything I need?" she asked.

"I'm sure it will, Maud."

"What do they make you wear?" asked Gregor. "Some ugly tunic, I bet!"

Maud eagerly told him all the details of her uniform. Aunt Jean helped Mrs. Hooper take out the tea things, and Uncle Rand left to write his sermon for the next day.

"You girls must be completely worn out," said Noni. "Would you like a nice hot bath? Then you can unpack and have supper on a tray and an early bedtime."

"Supper on a tray?" said Maud. "I'm fifteen!"

"Goodness, you look just like your mother when she didn't want to do something! Very well, Maud, after your bath you can come down in your dressing gown and join us for dinner if you like. But Polly must go straight to bed."

"I'd better go and deal with that wasps' nest," said Gregor. "Tomorrow I'll give you girls a tour of the island."

———

The rest of that long day was a blur. Mrs. Hooper filled the tin bath she had brought into their room. "You both look as if you need this!" she said. "I've left you extra water in those jugs. I'm off home now, girls, but I'll see you at breakfast!" She blew them a kiss.

Polly and Maud shared the blissfully hot water—they had to replace it twice it got so dirty. They washed each other's hair, got into their nightgowns and dressing gowns, and combed out their hair in front of the oil heater.

Noni brought up a tray of chicken soup and bread. While they ate, she put their clothes into drawers. "Tomorrow we'll repack the big suitcase for you, Maud," she said.

Polly managed a few spoonfuls of soup, but her eyelids kept drooping. Maud slurped her whole bowl.

When Noni sent them outside to the privy, Polly gripped Maud's hand all the way as they stumbled along the dark path. She was bursting to go, but when Maud showed her the deep, open hole she was supposed to sit over, she cried, "I can't! I'll fall in!"

"Don't be silly, Poll. Of course you won't. I'll go first and show you."

When it was her turn, Polly's urgent need overcame her fear. But she sat over the hole for as short a time as possible, terrified that something would rise up from below and bite her bottom. She held her nose until she came out. "Gregor was right," she said as they walked back. "It *stinks!*"

"Into bed with you, Polly," said Noni when they returned to their room. "Now, Maud, are you going to join us for dinner, or not? After all that soup you won't have room!"

Maud looked over at Polly huddled under her eiderdown. She yawned. "Well . . . I am a *bit* tired. I guess I'll go to bed too."

Noni smiled. "Good girl." She tucked them in and gave them each a brisk kiss. "Try not to be too sad, and don't forget to say your prayers."

Then her voice wavered and she cleared her throat, as if she were swallowing tears. "Oh, my dear bonnie girls, I'm so glad you are here at last!"

Polly barely heard her as she melted into sleep.

———

Hours later, Polly woke with a gasp. Where was she? Her bed wasn't swaying, so she was no longer on the train. Then she heard Maud's gentle breathing and remembered.

She sat up, pulled back the curtain, and looked out the window. The sea was glassy and the moon's reflection was a silvery path to the house. The dazzling stars made the black night even blacker—far darker than in the city.

Where was Daddy? How was it possible that she wasn't with him? It was a little over two weeks since he had left her—she'd never been away from him for even a day before that. Polly buried herself under the eiderdown and let some of her tears fall, pressing her pillow over her head so Maud wouldn't hear her.

Don't think about Daddy. What a stupid rule! How could she *help* thinking about him? Anyway, Maud couldn't control what was inside Polly's head. She tried to think of something comforting about Daddy, instead of what had happened.

When she was much younger, Daddy had often taken her for rides on his bicycle. He'd made a special wooden seat on the handlebars, like a basket with holes for her legs. Polly would clutch the sides of the seat and scream with laughter as the bike whizzed down hills, her hair blowing back into his face. Daddy would lean down and tell her about things they were passing. She always felt safe, even when they went over bumps, because Daddy was there to protect her.

Please, God, take care of Daddy, Polly prayed. She kept imagining being on the bike with him as she tried to sleep again, clutching one of the bed rails as if she were keeping herself from drowning.

CHAPTER THREE

SUNDAY

*S*he was skating, gliding across a lake. Daddy was zooming ahead of her and Polly laughed as she tried to catch up with him. Then Daddy fell through the ice and disappeared. Polly tried to scream, but no sound came.

A piercing whistle startled Polly awake. She sat up with relief. The whistle had come from Maud, of course.

Polly yawned away the bad dream. "What time is it?"

Maud grinned. "It's almost nine o'clock—I've been up for hours!"

"Who braided your hair?" asked Polly, stumbling out of bed.

"Noni. She called me into her room—she has breakfast in bed! She did a good job, don't you think?"

Maud helped Polly choose clothes for church. "Noni says we don't have to wear our mourning dresses any more. She doesn't believe in black clothes for children."

Polly smiled for the first time since she'd left Winnipeg. She'd worn her itchy black dress every day for the past week. The fabric was so cheap that it made dark smears on her skin, and the sleeves were split under the arms.

Polly had lots of other dresses; they were hand-me-downs from Maud. She picked out her favourite blue gingham one. Then she remembered that she hadn't worn coloured clothes since before it happened, and her delight in the dress vanished.

"It's nice to see you in that again," said Maud. "I wish I had something better to wear to church."

Since the depression had started there had been no money for new clothes. Polly remembered the day Maud had come home from school mortified because a well-off girl in her class had recognized the dress Maud had got from the Goodwill truck. Maud was wearing it this morning. It was too short for her and stretched tightly across her chest.

"Oh, well," said Maud. "Noni said she'd buy me new dresses in Victoria as well as my uniform."

"Is Noni rich, like Mrs. Tuttle said?" Polly asked.

"She must be. She has this big house and a housekeeper, and she's paying for my school."

"But she doesn't even have an indoor toilet!" Polly shuddered.

"That's just because this is an island." Maud began brushing out Polly's curls. "Noni asked why you're so silent, Doodle. She was relieved that you at least speak to *me*. I didn't know what to tell her."

"I just can't talk to them, that's all," said Polly.

"I guess you will when you're ready. That's what I told Noni. Come on, let's have breakfast. I waited for you and I'm starving!"

Maud was remarkably cheerful this morning. Had she forgotten why they were here? But Polly couldn't help feeling more cheerful herself on such a bright day.

The privy was a little less scary by daylight, but Polly still held her nose. On the way back to the house she paused to gaze at the view. This morning the sea looked like a wrinkled grey skin. Gulls soared and warbled and some black birds with long necks were perched on a log.

When she came in the kitchen door, Mrs. Hooper handed Polly a huge bowl of oatmeal and cream. "We need to fatten you up!" she told her.

Mrs. Hooper poured herself a cup of coffee and sat down at the table with Maud and Polly, gazing at them just as greedily as she had the day before. "All these years we've longed to see you, and here you are at last!" she told them. "Polly, you look so much like your mother it's uncanny! My, it's nice to have young ones in the house again."

Polly spooned soft brown sugar over the oatmeal. It was so delicious that she ate half the bowlful.

"What was our mother like?" asked Maud.

Mrs. Hooper chuckled. "Una was a scamp—loud and stubborn and determined to get her own way. Do you remember her at all, Maud?"

"I remember some things . . ." Maud stopped chewing. "We sat in a big chair and she would read me the funnies. Then we'd tickle each other and laugh so much that we cried."

"She was a tickler, all right! She would come up behind me while I was cooking and tickle my knees—she'd scare the living daylights out of me!"

Polly wished she could remember her mother. Whenever Maud and Daddy had talked about her, Polly had felt left out. But now she noticed how sad Maud looked. The trouble with remembering someone was that it made you miss them. Like Daddy . . . pain stabbed her insides, and she put down her spoon.

"Good morning, girls." Noni came into the kitchen, looking elegant in a grey silk dress with lace on the collar. She was carrying a fur wrap over her arm. "Are you ready for the service?" she asked. "Get your hats and carry your coats. I know it's summer, but the church is always frigid."

The little stone church was a short walk away, just past the rectory. People were walking up the hill to it from all directions, heeding the call of its tolling bell. Noni and Maud and Polly sat in the front pew with Aunt Jean. They all stood up for the first hymn as Gregor led the small choir up the aisle, carrying a tall cross. He wore a white robe, and his usually grinning face was solemn. As he passed them, however, he gave the girls a quick wink.

Uncle Rand, dressed in white and green robes, was the last in the procession. Words and music floated above Polly and she sat or stood or kneeled with rest of the congregation.

The church was a bright space of wood and stone. Clear windows framed the green and blue colours outside as if they were living stained glass. Every pew was filled with adults and children in their best clothes. Most of them stared at Maud and Polly, the adults discreetly and the children boldly. Polly avoided their eyes.

When Uncle Rand got up to preach, Polly tried to listen, but she couldn't understand what he was saying—something about "atonement." The rest of the congregation looked as mystified as Polly was. She rubbed her legs together.

"Are you cold, hen?" whispered Noni. She took off her fur wrap and draped it over Polly's knees.

Polly waited in the pew while Maud, Noni, and Aunt Jean went up to the altar for Communion. Maud crossed herself when she received the wafer and wine. Polly remembered going to the Ukrainian Catholic church in Winnipeg with Grannie. She and Maud had leaned on either side of her, half asleep, as the priest chanted the mass. Daddy had never come, and after Grannie had died, Polly and Maud had never gone to church again.

Until Daddy's funeral last week . . . *Don't think about it!*

Finally the long service was over. Everyone lined up at the door to shake Uncle Rand's hand. Aunt Jean led them to the parish hall behind the church.

Polly and Maud stood beside Noni as people poured into the hall for tea and cookies. "These are my dear grand-daughters," said Noni, as person after person came up to meet them.

"How do you do?" said Maud over and over again. Polly just held out her limp hand as if it belonged to someone else.

Most of the adults acted kind and pitying as they welcomed them to the island. "Poor little orphans," one muttered. The children who accompanied their parents looked suspicious.

"Alice is delighted to have a new girl coming to school," said a woman called Mrs. Mackenzie. "She'll take good care of Polly." She glared at her daughter, as if this were an order.

Alice, a scowling girl with red hair, didn't appear at

all delighted. She examined Polly so disdainfully that Polly moved closer to Noni.

"Polly won't be starting school for another week," said Noni.

A week was a long time. Polly lowered her eyes to shield herself from Alice's glare.

———

After church they went to the rectory for what Noni called Sunday dinner, even though it was at noon. The rectory was smaller and darker than Noni's house and much tidier. Polly was still worrying about all the staring children in the parish hall, especially that angry-looking girl. She thought of her friends in Winnipeg . . . especially Audrey, her best friend. Polly hadn't been able to see her since it happened. Audrey would be getting ready to start school in Winnipeg. What would she think when Polly wasn't there?

Polly pushed some dark meat around on her plate, trying not to cry.

"What *is* this?" asked Maud suspiciously.

"It's venison," said Gregor.

"Venison?"

"Deer. I shot it myself!"

Deer? Polly almost gagged as she put down her knife and fork.

"You shouldn't have told them that, Gregor," said Aunt Jean. "We eat a lot of venison, chickies. We're lucky to have such a plentiful supply of meat. And there are too many deer on the island. It's good for them to be culled, and it's delicious—try it!"

Maud did. "It *is* good!" She gobbled it up and asked for a second helping.

But Polly knew she could never eat it. Deer, like the graceful animals she had seen yesterday? She nibbled a few carrots and potatoes and left the venison on her plate.

Noni noticed. "At least *one* of you has a good appetite," she said, passing Maud her plate.

"It's swell to have so much to eat!" blurted out Maud.

All of the adults stared at her. "What do you mean, hen? Did you not have enough to eat in Winnipeg?" Noni asked.

Maud flushed. "Sometimes it was hard to find enough money for food, that's all."

"Oh, Maud, I am *so* sorry to hear that." Noni looked angry. "Why didn't your father write to me? I could have helped you out!"

"I don't want to talk about our father," muttered Maud.

There was an awkward silence until Uncle Rand asked Gregor about one of his courses.

After the meal Noni took Maud and Polly aside. "I noticed you crossing yourself in church today, Maud. You don't have to do that any more. You're Anglicans now, not Catholics."

Maud looked confused. "But our father was Catholic, and we were baptized as Catholics. Are we allowed to change?"

Noni smiled. "Of course you are! And your mother was Anglican, although she never thought much of church. Don't you think you should be the same religion as the rest of us?"

Maud shrugged. "I don't care, and I'm sure Polly doesn't either."

Gregor took them on a tour of the island. They shuffled along the dusty road while he showed them what he called "the village": a community hall, a gas station, the store, and the hotel. "My grandparents—that would be your *great*-grandparents, the MacGregors—ran the hotel when they first came to the island from Scotland," he told them. "After they retired, Aunt Clara and Uncle Gilbert took over, until Uncle Gilbert died."

Who was Uncle Gilbert? Polly wanted to ask. But she still couldn't make her tongue form words.

Maud answered for her. "Gilbert was our grandfather, right?"

"Right! He died when Una was fifteen. I was only five, but I remember the funeral—everyone on the island came. And I remember Uncle Gil. He used to read poetry to me that I didn't understand. He was kind, though."

"Are you called Gregor because your mother's last name was MacGregor?" asked Maud.

"Right again!" Gregor grinned. "Don't get my ma on about the MacGregors, though. You'd think she still lived in Scotland. When I was a kid I had to wear a kilt! In the Mac-Gregor tartan, of course."

Maud giggled. "You wore a skirt?"

"Yup. Only for church, but I got teased so much she finally let me stop. She'll probably make kilts for you as well—she's a good seamstress. And watch out for Robbie Burns Day. You'll have to eat the insides of a sheep! What do you think of *that*, Polly?"

Polly's insides lurched. First deer, and now a sheep's insides! But Gregor had such a mischievous glint in his eyes, maybe he was only teasing. She gave him a shy smile.

He softly pinched her nose. "Still not talking, are you, Pollywog . . . never mind, you will when you're ready."

They walked to the end of the long wharf and he took them out in what he called a "gasboat," a small open boat with a motor. It slowly chugged to the lighthouse and back. Polly sat in the front, her hair blowing back, while they passed bays and coves and a few houses dotting the shore. Cold water sprayed in her face. She tried not to imagine what would happen if the boat tipped and they fell into the depths below.

"Look, a seal!" cried Maud. A face like a grey dog's, with huge eyes, surfaced near them, then sank below the waves.

Gregor pointed out two eagles soaring high above. Polly had never seen such enormous birds.

After they returned, Uncle Rand took the boat over to Walker Island to conduct a church service there. Gregor left to play tennis with a friend, Noni went upstairs for a nap, and Maud and Polly took some books out to a swinging chair on the verandah.

There was so much to look at that Polly couldn't read. The sea was broken up by the sun into glittering jewels. Across the channel, on Walker Island, a man stood on the top of a cliff, so close that she could see his green hat. The only sounds were an occasional boat putting along the passage, a car and some horses and buggies on the road, and the voices of people strolling by. A woman looked up at the house and waved, but Polly turned her face away.

"Maud, look!" breathed Polly. A group of deer glided onto the grass and began to nibble it. One was a stag with velvety antlers. Then a passing buggy scared them away.

"I can't believe I'll actually be at St. Winifred's on Tuesday!" Maud said.

Maud had wanted to go to boarding school ever since she had discovered English novels about them at the library. In June, however, she'd thought she'd left school for good. This fall she had planned to start work as a housemaid for one of the rich ladies on Wellington Crescent.

Maud's eyes glowed. "Just think, Polly . . . I could be

dusting furniture and instead I'm going to boarding school! I'm so excited!"

"Aren't you nervous too?" Polly asked.

"A bit. But I'm sure to like it, the courses and sports are so excellent. There are thirty boarders—I wonder how many girls are in each dorm?"

Polly shuddered. "Thirty! That's a lot of new people to meet! Maud, you'll be here again next weekend, right?"

"Not this coming weekend—I'll only have been at school a few days. But after that, I'll be home every weekend. You'll barely notice I'm gone!"

Polly couldn't return her grin.

——

Aunt Jean arrived for tea, which they had on the verandah because the afternoon was so warm. "I'm looking forward to Tuesday," she said. "There are lots of things we need in Victoria. The four of us will have a grand time shopping without the men, right, chickies?"

Gregor came back and they all walked him to the wharf, where he was catching the steamer to Vancouver. "I'll see you in a few weeks, Pollywog!" he called.

Uncle Rand returned from his service and they made a light supper in the kitchen, since it was Mrs. Hooper's afternoon off. Then the adults gathered around a card table in the living room and played a game called Bezique. They tried to teach the girls, but Polly didn't understand it, and Maud was so excited about going to school that she couldn't concentrate.

"Where exactly *is* Victoria?" she asked.

Uncle Rand took down a map from the bookshelf and spread it on the tea table. "Here it is—on the southern tip of Vancouver Island. And here's where we took the ferry yesterday, and here's our island."

Polly leaned over Maud's shoulder and studied the map. Kingfisher Island was part of a group of islands about halfway between Vancouver and Victoria. They looked tiny compared with huge Vancouver Island.

"It looks like a pig," she whispered in Maud's ear.

"Did you say something, Polly?" Uncle Rand asked gently.

When she didn't answer, Maud said, "Polly thinks Kingfisher Island looks like a pig."

"So it does!" said Aunt Jean from the card table. "A little pig on its side. And we live along its tummy! Show the girls *your* map, Rand."

Uncle Rand got out a map that showed only the island. "I drew it myself," he said proudly. He showed them where he had marked X's for Noni's house and the rectory and the church.

Noni put down her cards. "Let's have a song or two," she

suggested. She sat down at the piano and they began to sing "Loch Lomond." Then she went on to "There's a Long Long Trail A-Winding."

Maud belted out the words, but Polly was silent. Daddy had always loved singing; this was one of his favourites.

"You two had better go to bed now," said Noni, and they were finally released.

———

That night Polly tumbled into sleep as if she were falling into a bottomless pit. She didn't wake up until almost noon. After lunch she tried to read, but she couldn't stop yawning. Noni suggested that she go back to bed. "Sleep is the best healer there is," she told her.

When she woke up, Maud and Noni were in the room packing Maud's suitcase. Polly sat up and watched them, trying to still the ache in her stomach. How would she ever cope without her strong, capable sister?

She stumbled through tea and dinner as if her numb body belonged to someone else. Finally it was time to go to bed again.

"Do you remember all the rules?" Maud asked Polly, after Noni had come up to kiss them good-night.

"Uh-huh," whispered Polly.

"What are they?"

"Don't tell anyone. Don't think about it or Daddy. Don't trust anyone except you. Be brave. Be polite."

"Good. You forgot the last one, though—no crying."

Polly exploded into sobs. "Oh, Maud, I don't want you to go! I don't want to stay here all by myself! I want to go *home!* I want everything to be like it was before!"

Maud got into bed with her. She cradled Polly until her sobs turned into hiccups. "Nothing will *ever* be like it was before, Doodle. I wish it could, but it can't, and you just have to get used to it."

"I want *Daddy!*" wailed Polly. "Oh, Maud, I want him so much!"

Maud stiffened. "Stop thinking about Daddy, Poll."

"But—" Polly tried to catch her breath. "Don't you—don't *you* think about him?"

"Never. I've put him out of my mind, and that's what you have to do. Go to sleep now, Doodle. Nothing is as bad as you think. Everybody here loves you. The island is a swell place, and I'll be back soon."

She rubbed Polly's back the way she used to when Polly was small, then she got into her own bed. Polly clutched the bed rail and tried not to think.

But it was no use. Her mind kept trying to return to what had happened. To quiet it, she again remembered an earlier, happier time.

One Saturday, just before what the adults called "the

crash," Daddy had taken Polly and Maud and Grannie to Grand Beach to celebrate Polly's sixth birthday. They'd had a car then. Daddy and Maud sat in the front seat and Polly snuggled up to Grannie in the back. For the whole long drive they bellowed out funny songs. Polly laughed so hard at "Yes, We Have No Bananas" that Grannie had to pat her on the back. They spent all day on the white stretch of sand or in the clear water. Daddy and Maud had swimming races and Polly paddled with Grannie. They ate the lunch Grannie had packed, and Maud helped Polly blow out the candles on her cake. Polly dozed all the way back, her head in Grannie's lap. The car was like a cradle as Daddy crooned lullabies and took them safely back to the city through the darkness.

CHAPTER FOUR

MAUD GOES TO SCHOOL

Polly watched a long, sleek steamer approach the wharf. A small crowd watched as well; Noni explained that they were waiting for the mail. The few people who were going to Victoria stood out in their best clothes.

"Jean, I wish you wouldn't wear that dreadful purple hat," Noni told her. "It's much too loud and it doesn't match your suit."

"Oh, Clara, don't be such a Victorian!" retorted Aunt Jean.

"I *am* a Victorian," said Noni.

"Nonsense, of course you aren't!"

"I am, and you are too. We were both born while the old Queen was still alive." She smiled. "Imagine that, hens— Jean and I have spanned two centuries!"

They climbed up a steep gangplank to the boat, which

was bigger than the one they had taken from Vancouver, even though it carried no cars.

"Goodbye! Have a good time!" Uncle Rand waved to them from the wharf as the steamer drew away.

"He loves being on his own," said Aunt Jean fondly as they settled into seats in the smoking room. "He gets so involved in writing his book that he forgets to eat!"

"He gets *too* involved," said Noni. "I didn't understand a word of Sunday's sermon and no one else did either. All that theory went over everyone's head! Can't you suggest that he make his sermons simpler, Jean?"

Cigarette smoke curled out of Aunt Jean's nostrils. "I've tried, but you know Rand. He's obsessed by atonement theory—whatever *that* means!"

"Well, he should put his obsession into the book, and those who are interested, like Gregor, can read it there. Sermons are for daily matters, like being kind to your neighbour. I could do better myself!"

"Of course you couldn't, Clara! And I think people are impressed by Rand's sermons. They come away with something to think about, like a meaty bone to gnaw on during the week."

"More like a *dry* bone," said Noni.

Polly listened to their banter. She was beginning to realize that it was like a friendly tennis match—they actually enjoyed it.

The room was so smoky that Maud and Polly went outside, clutching their hats in the breeze. They passed many
islands, some with houses on them and some uninhabited.
Maud pointed out a group of seals lounging on a rocky point.

But Polly stared at Maud instead, trying to memorize
her. Maud's braids were especially tight and her face was
shiny and pink. How could she look so happy when she was
leaving Polly?

They had lunch in the dining room, and then the
steamer approached Victoria. An enormous building like a
castle loomed in front of them. All the passengers crowded
onto the deck as it drew closer.

"That's where we're staying, chickies—the Empress
Hotel," Aunt Jean told them. "Isn't it posh? I don't know
why Clara wants to waste her money on such luxury, but she
insists, and who am I to argue with her? Anyway, the prices
have gone down so much that it's not so bad."

They disembarked and crossed the street to the hotel.
Polly gaped as they walked into the huge lobby, with its pil-
lars and chandeliers. A young man wearing a red jacket with
brass buttons carried their suitcases to their room.

The bedroom was even more splendid than the lobby,
with a fitted carpet and long drapes and satin counter-
panes on the twin beds. Just as Polly was wondering where
she would sleep, Noni told her that the hotel would bring
in a cot.

"Can we go shopping now?" asked Maud.

Aunt Jean laughed. "Yes, chickie, let's go and get your uniform! Otherwise you'll burst!" She and Noni powdered their noses, then they all went out.

———

Victoria was smaller than Winnipeg. The wide streets were flanked by low buildings and dotted with trees and street-lights. The fresh smell of the sea was everywhere. But, just like home, there weren't many cars on the streets, and they passed several men begging for money.

They went straight to the fancy store that stocked the St. Winifred's uniform. Polly sat in a chair while Maud tried on many things and checked them off on her list.

"I need *six* pairs of gymnasium hose," she told the saleswoman. "And a felt hat *and* a straw one. And this scarf is the wrong colour!"

"Oh, my, that's the scarf for Norwood House—I'm terribly sorry, dear," said the saleswoman, who seemed entirely cowed by Maud.

Maud tried on the whole uniform. "You look splendid," said Noni, but Polly thought she'd never seen such ugly clothes.

Maud wore a grey wool tunic that ballooned over its maroon belt. Under it was a stiff-collared white blouse and a mustard-coloured tie. A maroon blazer with a crest on its pocket, black stockings, and heavy, laced black shoes completed the outfit. On the chair beside her were a scratchy-looking grey coat, a maroon-and-mustard striped wool scarf, a mustard felt hat, and black gloves.

"Should I get the summer uniform now?" asked Maud.

"Let's wait," said Noni. "You may have grown by the summer term."

Maud needed other clothes as well as her uniform. Polly was glad for her as she watched her try on the "simple frocks for indoor wear" that were on the list. Finally Maud had clothes that fit!

"Would *you* like to get a new dress, Polly?" Noni asked.

Polly nodded with surprise. She had never had a store-bought dress. They found a pretty blue one with a pattern of small flowers on it. Then Noni bought her two brand new pairs of shoes: strapped black ones for church and brown oxfords for school. Polly couldn't help being pleased. "*Thank* you!" she whispered.

Maud insisted on wearing her uniform for the rest of the day. She held her head high as they walked along the street and in and out of stores. Aunt Jean bought Uncle Rand some underwear and Noni bought a special magazine about Scotland. Then they went to a grocery store and ordered a lot of food to be sent to the island.

Finally they took everything to the hotel and had tea in

the garden. Noni kept getting up to inspect the roses and the enormous dahlias. "Why can't mine be like this?" she said.

Maud tucked a napkin under her chin so she wouldn't spill anything on her tunic. She wouldn't take off her blazer, even though her face was beaded with perspiration. She devoured a piece of pie, but Polly shook her head at the tray of sandwiches and pastries. In a few hours Maud was going to leave her!

"Look, Polly!" Maud pointed out an older girl in a St. Winifred's uniform having tea with her parents. The girl glanced over at Maud and smiled.

"Oh, Noni, can't we go to the school *now?*" asked Maud.

"I told them not to expect us until six," said Noni.

"But the brochure says you can arrive any time after lunch. Please, Noni—I can't wait that long!"

"Very well, Maud," said Noni, "if you're sure that's what you want."

How could Maud want to leave them so soon? Polly clutched Noni's hand all the way to the taxi.

―――――――――

The school was on the edge of the city. The taxi drove through a stone gate and along a winding driveway, past woods and a large playing field.

"That must be where they play grass hockey," said Maud. "I'm sure I'll be good at it because I like running."

"Your mother liked running too," Noni told her. "She was also an excellent tennis player."

"She must have inherited that from Gilbert," said Aunt Jean. "Neither of *us* is athletic!"

Maud wasn't listening. Her eyes were fixed on the large stone house they were approaching. "That must be where the boarders live," she told Polly, "and the other two buildings must be the classrooms and the gym."

The taxi dropped them off at the entrance and the driver carried Maud's suitcase up the wide stairs and into a large, dark hall. One wall was covered with photographs of uniformed girls playing sports or in class groups. Three large oil paintings on another wall portrayed solemn women. They seemed to stare right at Polly.

"Former headmistresses, I imagine," said Aunt Jean, taking out a cigarette. "They look rather severe!"

Many girls were coming in and out, some in uniform and some in their own clothes. Other parents and girls stood in the hall in chattering groups.

A very tall woman hurried over to them. She was just as formidable as the women in the portraits. "This must be Maud Brown and her family!" she said.

Polly wished she could hide behind Noni, but that would be babyish.

"I'm Mrs. Whitfield, Maud's grandmother," said Noni.

The woman shook Noni's hand. "I am Miss Guppy, the

headmistress of St. Winifred's," she said grandly. Her voice was like a bark from a very large dog.

"This is my sister, Mrs. Stafford," said Noni.

Miss Guppy had bristly grey hair that stood out untidily from her bony face. She stared coldly down her long nose. "I'm afraid I'll have to ask you to extinguish your cigarette. We don't allow smoking here. It sets such a bad example, don't you think? You'll have to butt it outside—we have no ashtrays."

Aunt Jean flushed. She quickly left, then returned without the cigarette.

"And this is Maud!" For the first time, Miss Guppy smiled warmly. "I'm delighted to welcome you to St. Winifred's. You're the only new boarder this term, you know—I'm afraid our little population has shrunk in these hard times. We're delighted to have you join us." She shook Maud's hand and gazed hungrily at her. Then she spotted Polly and crushed her hand. "And you must be Maud's little sister. What is *your* name?"

Polly hung her head, trying not to rub her released hand.

"It's Polly," said Maud.

"I'm very sorry about your father, girls. I lost mine as a child as well." It was hard to imagine this strong, horsey-looking woman as a child. "It's a difficult trial God has sent you, but I know you'll be able to bear it. Let me show you around."

The next hour went by far too fast for Polly. Miss Guppy showed them a dining room with an ornate ceiling and the sitting room where the girls had free time in the evenings. She took them to a long building full of class-rooms. Another building contained a gymnasium and a science laboratory and two piano-practising rooms.

"It's so large!" marvelled Aunt Jean.

"We have all the modern conveniences," said Miss Guppy proudly. "Everything a young lady needs for a proper education."

They went back to the stone building. "The other mem-bers of your dormitory are already here," the headmistress told Maud. "I'll introduce them to you after your family leaves."

They sat in Miss Guppy's study while she told them how delighted she was to have a new student. "Many families can't afford private schools these days. I've had to take a cut in my own salary, but I would never leave, even if I had to work for free—St. Winifred's is my life. I know you will soon feel the same, Maud."

Miss Guppy frowned at Noni. "I was slightly confused when you told me Maud would be a weekly boarder."

"I thought I made it clear that Maud will be coming home every Friday after this one," Noni answered.

"That will be difficult for her. All of our boarders stay for the weekend, even if they live nearby. We go on special outings on Saturdays, and on Sundays we have spiritual discussions in the afternoons. The boarders are a tightly knit group at St. Winifred's. Maud will feel left out if she can't participate fully in their activities."

"Nevertheless, Maud will be coming home every weekend," repeated Noni firmly.

"Oh, but—" started Maud. Noni put up her hand and Maud was silent.

"Let's see how it goes," said Miss Guppy just as firmly. Maud turned to her with a relieved smile, and Polly's stomach hurt. Already Maud and Miss Guppy seemed to be in a private league that shut out the rest of them.

"Now, Maud, why don't you say goodbye to your family? I ordered a taxi for six o'clock and it must be here by now." Miss Guppy had them outside before they knew what was happening.

"Goodbye, hen," said Noni, kissing Maud. "Enjoy your new friends. You can tell us all about them when you come home."

"Have a good time, chickie," said Aunt Jean.

Then it was Polly's turn. She couldn't speak as Maud hugged her and whispered, "Remember the rules! See you in ten days!"

Maud turned and followed Miss Guppy back inside. The heavy door closed firmly behind them.

"Well!" said Aunt Jean in the taxi. "*There's* a woman who knows her own mind! She made me feel like a young girl!"

"She's terribly overbearing, but she appears to be an excellent and committed headmistress," said Noni.

"And Maud seems to like her," said Aunt Jean. "That's the most important thing."

"Yes, Maud seems to like *everything* about the school. I'm sure she'll be happy there. And of course she'll get a good classic education. I wish *I'd* had that opportunity."

On the way out they passed a group of uniformed girls walking up the drive. They were laughing and talking so intently that they didn't even glance at the taxi. They were part of a secret world, as alien as Maud now seemed to Polly.

———

To Polly's relief she was sent to bed early, after supper on a tray—which she hardly touched—that came to the room. She sat on her cot in her nightgown and watched Noni and Aunt Jean get dressed for dinner. "If you need anything, just phone the desk and they'll come and get us in the dining room," said Noni. She tucked Polly in and kissed her. "You go right to sleep, hen. Don't fash yourself about Maud—remember that you'll see her soon."

For a long time Polly lay on the bed, all the events of the day marching through her mind. Then she sat at the window and watched the lit-up boats in the harbour. People strolled by on the sidewalk, laughing and chatting. Everyone looked happy—everyone but her.

She got back into bed, burrowed under the blankets, and let herself cry.

Polly knew that Maud and Miss Guppy would prevail. Miss Guppy would persuade Noni to let Maud be a full boarder. She would come home a week this Friday, but then she'd stay for the whole term and Polly wouldn't see her until Christmas!

Now Polly had no one. No Maud, no Daddy, no Grannie . . . and no mother, even though she couldn't remember her. And she didn't understand what had happened in August and no one would tell her, not even Maud! She was tired of going on trains and boats and staying in new places. She didn't want to start a strange new school with scary-looking girls like Alice in it. The future was a dark tunnel she was being forced to enter, but it wasn't like the tunnels on the train because she didn't know when or if she would come out on the other side.

"Oh, oh!" sobbed Polly. Her tears choked her they came so fast.

"Why, chickie, what on earth is the matter?" Aunt Jean rushed in and sat on the edge of the cot. She took out her handkerchief and wiped Polly's face. Then she held her shuddering body. "Poor wean, this is so hard for you. Things will get better, I promise. We'll take good care of you, and you'll come to like living with us."

"I want to live with my *Daddy*, like I always have!" cried Polly.

"Whisht, now. You mustn't think about your father—it will only make you sad. Be a good lassie and try to go to sleep. Everything will look better in the morning."

Polly's sobs diminished to gulping breaths. She let Aunt Jean tuck her in. "Where's Noni?" she croaked.

"She ran into someone she knew, but she's coming up soon. Go to sleep now, chickie."

Aunt Jean rubbed Polly's back and began to sing:

Dance to your Daddy
My little babby
Dance to your Daddy
My little one.
You shall have a fishie
In a little dishie.
You shall have a fishie
When the boat comes in.

"Jean!" Noni hurried over from the door. "How can you sing that to Polly? It's completely inappropriate!"

"Sorry, Polly," said Aunt Jean. "I wasn't thinking. That was Gregor's favourite lullaby."

"I liked it," murmured Polly.

"Polly has been feeling sad," said Aunt Jean. "But do you know what, chickie? You're talking!"

"So you are!" said Noni. "I'm glad of that, but I'm sorry you're feeling sad." She took Aunt Jean's place on the bed and stroked Polly's hair.

Then *she* began to sing:

Lula lula lula bye-bye.
Do you want the stars to play with?
Or the moon to run away with?
They'll come if you don't cry.

Polly fell asleep to Noni's husky voice.

CHAPTER FIVE

a breather

Polly sat at the kitchen table and forced herself to eat a few mouthfuls of porridge, wondering what to do with herself. The rain drummed on the roof like a waterfall. Being without Maud was like being without a limb.

"Isn't it good to be home?" Aunt Jean had said the night before. But where *was* home? Polly wondered. It didn't feel like here, but neither did Winnipeg without Daddy. Maud's new home was her school, but Polly had nowhere.

"Why don't you take another pot of tea up to your grandmother?" suggested Mrs. Hooper, who was rolling out dough. "I'll set out a cup for you as well."

"All right," said Polly, since she didn't seem to have a choice.

She had to put the heavy tray down to knock on Noni's door.

"Come in," called the gravelly voice.

Polly felt shy going into Noni's bedroom. But Noni smiled at her, sitting up in bed in an embroidered dressing gown. Her loose hair made her face look softer. She put down her book.

"Ah, Polly, what a treat! And more tea! Come and sit beside me on the bed. Have you had breakfast?"

Polly nodded as she pushed off her shoes and scrambled onto the high bed.

"Why, look at your feet—they're sopping! You'd better take off your socks and get under the covers. How did you get so wet?"

"Going to the privy," Polly explained.

"We should have bought you gumboots in Victoria! Never mind, we'll find you some at the store. Now, hen, how many spoonfuls of sugar would you like in your tea?"

"Two, please." Polly was trying not to stare too obviously at Noni's things. "What are you reading?" she asked shyly.

"It's a book of poetry called *The Golden Treasury*. I read it every morning, and often during the night. I don't sleep very well. My arthritic hips make it hard to get comfortable, and I can't seem to turn off my mind. That's why I find it hard to get up in the mornings. Would you like me to read some poems aloud to you?"

"Yes, please."

Now Polly could stare freely. She slurped her sweet

milky tea and listened to Noni read a short poem about daffodils, then a longer one about going down to the sea.

Like the rest of the house, Noni's room was stuffed full
of objects: photos, cushions, books, magazines, and clothing were piled and draped everywhere.

Noni put down the book and picked up her cup. "Just
listen to that rain! Isn't it cozy, being inside in a warm bed?
Sometimes I think I could stay here all day! But the morning
awaits us. I'd better get dressed before Jean arrives, or she'll
be disgusted with me."

Polly wondered if she should leave, but Noni told her to
stay in bed. She tried not to stare as her grandmother peeled
off her dressing gown and nightgown and began to put on
many layers of underwear: drawers, a brassiere, a camisole,
a corset that had garters dangling from the bottom of it, and,
over it all, a slip. She sat on a stool to pull on her stockings
and fasten them to the garters. Finally she put on a brown
cotton dress.

"Now, hair!" she said, turning to her mirror. Noni
brushed her fluffy hair smooth and twisted it into a smooth
roll. Then she fastened the roll along the back of her head
with hairpins.

"There!" she said, turning around. "How do I look?"

Noni looked as if she had tied herself up tightly in a
brown package, but it would have been rude to say that. "You
look . . . tidy," said Polly.

"Thank you, hen! I try to at least be neat in my appearance, since I seem to have so much trouble keeping anything else tidy! Jean thinks I should get a bob, but I've had long hair all my life. I don't see any reason to change."

"Mrs. Tuttle told us we should get *our* hair bobbed," said Polly. "She said we looked old-fashioned."

"Nonsense! Your long hair is lovely. Would you like me to braid it?"

Polly shook her head. She always wore her hair loose, with barrettes or a ribbon pulling it back from her face. Its weight was like a comforting shawl around her shoulders.

"You're the image of Una as a child," Noni told her. "However, Una cut her hair short when she was twelve without my permission. How we argued about that!" She sighed. "Do you remember your mother at all, Polly?"

Again, Polly shook her head. "Maud does. Sometimes she tells me about her. She taught Maud how to whistle with two fingers!"

Noni smiled, although her sad eyes looked sadder. "Una often used to startle us doing that. Maud is so much like her, even though she doesn't resemble her mother at all."

They both flushed, realizing whom Maud did resemble.

Aunt Jean burst through the door. "Are you dressed, Clara? It's almost ten o'clock! Polly, I swear your grandmother is the laziest person on earth! I've been up since five! I've gathered the eggs, fed the chickens, and made your uncle's breakfast. *Some* of us can't afford help!"

"Help is cheap these hard times, Jean. You just prefer doing it all yourself."

"Well, I do like things to be done properly. Clara, I'm about to go to the store—do you need anything? Would Polly like to come with me? The rain seems to be letting up."

Noni smiled. "I'm sure she would—she can help carry things. I'll make you a list."

Aunt Jean chattered all the way to the store. "The Cunninghams live there," she said as they passed a large brown house. "Mildred was my first friend on the island. She thinks because she married a doctor she's a cut above me, but I think a rector's wife is higher than a doctor's wife, don't you? Gregor is good friends with Alec Cunningham. Alec is in Montreal right now, attending McGill, and Mildred never stops boasting about him—it's Alec this, Alec that, whenever we run into her. I can hardly get in a word about Gregor, and he's doing just as well."

Polly followed Aunt Jean up and down the aisles of the store as she filled her basket. Everything was here, from food to dishes to clothes to fishing gear.

"Clara has written 'Boots for Polly.'" Aunt Jean smiled. "Come and try these on."

She bought Polly a pair of green gumboots and some thick wool socks. "You can wear them home," she said.

Mr. Wynne, the storekeeper, gave Polly a piece of licorice. "Why aren't you in school, young lady?" he asked.

"She's not starting until next week," said Aunt Jean. Mr. Wynne waited for further explanation, but Aunt Jean went on to ask about his sick mother.

All the way back Polly stomped through puddles in her new boots. She helped put away the groceries in Noni's and then in Aunt Jean's kitchen. Uncle Rand came out of his study and joined them in the kitchen for a cup of coffee; Polly had milk and ate one of Aunt Jean's brownies.

Aunt Jean never sat still for long. She jumped up to wash their dishes, then took Polly over to the church. Polly helped her dust the pews until it was time to go back to Noni's for lunch.

The rest of the day was so filled with new things that Polly hardly had time to think about Maud. After lunch Noni went upstairs for a nap and Uncle Rand took Polly with him on a drive to visit an ill parishioner. She waited in the car while he went in, watching a sheepdog follow a man down the road. The dog paused and glanced at her; it had such an appealing face. Polly was about to get out and pat it, but then it hurried to catch up with its master.

"Sorry to take so long, Polly." Uncle Rand got into the car. "Mrs. Butler is a cross I have to bear."

"What do you mean?"

"She's constantly sending for me because she thinks she's dying. But there's nothing wrong with her, apart from her need to be the centre of attention. She's such a trial to her poor husband." He started the car. "Now I'll drive you all around the island."

The map Uncle Rand had shown Polly and Maud came alive. There were two main settlements of houses, some around the village where Noni's was, and more at Fowler Bay on the other side of the island. Other houses were on the farms or sprinkled occasionally along the shore. Uncle Rand pointed out a house on a cliff. "The Hays live up there—they had a challenging time building so high, but Captain Hay is so stubborn he wouldn't give up. They have an incredible view."

Polly was amazed at how quiet and empty the road was. They passed one other car, a man on a horse, a tractor putting along, and some fields full of oxen. On the water side of the road were farms enclosed by criss-cross log fencing. The other side was a dark fir forest.

"Where are all the people?" Polly asked.

Uncle Rand chuckled. "There aren't that many—only about one hundred and fifty."

A hundred and fifty! That was fewer than in Polly's old school! "Do you know them all?" she asked.

Uncle Rand nodded. "I've lived here all my life. And almost everyone is part of my congregation. I've baptized them and married them and conducted many of their funerals."

He turned the car down a bumpy lane and stopped in front of the house where he'd grown up. It was on a cove with a tiny island. "I spent hours on that island," he told her. "You can still see the fort I made."

Polly looked at the remains of a driftwood structure. It was hard to imagine bald Uncle Rand as a little boy playing there.

They turned back to the main road. "Don't go too fast!" Polly cried as a deer jumped in front of them.

"Don't worry, Polly, I'm always careful of deer. They're God's creatures, after all."

"Then why do you *eat* them?" asked Polly.

"Well, now that's a conundrum."

"A what?"

"A thorny question. I agree that it's a shame to kill such a beautiful, harmless animal, and the Scriptures do say 'Thou shalt not kill.' But there are too many deer, and we only kill what we eat. After all, we eat cows and pigs and lambs and chickens, as well. We just don't kill them ourselves, except for wild birds and chickens and geese."

Polly thought of the pretty chickens that scratched in the rectory yard. "You kill your chickens?"

"Sometimes. Some are for eggs and some are for meat. It's part of the cycle of life, Polly. But many people don't believe in eating meat—they're called vegetarians."

"From now on I'm going to be a vege—vegetarian too," she said firmly.

Uncle Rand didn't laugh at her. "You're free to eat whatever you want, my dear. Your grandmother and your aunt may object, but I'll stick up for you."

"Thank you."

As they headed back towards the village, Uncle Rand pointed out the school: a low, brown building at the back of a field. Polly shuddered as a bell clanged and children began running out. Red-haired Alice led the pack.

Polly counted on her fingers—still three and a half days before she had to encounter them.

The next two days were the same as Thursday. In the mornings Polly brought up Noni's tea and stayed to talk. Noni had many dressing gowns, all of them colourful and fancy. Polly tried them on and sashayed around the room while Noni got dressed. The long gowns trailed behind her and she pretended she was a princess.

For the rest of the day she was everybody's helper. She helped Aunt Jean polish church silver or pick vegetables or roll cigarettes. She helped Mrs. Hooper shell peas or make the beds. She drove around with Uncle Rand and he told her she was good company. This surprised Polly, because neither of them talked much. She supposed he liked their comfortable silence as much as she did.

On Saturday Noni said, "You're such a good helper, Polly, how would you like to have a regular task? You could replenish the woodbox every morning."

Polly filled a canvas sling with wood from the pile in the yard, carried it into the kitchen, and dumped it into a box beside the stove. The wood was heavy, and it took her several trips before the box was full, but she was proud of how much she could carry.

Noni was passionate about her flower garden. It was a mass of bright colour behind a wire enclosure. "Remember to always close the gate," she warned Polly as they watered and weeded. "The deer would gobble these up in a minute!"

Every evening before dinner Noni played the piano. "I'll teach you if you like," Noni told Polly. She had already offered to show Polly how to paint with watercolours. Soft paintings of island scenes dotted the walls. Polly liked painting, but she had used up her paints long ago and Daddy couldn't afford to get her new ones.

Aunt Jean and Uncle Rand always came to Noni's for dinner. Then the adults would play Bezique. Polly pretended to read, but she only stared at the page, wondering what Maud was doing.

"Didn't you like the toys I put in your room, chickie?" Aunt Jean asked her on Saturday evening. "They used to be

Gregor's. I'm sorry I couldn't find more, but most of his toys were trucks and cap guns, not suitable for girls."

"I like the logs," said Polly. "I made a house out of them."

"I wish I'd saved Una's dolls, but I gave them all away after we left the hotel," said Noni. "She never played with them much. We should have bought you a doll in Victoria, Polly—I'm sorry I didn't think of it."

"I *have* dolls!" said Polly. She ran upstairs and pulled out the small suitcase she'd shoved under her bed.

One after another she lifted out her five dolls. Some-one—the social worker?—had packed them so carefully in newspaper that their faces were undamaged. Polly lined up the dolls on her bed and they gazed at her reproachfully. After it had happened she had completely forgotten them.

"I'm sorry," whispered Polly. She picked up a draw-string bag stuffed with dolls' clothes, bundled up the dolls, and took them downstairs.

"What bonnie dolls!" said Aunt Jean, coming over to look while Noni added up the Bezique scores. "What are their names?"

Polly shyly introduced them: Betsey, Bobsy, Arabella, Peaches, and Elizabeth, her favourite, who had real hair and eyes that opened and shut.

"Clara and I had lovely dolls in Scotland—Mother made all their clothes. But we gave them to our cousins when we moved to Canada," Aunt Jean told her.

"How old were you?" asked Polly as she fastened a tiny dress onto Peaches, the baby.

"I was thirteen and Clara was fifteen—too old for dolls."

Polly wondered when she would be too old. Maud had never shown any interest in dolls, but Polly had always enjoyed them. Their faces of bisque or rubber or cloth seemed to come alive now that they were being paid attention to again.

"I could knit some more clothes for them, chickie," said Aunt Jean. "In fact, I could teach *you* how to knit— would you like that?"

"Yes, please!"

Maud could knit. Grannie had taught her, and she had always said she would teach Polly one day, but she had died before Polly was old enough.

Polly played with her dolls all evening, murmuring to them as the adults resumed their card game. At bedtime she dressed them all in their nightgowns and tucked them into the foot of her bed; except for Elizabeth, who snuggled up beside her. Now the room didn't seem nearly as empty.

As usual, however, memories of Daddy flooded her mind as soon as she laid her head on her pillow. She could hear his proud voice praising her for winning the school spelling bee. She could feel his warm hands rubbing her back or carefully bandaging her knees when she fell off her bike. She could smell his hair cream.

Polly said a little prayer for him and cried herself to sleep.

———

Church was exactly the same as the week before, except that Gregor wasn't there to carry the cross; he'd stayed in Vancouver this weekend. Uncle Rand's sermon was even more obscure.

At coffee hour the same children stared at Polly, and Alice gave her the same disdaining glance. Polly shuddered; tomorrow she'd have to face all of them!

At Sunday dinner her stomach hurt so much she couldn't eat. Noni sent her to her room for a nap. Polly woke up to find her grandmother sitting on the edge of the bed, stroking her hair.

"Wake up, sleepyhead! It's almost time for supper. Do you think you can eat anything?"

Polly sat up and shook her head. "I'm not hungry."

Noni's grey eyes studied her. "I've been wondering, hen, if you need another week before you're ready for school. What do you think?"

"Oh, yes, please!" Polly was so relieved she felt dizzy. Then she looked worried. "But Noni, Maud won't like that! She'll think I'll get too far behind."

"I am in charge of you now, not Maud. And it won't be

hard for you to catch up. We'll read to each other every morning." Noni smiled. "Now are you hungry?"

"A little," said Polly. "What's for supper?"

———

On Friday Polly awoke with dread. The week had gone by far too fast, and she didn't feel any more ready for school. Then she remembered: Maud was coming today! She would arrive on the steamer after dinner. Polly skipped downstairs and ate her entire bowl of porridge for the first time.

Every morning she and Noni had taken turns reading aloud a very hard book called *Waverley*. Polly didn't understand much of it, but Noni said she was an excellent reader. This morning, to Polly's relief, they talked instead.

"Where did you and Aunt Jean live in Scotland?" she asked as she and Noni sipped their tea.

"A place called Stirling. It's a beautiful town between Edinburgh and Glasgow. I really missed it at first. But on the only occasion I went back to visit, after Gilbert and I were married, I realized I belonged here."

"Gilbert is my grandfather, right?" asked Polly, remembering what Gregor had told them. She curled up on the pillow next to Noni. Listening to her was like reading a story.

"Yes, he was. How I wish he could have met you and Maud! He was a dear man, gentle and witty. But he died when your mother was fifteen. Una became uncontrollable after that. She adored her father. She never listened to me, but when Gilbert asked her to do something, she usually obeyed him."

Noni was speaking to her as if she were a grown-up! "Was my grandfather from the island, like Uncle Rand?" Polly asked.

"No, Gilbert was English. He came to British Columbia as a young man and taught in one of the boys schools in Victoria. Jean and I were spending the weekend there with our parents and I met Gilbert at a dance at the Empress Hotel. After we married he helped my parents with the hotel, and after they died we both ran it. He also tutored young people who were applying for university. When Gilbert's parents died and he came into his inheritance, he wanted us to move to Devon and live in the family home, but I couldn't bear leaving here. Sometimes I wonder if I was wrong. Gilbert really missed the theatre and concerts and the cultured life we would have had in England. He was a very intelligent man. He's the one who got me interested in poetry—he knew a lot by heart, and he wrote some poetry himself." Noni's voice was animated. "Pass me those albums on the table, Polly—I'll show you some photos of Gilbert and Una."

Polly gazed at long-ago images of her grandparents and her mother. They had all been taken on the island—

standing outside the hotel, or picnicking, or waving from the steamer. Gilbert and Noni made a handsome couple. He was tall and distinguished with a curling moustache. Noni looked much more relaxed, with her long hair around her shoulders, always smiling or laughing at the camera.

Seeing Una through the years was like gazing into a mirror. She looked almost exactly like Polly, except that Una's expression was often sullen and rebellious. The last photograph was of Una dressed in a coat and hat and carrying a suitcase.

"That's when she was leaving to visit Blanche Tuttle in Winnipeg," said Noni. "She was just seventeen," she added tightly.

Polly closed up the album. "Are there any more?" she asked.

"That's all," said Noni.

"But what about my parents' wedding?" asked Polly.

Noni looked away. "I'm sorry, hen, but we didn't get around to taking any photographs at the wedding."

If only there had been a photo of Daddy! Polly didn't have any of him. There were a few albums in their house in Winnipeg, but no one had thought of packing them.

Noni's voice trembled. "Every night I lie awake and think about Una and Gilbert. You never stop missing people, Polly—but you know about that. And now I have you and Maud to love."

She took Polly's hand. "Let's think of something more cheerful than missing people. Do you know what I do when I get too sad? I think about all there is to *learn* in this world—poetry and flower names and songs, all the things I want to paint. But enough about me! Tell me, hen, is there anything special you'd like for your birthday?"

Her birthday! Polly had completely forgotten that next Thursday she would turn ten. She shook her head. The only present she wanted was Daddy—and that was impossible for anyone to get.

"Well, you let me know. Now, I must get up. You can help me pick some flowers to welcome Maud."

The day went by far too slowly. Polly helped Noni pick flowers. She swept out her and Maud's bedroom, and helped Mrs. Hooper make a chocolate cake. After dinner she sat on the verandah, willing Maud's boat to appear.

Finally she and Noni walked to the wharf. The sky was streaked with pink as the steamer glided around the point. As it grew nearer, Polly spotted Maud standing on the deck. She was in her uniform, waving madly.

"Maud, Maud!" called Polly, jumping up and down.

A few minutes later Maud's strong arms were around her.

In ten days Maud had become as jolly a schoolgirl as a character in one of her books. All she talked about was St. Winifred's.

She told Polly every detail about the five other girls in her dorm: Mary, Sylvia, Edith, Sadie, and Ann. "Sadie's such a brick—we're already best friends. She's really good at games and she thinks I can get on the hockey team—isn't that nifty? Her parents live in Duncan and she has a horse! She's going to ask me there for part of the Christmas holidays—do you think Noni would let me go?"

They were walking along the beach. Polly picked up a stone and hurled it into the water. All week she had hoped that Maud would dislike St. Winifred's so much she'd decide not to go back. But now Maud seemed to belong to her school more than to Polly.

"Some of the matrons are really grumpy, but our dorm has the nicest. Her name is Miss Jacob and she's in love with a man who works in a store—she sees him every Sunday. Miss Jacob braids my hair for me. Oh, and Poll, the Guppy had me for tea in her study on Wednesday afternoon! Four other girls came too. Edith says that if you're asked for tea, it means you're one of her favourites! Imagine me being asked so soon, and I was the youngest! Two of the others are prefects! And I'm going to have special Latin classes with the Guppy because I've never taken it before. She's really pleased with how I'm doing in my other courses, though."

Polly decided she hated the Guppy. "Don't you think she's kind of bossy?" she asked.

"Not at all! She's strict, but that's because she's helping us live up to St. Winnie's ideals. Some of the day girls are afraid of her, but all the boarders know how kind she really is. At tea she told us stories about her boarding school in England. She had to go when she was only five, because her mother was ill. Isn't that sad? She loved the school, though, and she became games captain *and* head girl."

Polly thought of a way to change the subject. "Guess what, Maud. I'm a vegetarian now!"

"What?" Maud frowned. "That's not good for you, Doodle. You're skinny enough as it is. You need meat."

"I won't eat it!" said Polly proudly.

"What does Noni think?"

"She hasn't said anything—maybe she hasn't noticed yet."

Maud shrugged. "Well, she'll probably stop you when she does. Poll, next week I get my house pin! I'm so glad I'm in Sussex. Sylvia is too, and she says it's the best house. Agnes Cooper is my house captain, and she's swell."

Polly finally got Maud's attention by telling her how afraid she was to start school on Monday.

"But haven't you gone yet?" Maud asked. Polly explained how Noni had let her stay home another week.

Maud frowned. "That's not right—you're going to be

really far behind! You *knew* I didn't want you to stay home, Poll. You should have remembered that, not listened to Noni."

"Noni says *she's* in charge of me now, not you," said Polly haughtily. "Anyway, you're not here."

Maud looked guilty. Then she began telling Polly how she was going to try out for the house play.

Listening to Maud talk about St. Winifred's was like learning about a foreign country she didn't want to visit. Polly was almost relieved when Gregor arrived on Saturday morning.

Gregor had to work hard on the weekends he came home from Vancouver—he cut wood and shot grouse and did whatever other jobs his mother had waiting for him. After he'd finished his work he announced that he was going to teach Maud and Polly how to row.

Maybe this was just another task on Aunt Jean's list, but Polly was glad to have an excuse not to listen to Maud's monologue. And she was beginning to enjoy Gregor. He was easy to be with, and she liked how he called her "Pollywog."

Maud was good at rowing, but Polly kept splashing the heavy oars. Gregor had brought along fishing rods. He showed them how to bait their hooks with cut-up herring. Maud was explaining St. Winifred's house point system to Gregor. "If you get five order marks—that's for doing something against the rules—you get a conduct mark. Then you have to—oh! I got a bite!"

Order marks were forgotten as Maud eagerly reeled in her first cod. Then she got three more. "You're a born fisher-woman!" Gregor told her.

Then Polly caught a fish. It was exciting to feel its sharp tug and to shorten the line until Gregor scooped it into the net. But when Gregor banged its head on the side of the boat, its bright eye turned dull.

I promise I won't eat you, vowed Polly.

"It's so hot!" said Gregor, wiping his brow after they landed the rowboat. "What do you say to a swim? The sea can be quite warm in September. Do you have bathing costumes?"

Maud nodded.

"Meet me here in ten minutes," said Gregor as they helped him pull the boat to the shore.

Polly pulled her towel around herself and shivered, despite the hot afternoon sun. The sea looked so cold and wavy and deep—what lurked under it?

"Come on, Pollywog!"

"I don't know how to swim," said Polly.

"Then I'll teach you!" Gregor held out his hand and Polly had no choice but to drop her towel and wade in beside him. Maud held her other hand. The water was icy but bear-able, and she got used to it as they waded deeper.

Maud dropped Polly's hand and lunged into the water, kicking vigorously as she swam away.

"Lie out flat on the water," Gregor told Polly. "I'll hold my hand under your tummy."

"I don't want to," said Polly.

"There's nothing to be afraid of, Pollywog. I'll hold you up and I won't let you go unless you tell me to."

"No, thank you," said Polly.

Maud swam back. "Come on, Doodle, it's easy! How about if *I* hold you?"

Polly looked at their eager faces and tried to be brave. Then she gazed down at the clear greenish water. Tiny fish were swarming in it—what if they bit her? She turned her back on Maud and Gregor and splashed to the shore.

———

At Sunday dinner Maud put down her knife and fork and made a plea. "Noni, do you think I could stay at school next weekend? The boarders are going to Sooke for a picnic—I'll be the only one to miss it."

"Next weekend? But on Saturday we're celebrating Polly's birthday!"

"Oh, Polly, I'm sorry—I completely forgot!" Polly watched Maud struggle to conceal her disappointment.

It was one thing for Polly to forget her own birthday. It

was quite another for Maud to! And Polly could tell that she would rather stay at school. "You don't have to come," she mumbled.

"Of course she'll come!" said Noni. "You are a weekly boarder, Maud, not a full-time one. I know there are events at the school on weekends, but your family is more important."

"Yes, Noni," said Maud, but she looked what Daddy used to call "Maudish."

"Polly, you haven't touched your pork! Eat up now—we need to put some meat on your bones," said Aunt Jean.

For many days Polly had got away with not eating meat, but now she felt too glum to resist. She put a bit of crackling into her mouth—it was delicious. *I'll tell them I'm a vegetarian later,* she decided.

———

Maud was travelling back to Victoria with Bill Forest, a friend of Gregor's, who was attending university there. "You watch him, Maud," teased Gregor. "He's likely to load you up with cigarettes for your chums."

"Gregor!" scolded his mother.

"Smoking is against the rules," said Maud primly.

Polly sat in their room and watched Maud pack. Mrs. Hooper had given her a lot of good things for her tuck box: cookies and apples and a lemon cake.

"What's a tuck box?" asked Polly. She didn't care what it was, but she had to squeeze every bit of Maud she could out of this last hour.

"It's a box I keep in the dining room cupboard," explained Maud. "Every Thursday before we go to bed we're allowed to share what's in our boxes. Last week I didn't have anything, so I'm glad to have this cake! Ann's mother sent her one, but it crumbled in the mail. Did I tell you that Ann's from Portland? She's the first American I've ever met."

"Maud, I really wouldn't mind if you stayed next week-end," Polly lied.

"That's all right, Doodle. I wouldn't miss your birthday party for anything!" Maud sounded sincere, and Polly felt better. But then Maud added, "After next weekend, though, I'm going to try to convince Noni to let me be a full-time boarder. I'll get Miss Guppy to write her a letter. I'm the only one who doesn't stay, and I miss too much. I'm sure Noni will realize that when the Guppy writes."

"But Maud—"

Maud looked at her. "I know you want me here, Doodle. But you're just going to have to accept it. Anyway, you seem fine. You're talking to them now, and you're eating more, even meat! How about the rules—are you keeping them? *I* am. And I *never* think about Daddy. Do you?"

"Sometimes." *Always*, Polly added to herself. "Oh, Maud, how I can help thinking about Daddy, when—"

"Polly! You promised! You can't think about him *at all*, do you understand?"

Polly nodded, but pain stabbed her insides.

"Once you start school tomorrow it will be easier," Maud told her. "You'll have new friends to think about instead, just like I do. What's rule number four?"

"Be brave," whispered Polly.

"Right. Just be brave and you'll be fine!"

How could Maud find everything so easy? Just as Polly had begun to feel a little bit safe, everything was scary again.

CHAPTER SIX

POLLY GOES TO SCHOOL

Polly couldn't eat more than a few spoonfuls of her porridge.

"Poor mite, you're nervous about school, aren't you?" said Mrs. Hooper. "Don't you worry. My grandsons, George and Percy, go there and they like it fine. The new teacher isn't at all strict, they tell me."

All Polly could think of was Alice. "I couldn't eat my breakfast," she told Noni as she brought up her tea. "Do you think I should stay home from school another week?"

Noni felt her forehead. "Do you feel sick?" she asked.

Polly couldn't lie to those clear grey eyes. "Not really . . ." she mumbled. "I guess I'm just scared."

"Of course you are, hen! It's a whole new experience for you, on top of everything else. But I think you're ready for school now. You've had a good long rest and you're looking much better. I guarantee that once you get used to it you'll like it. And that nice Alice Mackenzie said she'd take care of you. Will you be brave and try? I tell you what—if you find it too much after today, then we'll talk about keeping you home longer."

Be brave . . . Noni and Maud kept saying this, but how could Polly be brave when she felt like throwing up the little she had eaten? All she could do was nod and get ready to go.

Mrs. Hooper had ironed a freshly washed pink dress for her. Polly put on her new oxfords, picked up her lunch bucket, and went over to the rectory to meet Uncle Rand, who was going to take her in his car this first morning.

The three-mile drive went far too quickly for Polly; it seemed more like three inches. Uncle Rand kissed her goodbye. "I'll pick you up after school. Have a good day!"

Polly stood alone at the side of the road. A noisy group of children milled around the schoolyard. A woman came out and rang a handbell. Polly waited until everyone had gone in, then forced herself to walk across the field and enter the building.

"Are you Polly?" a friendly-looking boy asked her in the hall. "Come on, I'll show you where our classroom is."

Our classroom? How could she possibly be in the same room as this big boy?

Polly quickly found out that there was only *one* classroom.

She stood in the doorway and quickly counted twenty-two children of all ages. As they gradually noticed her, they all stopped talking and stared.

A nervous young woman who said she was Miss Hunter showed Polly where to hang her coat and lunch bucket.

"Now, let's see where we can put you . . ." she murmured. Polly had never seen a teacher look so anxious.

"Dorothy, you go and sit with Alice, and Polly can sit with Biddy," said Miss Hunter.

Alice . . . Polly watched the red-haired girl from church glower at the teacher.

"But Miss Hunter, you *know* I need to sit by myself! I can't concentrate unless I do."

"I'm sorry, Alice, but there aren't enough desks." Miss Hunter's voice came out in a strained bleat.

Alice looked around. Each desk had two students except hers. "All right," she said angrily, "but I don't want Dorothy. I want Hana."

"Very well. Hana, you move beside Alice, and Dorothy can sit where you were."

The girl who had to join Alice looked terrified, and the one who moved to her place looked relieved. Polly waited until they were settled, then slid in beside Biddy.

"*Hi*, Polly!" said Biddy as the room's noisy din resumed. She was fair-haired, and freckled all over, even on her ears and fingers. Polly remembered her smiling in church.

Polly tried to smile back. But she wondered what her grade five class in Winnipeg was doing. Did Audrey miss her? Did she already have a new best friend?

Be brave, don't cry . . . Polly looked around at the walls covered in maps and lists of numbers and spelling words. What if Maud was right and she was too far behind?

"Order, now," called Miss Hunter.

No one listened. Desk lids slammed and chairs scraped as everyone continued to chatter. Two of the boys were tossing erasers at each other, and Alice was beating a ruler on the edge of her desk in time to singing, "'Hail, hail, the gang's all here!'" at the top of her voice.

"*Order!*" shouted Miss Hunter, rapping her pointer hard on the floor. The students stopped talking, although Alice kept singing softly under her breath. Miss Hunter's face was flushed. Polly realized that her new teacher, who seemed hardly older than the oldest girls, was even more frightened than she was.

Everyone stood and sang "God Save the King" in thin voices, then bowed their heads while Miss Hunter recited the Lord's Prayer. A few students mumbled along with her.

"This morning I'd like to welcome Polly Brown to our school," said Miss Hunter after they had sat down. She smiled at Polly. "Polly's father has recently passed away. She and her older sister have moved to the island from Winnipeg to live with their grandmother, Mrs. Whitfield. We're

very sorry about your father's death, Polly, but we hope you
will be happy here."

"How did he die?" asked Alice.

"That is an inappropriate question, Alice," said Miss
Hunter. "Now, Polly, let me introduce you to your new
classmates."

Polly tried to match names to faces she had seen in
church or in the store. She noticed Mrs. Hooper's grandsons: George was older than she was, and Percy younger.
The friendly boy who had welcomed her was Chester. At the
desk on one side of her sat two little girls called Margaret
and Doris. Luke and Seiji were on the other side. "Luke's
my younger brother," whispered Biddy. At least Alice was in
the far back corner.

Miss Hunter divided them into two groups. The older
ones were told to copy the spelling words into their note-
books while she took the younger ones to the back of the
room and listened to them read. But she kept having to leave
them to quiet down the older children.

"Wallace and Fred, if you don't behave, you'll have to
stay after school!" she warned.

Peace prevailed for a short time, but then the whisper-
ing and giggling started again. Finally it was time for recess.
Miss Hunter looked relieved as she picked up the bell.

Everyone dashed into the field. The older boys began
a game of football and the older girls surrounded Polly so

closely she felt suffocated. Behind her, the little ones were
playing on the swings and teeter-totter.

"So, Polly, tell us how your father died," said Alice,
while the others stared at her.

"He drowned," said Polly.

"Oh, no!" gasped Biddy. The other girls—except for
Alice—looked sympathetic as well. They waited for her to
say more.

Polly remembered Maud's advice on the train. She
hung her head and whispered, "I don't want to talk about
it."

"Where's your sister?" asked Dorothy.

"She's a boarder at St. Winifred's. It's a girls school in
Victoria."

"We *know* about St. Winifred's, dummy," said Alice.
"I'll be going there next year. My mother is making my
grandfather pay for it so she can get rid of me."

"Polly, do you want to come and swing?" asked Biddy.

"Wait!" ordered Alice. Biddy obeyed her. "Polly, we
know that your mother is dead too. What happened to *her*?"

"She died in a car accident," whispered Polly.

"How old were you? Who took care of you after she
died?" asked Hana.

"I was two. My other grandmother took care of me. But
she died a few years ago."

"Oh, you poor thing!" said Biddy.

"She's *not* a poor thing," said Alice. "She was only two, so she probably can't even remember her mother. Lots of people's grandparents die, and *my* father is dead as well." She glared at Polly. "Don't think you're going to get a lot of sympathy just because you're an orphan."

"Can we go now?" asked Biddy.

Alice shrugged. "If you want."

Polly followed Biddy to the swings. "I'm so glad there's finally another girl in grade five!" said Biddy. "Alice and her special group have always left me out, and I get so tired of playing with the younger girls. Will you eat lunch with me?"

Polly gratefully nodded yes.

As the morning went on, Polly's fog of confusion began to clear a little. She bent her head over long columns of numbers to add up, relieved that they were easy. She took her turn reading aloud and Miss Hunter praised her as much as Noni had.

At lunch, she and Biddy took their buckets far away from the older girls and perched on the school woodpile. Biddy flitted from one subject to another and all Polly had to do was listen. She munched on her cold pork sandwich, not even noticing that she was eating meat.

"We live really close to you," Biddy was saying. "Only a bit down the road—you know that red house across from the meadow? I've been watching you and your sister since you arrived and I wanted to ask you over, but my mum said to let you get settled first. Your sister has the longest braids I've ever seen! My dog, Bramble, had six pups! Would you like to come to my house after school and meet them?"

Biddy was already assuming they were friends! "I guess so," Polly finally answered. *As long as you don't ask too many questions*, she added to herself.

Finally the long day ended. Uncle Rand was waiting outside the field. "How was it?" he asked her.

Alice glanced at Polly disdainfully as she and Milly walked past the car. Polly watched Biddy and her brother Luke speed away on their bikes. Biddy had asked her to walk over to her house later.

"It wasn't *too* bad," said Polly slowly. "There were some good things and some bad things."

"That sounds like anything else in life," said Uncle Rand.

———

Biddy seemed the only calm person in her chaotic family. Besides her and Luke there were twin toddlers, William and Fanny, and a baby called Shirley. Mrs. Taylor dangled the baby from her side and darted after the twins in between plucking a chicken. Polly gulped; the pile of feathers on the floor was evidence of how recently the chicken had been alive.

"Hello, there, Polly!" Biddy's mother said cheerfully. "Welcome to our busy household! You'll have to forage for something to eat yourselves, girls."

Biddy found some leftover cake and took Polly out to the barn. The puppies were a warm heap of fur, whimpering in the straw as they competed for Bramble's milk. Biddy put one in Polly's arms; it smelled like skunk. Its tiny mouth opened as it squeaked for its mother and she put it back.

Polly had wanted a dog for as long as she could remember. Grannie had been allergic to them, however, and then times had got so hard that Daddy couldn't afford one. Her desire for one of these squirmy pups was so strong that she felt sick.

"I wish we could keep one, but my parents are going to sell them because they need the extra money," said Biddy. "They're purebred border terriers," she added proudly. "My uncle owns their father."

Polly stroked Bramble's whiskery face. She had never seen a dog that looked like this. Bramble's fur was wiry and brindled. She had a white ring around her tail.

"Polly, maybe your grandmother would buy you one! Then it would grow up near its mother and we could walk them and play with them! Could you ask her?"

Polly's heart leapt. Noni had wondered what she wanted for her birthday. Did she mean *anything*? "I'll ask her!" she said. "Are they very expensive?"

"I don't know—she could find out from my parents. Oh, I hope you get one!"

"So do I!"

Then Biddy asked, "Do you get along with your grand-mother, Polly? I'm a bit afraid of her! Mum really admires her, though. She calls her the queen of the island!"

"I like her a lot," said Polly. "She *looks* scary, but she isn't at all."

Biddy led Polly out of the barn. She showed Polly her room, which was the only neat place in the house.

"Oh, look!" cried Polly. On the floor in a cradle lay the biggest baby doll she had ever seen.

"You can pick her up if you want," said Biddy. "Her name's Margaret Rose, after the princess."

"She's the same size as a real baby!"

"She can wear Shirley's newborn clothes. Mother gave me all of them because she says she's not having any more babies."

"You're so lucky to have younger brothers and sisters," said Polly.

Biddy shrugged. "Shirley cries a lot. And the twins are awful, always getting into my stuff. I prefer Margaret Rose. *She* never cries or dirties her diapers."

Polly continued to admire Margaret Rose's lifelike moulded curls and her blue glass eyes. Biddy pulled out a box and showed Polly all her clothes.

"I have five dolls," said Polly shyly. "One of them is

called Elizabeth, after the other princess. Maybe you could bring Margaret Rose over and we could play with them all."

"Sure!" Biddy accepted this as easily as she did everything else about Polly. She acted as if they had always been friends, instead of only meeting that day.

"Isn't Alice awful?" said Biddy as they changed the doll's dress. "I don't see why she always has to be the boss, but even Chester is afraid of her, and he's the oldest. Dorothy and Hana and Milly are like her slaves—they do exactly what she says. Sometimes they're mean to me, as if they belong to a secret club that I can't join. But now that you're here, Polly, we can be our *own* club!"

Polly glowed.

Biddy stood up. "Do you want to see the fort that Luke and I are making?"

Polly followed her through the field and onto the beach. They played in the driftwood fort until it was time for her to go home.

———

"How was school, Polly?" asked Noni before dinner.

"It wasn't too bad," said Polly again. "Some of the older kids don't listen to the teacher, though." She had decided not to say anything about Alice, since Noni was friends with her mother.

Noni sighed. "That poor lass. I know her family—they

live on Valencia Island. Mabel is far too young to be a teacher. Well, I know *you* will listen, Polly. And I'm delighted you have a new friend! Biddy Taylor is a nice bairn—I've known her all her life. We buy our milk and cheese and lambs from her father. Would you like to invite her over here tomorrow?"

"Yes, please!" said Polly.

Finally she got up the courage to ask the question that burned in her mind. She took a deep breath. "Noni . . . remember when you asked what I wanted for my birthday? May I—may I have a puppy? Biddy's dog has six!"

"A dog? I don't know, hen. Would you be able to take care of it? I don't want Mrs. Hooper to have any extra work."

"I would do *everything!*" breathed Polly.

"It would be pleasant to have a dog again," mused Noni. "Gilbert and I had one for years—a Scottie called Angus. He was a terror! I'll think about it, hen."

That sounded like yes! "Thank you!" said Polly. She was so thrilled that at dinner she again forgot she was a vegetarian and ate some of her chicken.

Oh, Daddy, Daddy, I might get a dog! she whispered into her pillow that night. She longed so desperately to tell him in person that her joy turned to tears. Then she stopped crying as a wonderful idea came into her head.

CHAPTER SEVEN

LETTERS AND A PUPPY

Polly had to wait until the weekend before she could carry out her plan. Noni had started to give her a small allowance every Saturday. Late that afternoon she emptied the previous week's money out of the flowered china pig on her chest of drawers. She took it, and this week's allowance, to the store and bought a thick pad of paper and some envelopes.

On Sunday evening after supper Polly finally had some time to be alone. She told the grown-ups she was going to read in her room. Then she found a pencil, went upstairs, and leaned against her pillow.

She examined the tip of the finger that Maud had pricked with a needle. They had made a pact never to tell anyone their secret. Polly's finger was long healed, but the secret festered inside her like a much bigger sore. She could never reveal it, but no one would hear her if she just said it to herself.

"Daddy is alive. Daddy is alive. Daddy is *alive!*" she whispered. The truth seemed to whizz around the room, as though she'd suddenly let go of a balloon that she'd blown up but not tied. How good it felt to release those words into the air!

She blinked back tears, picked up her pencil, and began to write.

September 25, 1932

Dear Daddy,

Maud says I'm not supposed to think about you, but I can't help it! I have thought about you every moment since you left. I wish so much I could send you letters and you could write back. I'm going to write to you anyway, and when I see you again, I'll give you the letters.

Oh, my Daddy, I miss you so much! I hope that wherever you are you are warm and have enough to eat. It is so hard to pretend you are dead! Sometimes I want to tell someone you are alive, but Maud pricked our fingers and we made a solemn promise not to.

So much has happened since that terrible day when you went away, Daddy! When you didn't come home, the police came and said you had drowned.

Then Maud got your letter that said you had only pretended to drown, and that you had gone to Ontario to look for work. Maud and I had to live with a foster family for two weeks until Noni's friend Mrs. Tuttle was coming back on the train and could take us to Vancouver with her.

Now we live on Kingfisher Island like you wanted us to, with Noni (that's what we call Grandmother) and Aunt Jean and Uncle Rand and Gregor. Maud goes to boarding school in Victoria, and Gregor only comes home on some weekends.

At first I didn't like being here, but now I'm getting used to it. Everyone here is nice to me. They use strange words sometimes, like "hen" and "bairn" and "wean" and "whisht" and "fash," but that's because they used to live in Scotland.

I have a new best friend called Biddy. She lives on a farm and she has lots of younger brothers and sisters.

Daddy, I'm getting a dog! On the morning of my birthday Noni told me that I could have one of Biddy's dog's puppies when it's old enough to leave its mother. I'll choose one this week. When Noni told me I could have a dog, I was so happy that I danced around her room and shouted!

I bet you thought about me on my birthday, Daddy. Now I'm ten! We had my party yesterday. Maud and Gregor both came home for it. I got a lot of swell presents. Aunt Jean and Uncle Rand and Gregor gave me a new bicycle! Gregor brought it back from Vancouver. I was riding my mother's old bike to school, but it's so rickety that the chain kept falling off and the tires went flat. Sometimes I had to walk it to school and I was late two times.

My new bike is shiny red, with a bell. It has a leather seat and a wicker basket. I rode it to Biddy's and back and it's really smooth.

Maud gave me a book of paper dolls, Mrs. Hooper knitted me a green hat with yellow stripes, and Biddy made me a felt bookmark.

I'm really upset with Maud, Daddy. She likes St. Winifred's School so much that she almost forgets about me! Miss Guppy (that's the bossy headmistress there) wrote Noni a letter saying that it was important for Maud to stay at the school on the weekends. Maud has a part in the school play, but if she can't stay on Saturdays to rehearse, she won't be able to be in it. So Noni had to give in and say Maud didn't have to come home on the weekends. That means I won't see her until we go to see the play in November! She says she'll write every week, but that's not the same.

When I blew out all the candles on my birthday cake, I wished I would see you again, Daddy. When

will that be? It's so sad that you had to go away
because you couldn't afford to take care of us. You said
in the letter you wouldn't see us until we were grown
up, but I can't wait that long!
      Much love,
      Polly

There! Polly had never written such a long letter. What a relief to be able to acknowledge that Daddy was alive, and to tell him things!

She put the letter into an envelope, dated it, and looked around the room. Where could she hide it?

A small wooden chest stood against the far wall. Polly lifted the lid; it smelled of cedar and contained woollen hats and scarves. At the bottom was a pile of old magazines. Polly hid the envelope under them and closed the lid.

———

Polly woke up on Monday with a dull ache inside her. She remembered why: she was not going to see Maud again until they went to the play in November. The ache disappeared, however, when she also remembered she was now ten—and she was going to get a puppy.

Biddy called for her as usual and they set off for school. Polly's new bike was so efficient that she scarcely puffed as they went up the hills. She whizzed down them much faster than Biddy, the wind blowing back her hair.

At school Polly and Biddy were inseparable. Since they were so well-behaved, Miss Hunter was happy to let them do much of their work on their own as she tried to cope with the others. She gave Polly and Biddy lists of sums or spelling words or poems to memorize, or something to read in a history book to quiz each other on.

They found the work easy and finished it quickly. Then they whispered and drew and giggled over secret games. They pretended they were princesses doing their schoolwork in the royal nursery; or they made lists of fairies and elves and drew clothes for them.

Alice and her subordinates tried to boss them at recess and lunch, but Polly and Biddy found hiding places they would run to as soon as the bell rang: behind the woodpile, a clearing in the woods, or inside the tool shed.

Today Alice strolled over to them as they were leaning their bikes against a tree. "Where'd you get the nifty bike, Miss Richy-boots?"

"From my grandmother," whispered Polly.

"Let's take a look at it."

Polly flinched as Alice examined every inch of the bike. Would she damage it?

"Very fancy," said Alice. She brushed one of her red curls out of her eyes. "It looks too big for a little girl. I tell you what, Polly, I'll trade you. My bike is too small for me, but this one would be perfect if I raised the seat. How about it?"

"No, thank you."

Alice pinched Polly's arm hard. "Did I hear you refuse such a kind offer?"

"Yes, you did!" cried Biddy. "Leave her alone, Alice! She doesn't *want* to trade!"

Polly thought of Maud. *Be brave* . . .

"If you make me trade, I'll tell my grandmother," she said, trying to keep her voice from wobbling. "Then she'll tell your mother."

A flicker of fear passed over Alice's face. "I didn't say I was going to *make* you trade, stupid. I just said it would be a good idea. But if you don't want to, that's fine." She stalked away.

"Good for you, Polly!" whispered Biddy. "You were so brave!"

"So were you!" They walked into school with their heads high.

That day after school Polly picked out her dog. She and Biddy carried all the pups out into the sunshine and watched them play. Now they were five weeks old. They stood in their dishes of mushy food, chased and pounced on one another, and made tiny growls and barks.

"How can I ever choose?" Polly asked Biddy. "They're all so sweet!"

"Well, first of all, do you want a boy or a girl?"

"A boy."

"Then you only have four to choose from." Biddy picked up each of the male pups one by one and passed it to Polly. The first wriggled impatiently. The second nibbled her hand with his sharp teeth. The third trembled with fright until she put him down. But the fourth snuggled into her neck and licked her chin.

"This one," said Polly. He had chosen *her!*

"He's my favourite too."

Polly studied him closely. He had a dark saddle on his back, but so did many of the others. This puppy, however, was the only one with a black V between his eyes.

"Will you remember that he's mine?" she asked Biddy anxiously.

Biddy nodded. "And my dad's going to put different-coloured ribbons around their necks, because some people are coming to choose this weekend." She took the puppy from Polly.

Polly was sure that it looked back at her pleadingly. "Oh, I wish I could take him home this minute!"

"Mum and Dad said they won't be ready to go for another three weeks. What will you call him?" Biddy asked.

"I don't know. Let's make a list!"

They ran to Biddy's room and started to write down dog names.

"'Bingo,' 'Badger,' 'Lucky,' or 'Pickles,'" Polly told the adults a few days later. "Biddy likes 'Rex' as well, but I think that's too ordinary."

"I like the name 'Badger,'" said Aunt Jean. She and Noni had gone over to inspect the new pup. "Bramble is a bit like a badger, with her scruffy fur."

"She looks more like an otter," said Noni.

Polly thought of the otters she watched play on the beach, with their whiskery faces and supple bodies. "How about 'Otter'?"

"One of my favourite books is called *Tarka the Otter*," said Uncle Rand. "What about 'Tarka'?"

"Tarka . . . I like that!" said Polly. "Is Tarka a boy or a girl?"

"A boy. You'd enjoy the book, Polly. I'll lend it to you when you're a bit older."

Polly thanked him, and thought about the name a little longer. *Here, Tarka!* she imagined calling. Her dog would come to her instantly and sit at her feet. He would never bark too loudly and he would never nip. He'd walk quietly at her side without a leash. Every night he would sleep in a basket beside her bed, and he would go everywhere with her, except to school. He would be perfect.

Then Polly had an awful thought. "Noni," she said, "I know I said I would take care of my dog all by myself. But what about when I'm in school? When I get him, he'll still need to be fed four times a day! Who will do that?"

"Don't you worry, hen. I'll be happy to feed him and walk him when you're not here."

"It will get her up in the mornings!" said Aunt Jean.

Noni ignored her and continued to smile at Polly. "Are you going to call him 'Tarka'?"

"Yes!"

"We look forward very much to welcoming Tarka into the family," said Aunt Jean. Her voice had the tone grown-ups used when they were laughing behind their words, but Polly didn't care. She started to plan everything she needed to have before Tarka's arrival.

When Polly arrived home from school on Friday afternoon, a letter from Maud had arrived. Polly sat beside Noni as she read it aloud.

"'I knew you would be wanting to hear from me, so I'm writing early.'" Maud's clear handwriting described in detail every hockey game and play rehearsal. "'Pamela, a girl in the upper sixth, told me I was a natural born actress!'" she wrote. The letter filled four pages, but there was not one word about missing them, just "Much love from Maud" at the end.

"What does 'upper sixth' mean?" asked Polly, taking the letter from Noni and studying it.

"The second part of the sixth form—it's the same as grade twelve. St. Winifred's models itself on an English school, where they use forms instead of grades."

"That's stupid!" said Polly. "It's not an English school— it's in Canada! I'm glad I don't go there."

"You will one day, though," said Noni quietly.

Polly stared at her. "What do you mean?"

"Exactly what I said. You know your school only goes up to grade seven. Many children on the island attend a public high school in Sidney or Victoria or Vancouver and board with relatives or friends during the term. But we don't know anyone you could live with, and I think you'd get a better education at St. Winifred's than at a public school."

"I have to go away?" She had just *gone* away, to come here! "But Noni, why couldn't I have a governess? Or *you* could teach me!"

Noni laughed. "I've actually thought of that myself, hen. I could teach you literature and music and art, but I could never cope with mathematics or history or geography or any of the other subjects you need to know."

"Uncle Rand could! He knows everything!"

"Not quite everything, although he'd be very flattered to know that you think that. And yes, we could easily find you a governess—many young women would be glad to get a job. Jean and I never learned much from our governess, however. And I don't like the idea of you being isolated at home. You'll be shy at boarding school, but you'll soon get to like it and you'll make good friends. Let's stop worrying about this now—it's still three years away."

Polly hung her head. "Maybe I won't be here in three years," she mumbled.

Noni lifted her chin and looked at her sharply. "Polly, of course you'll be here. Your father has *died*. I know that's difficult for you to believe, but you're always going to live with me. I'm your guardian now."

"But Daddy—" Polly gulped down her words. She had almost given away the secret!

Noni kissed her. "Polly, I'm sorry I brought up the subject of boarding school, but you're ten now—you're old enough to know and be brave about what's going to happen. But not for three more years! So cheer up. Shall I ask Mrs. Hooper to bring us some tea?"

Polly nodded, trying to recover. Three years was a long way off. Surely by then she could think of a way not to go.

When they were sipping their tea and Polly had eaten one of Mrs. Hooper's delicious cookies, she looked at Noni.

"Can I ask you something?"

"Ask away, hen!"

"Did you like my father?"

Talking about Daddy was against the rules, but Maud would never know.

Noni flushed. "Of course I did!" she said, much too fast. "I only met him twice, but when I did I thought he was a—a charming man."

"When did you meet him?"

"When he and your mother got married and at your mother's funeral."

"Why didn't you come and see us any other times?"

Noni looked even more flustered. "Polly, the day before her wedding, your mother and I had a dreadful quarrel. She refused to have anything to do with me after that, although she let me write to you and send you presents."

"What was the quarrel about?"

"I can't tell you," said Noni firmly. "Perhaps I will one day. But you're not old enough yet."

Polly put down her cup. She walked out of the room with her head held high. "I'm going over to visit Tarka," she told Noni haughtily.

Another secret she was not old enough to hear! Polly consoled herself with the thought that *she* had a secret too.

Imagine if Noni knew Daddy was alive! That secret was so enormous that the world didn't seem large enough to contain it.

_____

Dear Daddy, wrote Polly that evening. *Noni has a secret about our mother, but she won't tell me. And Noni and Maud and Mrs. Tuttle know something about you that I don't. It makes me so mad!*

Daddy, why did you leave us? Don't you love us any more? Maud said you wanted us to live with Noni because you couldn't take care of us. But you never asked me if that was what I wanted! I would rather be poor and still live with you than live on the island. I don't think you were fair to leave without telling us.

Polly stopped writing, her hand shaking. She couldn't say things like that to Daddy! On the way to the privy she burned the letter in the stove.

_____

Polly saw Tarka every day during the weeks before he came home. She and Biddy would stop at Noni's for milk and cookies and tell Noni about their day at school, and Polly would change into her overalls.

"Your grandmother *is* nice," Biddy told Polly. "I'm not afraid of her any more."

After their snack they crunched through the arbutus bark and pine needles that littered the road to Biddy's. Polly rushed straight to the barn and Biddy joined her as soon as she had changed.

Tarka knew his name and he knew Polly. When she called him, he pranced over and licked her hand. The puppies were eating some meat now and Polly held bits out to him. She and Biddy laughed as the six pups tumbled over each other. When Bramble appeared they all attacked her, still trying to nurse, but she growled them away.

When the pups fell asleep in a heap, Polly and Biddy, and often Luke, would go to the beach. They worked on the fort until every piece of driftwood was firmly in place.

Luke was eight and as easygoing as Biddy; he was always nice to Polly. His best friend, Seiji, was also eight and sometimes joined them in the fort. Seiji was friendly, but when he was there, he and Luke only wanted to do boring boys things, like aiming at gulls with their slingshots. Polly was worried they would actually hit one.

"Luke, when we started the fort, you said that it was just for us!" Biddy told him one day when Seiji wasn't there.

"You let Polly play in it—why can't Seiji?" Luke retorted.

The problem couldn't be resolved. Finally, on the days when Seiji came, Biddy and Polly did other things. If it was calm they took out the rowboat. Or they climbed the big tree in the meadow, or, if Biddy had to babysit the twins, they walked them to the store. On rainy days they played with their dolls.

Biddy often asked Polly about her life in Winnipeg. Polly told her about her school and her friends there, about making snow forts and travelling downtown on the streetcar.

"Did you have movies in Winnipeg?" Biddy asked.

"Of course!" said Polly. "Maud and I went every Saturday afternoon. If it was a western, all the boys would take out their cap guns and shoot when the cowboys did. The movie theatre got really smoky and stinky."

"You're so lucky," said Biddy. "I've only seen one movie in my whole life! That was last year in Victoria. It was Charlie Chaplin in *City Lights*. It was so funny!"

"I saw that," said Polly.

She hadn't told Biddy that Daddy usually went to the movies with them. Even when he was out of work, he would manage to find enough change to go. On the way home he would do such accurate imitations of the actors that everyone on the streetcar would laugh at him.

"Did you have a big house in Winnipeg?" Biddy asked her.

"Oh, no! Our house was small, and it wasn't really ours—it was rented."

"But why?"

"Because we didn't have much money."

Biddy looked astounded. "You didn't? But you're rich! Mrs. Whitfield's the richest woman on the island—everyone knows that."

"My grandmother may be rich, but we weren't. Sometimes we were so poor we had to go on the dole."

Polly began to tell Biddy how hard it was for Daddy to find jobs, how they sometimes went to bed hungry, and how they never had money for new clothes. Biddy listened with wide eyes. She wanted to hear more, but Polly had to stop. Talking about her former life was like peeling off a scab.

She kept expecting Biddy to ask about Daddy, but she didn't for a long time; her parents must have told her not to. Finally one day she said, "You must *really* miss your dad, Polly."

Polly was ready. "I don't want to talk about it," she said quickly. Biddy flushed and changed the subject.

If only she could tell her that Daddy was alive! If only she could prick the secret inside her and let it burst! But she'd made Maud a solemn promise, sealed with blood.

———

October 9, 1932

Dear Daddy,

Tarka is home! I went to get him yesterday and carried him here in my arms. I had everything ready. He has a basket, a leash, and a collar, two bowls for

*water and food, and some knotted old socks to chew
on. He gets four meals a day of bread and milk and a
little meat.*

*He sleeps in my room. The first night I tried to
keep him in his basket, but he cried and cried so I took
him on my bed and he settled right down and went to
sleep. So now he sleeps with me every night.*

*Sometimes he puddles on the floor, but I scold him
and take him right outside. He chews on my shoes and
dolls and he almost ate my toothbrush! He follows me
everywhere and he licks people and wags his tail. He
looks like an otter and that's why his name is Tarka.*
Tarka the Otter is a book that Uncle Rand likes.

Oh, Daddy, I wish you could meet him!
Your Polly

Polly read over the letter, then sealed it in an envelope,
dated it, and put it with her first letter in the chest. Then
she sat on the floor and gazed at Tarka, peacefully sleeping
in his basket.

He was beautiful, from his dear little black ears to the
matching dark lines that extended from each eye. His brindled fur felt as wiry as Bramble's. When he was asleep, he
looked innocent, but as soon as he woke up he would race
around and steal Polly's underwear and bark at all the new
things he didn't understand, like Mrs. Hooper sweeping the
floor or Noni's umbrella.

Puppies *were* a lot of work! And they weren't as perfect as Polly had imagined. She had to keep trying to wear Tarka out so he would sleep and give the household some peace. Polly worried that Tarka was too much trouble for Noni when she was at school, but Noni kept him locked in the kitchen or tied up outside when she was busy, and she said he was fine.

"Tarka, my little Tarka-dog," whispered Polly, bending down to him and breathing in his skunky smell. Sometimes she pretended he was her little brother, although a brother would probably be easier to take care of—and at least he would wear diapers!

"Out you go, now!" she said as Tarka opened his eyes and stumbled out of his basket, sniffing the floor. She was too late, and wiped up his puddle with the rags she now kept in her room. "Oh, Tarka, you bad boy. When will you learn?" She carried him downstairs and out to the yard, and when he squatted again, she praised him hugely. "That's a *good* dog!"

———

October 23, 1932

Dear Daddy,

Tarka is now ten weeks old! He doesn't have as many accidents as he used to, although sometimes he still doesn't remember. Noni had some ladies for tea and Mrs. Cunningham said what is that awful smell and Tarka had done his business right under the chair where she was sitting! I'm trying to teach him how to sit, but he doesn't understand yet.

Biddy and I are going to dress up as ghosts for Hallowe'en. They don't do trick-or-treating here. They just have a big party in the hall.

Oh, Daddy, where are you?

Love from Polly

November 4, 1932

Dear Daddy,

Tarka has grown so much! I'm trying to teach him how to walk on a leash, but he chews the leash and he chewed the rope when Noni tied him up in the yard. He got away in the road, but Mr. Lewis found him and brought him home. So Gregor is making him a leash out of a chain. Tarka hardly ever has an accident in the house now and he loves to chase balls, so I bought him four little ones with my allowance. He tosses them in the air and tries to catch them. I wish you could see him!

The Hallowe'en party was swell. There were just as many grown-ups there as children and they all dressed up too. Noni and Aunt Jean were twin babies— they wore bonnets and tablecloths as diapers! Some-one played a fiddle and everyone danced. I fell asleep on the pile of coats and Uncle Rand carried me all the way home—I don't even remember!

Noni and I are painting pictures of fall leaves. She lets me use her watercolour paints. My leaves don't look as real as Noni's, but she likes them.

Noni is also teaching me how to play the piano. I can do "Twinkle Twinkle" with one hand.

There's a really mean girl at my school called Alice Mackenzie. She sassed Miss Hunter so much that Miss Hunter told Alice's mother. Hana told us that Alice's mother whipped her! Now Alice is horrible to everyone. She pulls Biddy's hair and she pinches me whenever she can.

If you were here, Daddy, you could tell me what to do about Alice.

Love from Polly

———

Alice's campaign against Miss Hunter was too awful to write about. She put tacks on Miss Hunter's chair or worms in her tea. She asked her sweetly if she had heard from her beau lately, when the whole island knew that he had jilted her.

Miss Hunter's cheeks would redden and her eyes would fill with tears. She knew now what had happened when she'd told on Alice, and all she could do was try to ignore her.

The rest of the class was so shocked at Alice's behaviour that they became much quieter themselves. This infuriated Alice. "All right, everyone, at my signal rock your desks," she ordered them before Miss Hunter came in.

No one would. Alice retaliated with sharp comments or vicious pinches, but the class continued to support Miss Hunter. Polly brought her asters from Noni's garden, and the younger ones began to escape from Alice and eat their lunch in the schoolroom while Miss Hunter read to them.

———

November 15, 1932

Dear Daddy,

Tarka is behaving better on the leash now that he can't chew it. Biddy and I go for long walks with him and Bramble. We let Tarka run loose on the beach or in the meadow, but he eats barnacles and cow pies and throws up, and he rolls in otter doo and then I have to give him a bath.

Noni and Aunt Jean and I going to Victoria to see Maud's play! We're leaving Friday evening and we'll go to the school on Saturday morning. Uncle Rand won't be there because he can't miss church. I can hardly wait to see Maud! We're bringing her a cake.

Much love from your Polly Wolly Doodle

CHAPTER EIGHT

DAYS DRAWING IN

Maud had expanded. Her face was broader and her bosom and tummy pushed out her tunic. She crushed Polly in a fierce hug. Then she grinned at all of them, so welcoming that her tight braids seemed to wave like extra arms.

"All the other boarders have gone for a walk, but Miss Guppy said I could stay and wait for you. Is this a *cake?*" Maud led them to the dining room and reverently placed Mrs. Hooper's cake in her tuck box. "Now I'll show you my dorm!" she called over her shoulder, almost running ahead of them.

They followed her upstairs. Polly grimaced at the six narrow white beds, at the bare floor and the uncurtained windows. The room looked stingy.

"And this is where I keep my clothes," said Maud, pointing to a small chest of drawers.

"But Maud, you have hardly any room!" said Noni.

Aunt Jean frowned. "This floor looks as if it has splinters—can't you ask for a carpet?"

Maud laughed. "It's fine. None of us cares if it's comfortable—we just have larks! Look, here's a snap of Sadie with her horse. His name is Midnight. When I visit her after Christmas, she'll let me ride him!"

"Are you really going there after Christmas?" Polly asked.

"I hope so. Can I, Noni? Sadie's parents have invited me. They'll be here for the play, so you can meet them."

"We'll see," said Noni.

Feet thundered on the stairs and five girls burst into the dorm. "These are my roommates!" said Maud proudly.

Polly wished Maud had said *This is my family!* first. She stared suspiciously at the strangers who had taken over Maud's life.

The American girl, Ann, was the prettiest. Edith was giggly, Sylvia looked haughty, and Mary shy. Sadie smiled at Polly and said, "Hi, there, kiddo!" She had twinkly blue eyes and a large mouth. Polly couldn't smile back.

A bell clanged and Maud led them downstairs. Miss Guppy sailed out of her study and extended her hand to them. "How very nice to see you again, Polly!" she blared.

"I'm looking forward to the day when we have *you* at the school as well."

Polly stepped behind Noni, out of the Guppy's hungry gaze. She would *never* come to this place—it was like a prison! And she could never leave Tarka! She'd have to figure out a way to convince Noni not to send her. At least she had almost three years to think of something.

"We'll let you go to lunch now, Maud," said Noni. "After the play we'll take you out to dinner."

"Break a leg, chickie!" said Aunt Jean merrily.

Polly was shocked. "Why did you tell Maud to *break a leg?*" she asked when they were in the taxi.

"Oh, that's just a theatre expression—it means good luck," laughed Aunt Jean.

The three of them had lunch at the hotel, where they had arrived late the night before. The waiter was carving a delicious-smelling roast and Polly couldn't help accepting a piece.

This is a cow, she told herself sternly, but the beef was so juicy and delicious that she kept eating.

They went up to their rooms to rest before the play. Noni and Aunt Jean slept, but Polly knelt on a chair by the window. A gull hopped right onto the stone sill and cocked his head expectantly at her; she wished she had some crumbs to give him.

Polly remembered the last time she'd been in this hotel

and how she couldn't stop crying. Now tears threatened her again. If only Maud hadn't become a hearty schoolgirl, and if only Daddy could return! Maybe he could live on the island! Then Polly would have her old family together with her new family and everything would be perfect.

Noni and Aunt Jean woke up and got dressed for the play. Aunt Jean fastened the back buttons on Polly's best dress and brushed out her tangled hair.

"Maud's roommates seem like nice girls," she said. "Did you like them?"

Polly shrugged. "I guess so."

"You know, hen, friends are everything to girls Maud's age," said Noni. "They get so involved with one another that their families don't seem to exist. Una was like that with Blanche Tuttle. When Maud comes home for Christmas, she'll pay more attention to us—I'm sure of it."

Polly remembered Maud's hug. "She seemed glad to see us, didn't she?"

"Yes, she did. I'm sure she misses us—especially you— more than she realizes. And tonight we get her all to ourselves for dinner! She's so nice and plump I bet she'll taste good!" Noni added, making Polly laugh.

A string quartet was playing in the lobby and people were having tea, but Noni led them across the street to the Crystal Gardens—a large building with a glass roof enclosing a swimming pool. They had tea in the arboretum, breathing in the humid air while they watched the swimmers below them.

"The next time we come to Victoria we'll bring our bathing costumes," said Aunt Jean. "You would love the pool, Polly—the water is much warmer than the sea."

Gregor must have told her how Polly was afraid of swimming. "Thank you," she whispered. She couldn't tell Aunt Jean that it wasn't the sea's coldness she feared, but the scary depths underneath the surface.

The play was *A Midsummer Night's Dream* by William Shakespeare. Maud had warned Polly that she might not understand the words, but Noni had already read aloud some of the play to Polly and she enjoyed its lilting lines.

Polly almost forgot that all the male parts were acted by girls. Maud, a chubby Peaseblossom, made the most of her small role, leading the other fairies around bossily and scratching Bottom's head in an exaggerated manner. Polly sat on the edge of her seat, enthralled by the love stories and laughing so hard she almost choked. She clapped and clapped at the end, her eyes riveted proudly on Maud as the cast bowed.

The family pounced on Maud when she emerged from the dressing room. "You were excellent, hen!" said Noni. "I didn't know we had an actor in the family!"

Polly flinched, remembering Daddy's funny imitations of Buster Keaton and Boris Karloff.

Sadie came up and introduced her parents, Mr. and Mrs. Harvey. "We're hoping Maud can join us for a week after Christmas," Mrs. Harvey told Noni. "The girls are such good friends, and Sadie is longing to show Maud everything."

"We'll see," said Noni again. "I'll think about it and write to you."

Mrs. Harvey looked as disappointed as Maud, but she smiled and said that she'd wait for Noni's letter.

They drove to a fancy restaurant nearby. Almost every table was filled with boarders and their families; Maud and her roommates kept turning around and waving to one another.

"Chickie, they must hardly feed you at school!" teased Aunt Jean, after Maud had eaten two desserts and finished Polly's.

"They do, but it's not nearly as good as this," said Maud. "The worst meal is liver and onions, and we have it every Tuesday! The best is the roast we get on Sundays."

Maud chattered unceasingly about the play, about every mistake and every triumph. Finally she turned to Polly and asked, "How's your puppy?"

Polly talked quickly, so Maud couldn't interrupt with something else about school. "He's a *wonderful* dog!" she said proudly. "He can sit and lie down on command and he never has accidents in the house any more."

"He's no angel, though," said Noni dryly. Yesterday he had chewed one of her best shoes.

Polly and Maud went to the ladies' room. "If only Daddy could have seen you in the play!" Polly said as they were washing their hands. "He would have been so proud!"

"You're not supposed to be thinking about Daddy, Poll!"

Polly bent over the sink. What if Maud knew that she wrote letters to him? "In a month you can finally meet Tarka," she said, to change the subject.

A month was a very long time, Polly thought as they drove Maud back to school and kissed her goodbye. But after that she'd have Maud to herself for all of the holidays— unless Noni let her go to visit Sadie.

———

The weather became colder and darker. Polly kept expecting it to snow, but it only got wetter. Even when she wore her gumboots and raincoat to school, she would often arrive home soaked and bone cold—far colder than in Winnipeg, where the temperature had been lower but the air much dryer. It was so misty that she couldn't see the other islands, and at night the fog bell clanged through her dreams.

"The days are drawing in," said Aunt Jean one evening. "Christmas will be upon us before we realize it!"

"I want to talk to you and Rand about that," said Noni. "Today I received a rather unsettling letter. Lydia Tuttle wants to come for part of the holidays."

Aunt Jean put down her cards. "I *told* you you shouldn't have asked her!"

Polly was sitting in a chair, working on her knitting. The Turtle! She'd thought she would never see her again!

"I had to be polite, Jean. And we can't refuse her request, not after how kind she was, bringing the girls on the train."

Aunt Jean sighed. "How long is she staying?"

"She wants to come for a week, starting on December twentieth."

"A week!" said Aunt Jean. "That's much too long. And why would she want to come at all? She's never liked the island."

"She says she wants to see the girls again. And her daughter and her son-in-law will be away for Christmas—I suppose she has nowhere else to go."

"But she's such a busybody and she never stops talking!" said Aunt Jean. "This is the girls' first Christmas with us—it's not a good time to visit. Does she know?"

Polly held her breath. Does she know *what?* Sometimes,

if she sat very still in her chair, the grown-ups talked as if she weren't there. She kept her head down.

"Of course she knows," said Noni in a low voice. "I knew she'd find out in Winnipeg, so I told her before she went. Don't worry, she won't breathe a word about it."

Uncle Rand patted his wife's arm. "Now, my dear, we'll just have to make Lydia feel welcome. We wouldn't want her to be alone at Christmas."

"She's a lazy old cow," said Aunt Jean.

Polly tried to smother her gasp.

"Jean, remember the bairn!" said Noni. "Polly, it's getting late. Take Tarka out to do his business and then go up to bed."

———

December 15, 1932

Dear Daddy,

I'm getting so excited about Christmas! We spend every afternoon at school rehearsing for the carol concert. A woman called Mrs. Waddington is leading us. She used to be a singer and she told Alice that she has a beautiful voice. Alice is going to sing the solo part of "O Holy Night." She's so busy practising that she leaves us alone.

We're also rehearsing the Nativity play at church. Aunt Jean and Mrs. Cunningham are directing us. Biddy and I are shepherds and Tarka and Bramble are going to be sheepdogs! We've promised to keep them on their leashes.

I helped Mrs. Hooper make Christmas cake and cookies and I helped Aunt Jean decorate the church with boughs and I helped Noni cut holly for the house. Gregor is home for the holidays. I stayed at the rectory with him and Uncle Rand while Noni and Aunt Jean went to Victoria for three whole days. We had a lot of fun—they never made me go to bed and we played checkers every night! Noni and Aunt Jean came back with lots of boxes. I wonder what is in them?

Gregor's best friend, Alec Cunningham, is home too. He's a friendly boy, and very handsome. Gregor is going to be Herod in the play and Alec is going to be Joseph. A girl from the island called Cynthia is going to be Mary. She goes to university in Montreal with Alec.

Aunt Jean thinks that Alec is carrying a torch for Cynthia! Gregor says they are just friends. He and Alec and Cynthia are always in the rectory living room playing jazz records or strumming on their ukuleles. They let Biddy and me listen. We think that Gregor and Alec both like Cynthia!

I've made all my presents. Aunt Jean taught me how to knit! I can only do the garter stitch so far, but

I knit bookmarks for Biddy and Gregor and I made
a striped scarf for Maud. It's in the school colours of
maroon and mustard. I think those colours are really
ugly, but she'll like it. I painted pictures for the grown-
ups—one of Noni's house and one of the church.

Daddy, I've made a present for you too! I'll give
it to you when I see you again. That won't be long, I
hope! Daddy, please come back to me before I'm grown
up—I can't wait that long!

Much love,
Polly

———

Polly jumped up and down to keep warm as she watched the
steamer carrying Maud come around the point.

"You're going to be the Angel Gabriel in the Nativity
play!" she told her, hugging Maud so hard that Maud begged
for mercy.

"Gabriel?"

"Yes! Aunt Jean says you're such a good actress that you
won't have any trouble learning your lines. We're having a
rehearsal in half an hour!"

Maud was going to be a splendid Gabriel, Aunt Jean
said, after Maud had run out from the side of the church and
shouted "Fear not!" to the shepherds.

Polly sat beside Maud at the manger as all the little

angels came shyly up the aisle. "Walk faster and speak louder!" begged Aunt Jean as they whispered "Glory to God in the highest."

"I'm so glad you're home," Polly told Maud. "Isn't Tarka nice?" Tarka was licking Maud's face.

"He's very nice. And I'm glad to be home too," said Maud.

Polly grinned. Now everyone she loved—except Daddy, of course—was on the island. Noni had given Maud permission to visit Sadie, but that wasn't until the day after Boxing Day. Until then, Polly had her all to herself. It was going to be an almost perfect Christmas.

But Polly had forgotten about Mrs. Tuttle.

———

The Turtle arrived three days later. "Now, I don't want to be a bother," she told them, after she and her large suitcase were shown to the spare room off the living room. "You just carry on with your Christmas preparations as if I wasn't here."

But she *was* a bother. Her constant appetite meant that someone was always having to bring her cups of tea and cookies. She wanted to see several old friends on the island, so one of the adults had to interrupt what he or she was doing to drive her somewhere. Whenever she was alone with Maud and Polly she was nosier than ever, as if they were still on the train.

"Why, Maud, look how fat you've become!" the Turtle said. "You'd better be careful—you don't want to look like me! And Polly is still much too thin. The two of you are like Jack Sprat and his wife!" She chuckled at her own joke.

Maud flounced out of the living room. Polly couldn't think of an excuse to leave. She had to spend the next hour nodding politely while Mrs. Tuttle gave her an endless description of how she was redecorating her house in Vancouver.

"She's like a tap someone has forgotten to turn off!" said Aunt Jean when they were walking to a rehearsal. "I don't envy you girls, having her in the house all the time. At least I can escape."

"Noni, do you think I'm too fat?" asked Maud, when she and Polly were in Noni's bedroom one morning. "The Tur—I mean, Mrs. Tuttle said I was."

"Of course not, hen! You're just pleasingly plump. You'll fine down when you're older. Mrs. Tuttle shouldn't have told you that." She sighed. "Our guest is rather wearing, isn't she? But never mind, at least she has a lot of naps, and she's leaving on Boxing Day. Thank you for putting up with her, girls. I'm proud of you both for being so polite."

On the last day of school, all the island families gathered in the community hall to hear the concert. Polly stood beside

Biddy and watched Mrs. Waddington carefully as they struggled through each carol. They were mostly familiar ones like "Silent Night" and "The First Noel," but some had complicated parts that no one quite managed to get note perfect; Polly was thankful that she was a soprano and had the familiar tunes to sing.

After "Away in a Manger," Polly's favourite, Alice went to the front for her solo. Her crystal voice climbed higher and higher, as if it were rising through the ceiling and becoming part of the starry night. Polly watched Alice's mother. She looked astonished, as if she hadn't known that her daughter was capable of such a feat.

The rest of the choir sang the chorus. "O night divine!" they rang out in perfect unison. Mrs. Waddington looked proud.

After the concert they had hot cider and cake. "That child has a remarkable voice," said Mrs. Tuttle as they walked home. "She should be properly trained."

The Turtle was not so positive about the Nativity play on Christmas Eve. "I hope you don't mind me saying this, but it was more like a rowdy pub scene than the story of our Lord's birth!" she said afterwards.

She was referring to the part when one of Gabriel's wings fell off, and then Tarka wriggled out of his collar, grabbed the wing, and tore down the aisle with it. Noni finally caught him, and he spent the rest of the play on her knee. Aunt Jean tried to restore order, but giggles kept erupting from the cast and audience and it was difficult to get back to the mood of the story.

Aunt Jean had knit Polly and Maud Christmas red-and-white striped stockings to hang under the mantel. They had never had specially made stockings before; they'd always just used Daddy's socks. After the play they hung up the stockings.

"Now off to bed, you two!" Noni smiled. "Santa won't come until you're sound asleep."

"How will he know we live here now?" asked Polly.

Aunt Jean smiled. "Santa is magic, chickie—he always knows where to find you."

Maud fell asleep at once, but Polly lay in bed and listened to Noni playing carols on the piano while the others sang softly.

She couldn't help remembering last Christmas with Daddy. There hadn't been much money for presents, but Santa had managed to fill their socks with an orange, toffee and popcorn, red ribbons for Maud's hair, and a blue one for Polly's.

Where *was* Daddy? Was he somewhere warm and dry? Was he lonely and was he thinking of them? *Please take good care of him, God,* she prayed. Then she wept into her pillow until sleep overtook her.

———

The next thing she knew, Maud was whistling her awake. She bounced on the bed, dangling Polly's stuffed stocking. "Merry Christmas, Doodle!"

Polly sat up. Santa had come as usual, the sun was sparkling on the sea, and a delicious smell of bacon wafted up from the kitchen. She tore into her stocking, then admired Maud's loot. They each had a pile of candy, nuts, handkerchiefs, pencils, and hair ornaments. Maud was thrilled with a pair of real silk stockings; Polly got a tin harmonica and a rubber dog bone for Tarka. Her heart tingled with the Christmas glow that came every year . . . even this one.

Noni was in the kitchen cooking bacon. Polly decided that, even though bacon came from pigs, she could have two pieces because it was Christmas. Aunt Jean, Uncle Rand, and Gregor appeared at the back door bellowing, "We Wish You a Merry Christmas!" They all had to wait until the Turtle finally got up and ate her breakfast. Then they had the tree.

Polly got more presents than she had ever had in her life: books and paints, a board game called Parcheesi, new knit clothes for Elizabeth, sheepskin slippers, and a rabbit fur muff. Aunt Jean had altered Gregor's kilt for her. Polly wore it and the muff to church and showed them to Biddy on the porch.

"I got a Mickey Mouse doll," said Biddy, "but Mum wouldn't let me bring it."

Biddy's family sat behind Polly's. Biddy kept poking Polly until Noni frowned at them. The church smelled piney. As usual it was freezing, but Polly kept her hands in her muff and snuggled into the side of Noni's fur coat. "'All is calm, all is bright,'" she sang when they stood for the last carol. When they emerged from the church, the words were true: the smooth sea glistened and the orange bark of the arbutus trees looked as if it were on fire.

They had Christmas dinner at noon: a long feast of roast goose, mashed potatoes, turnips, Brussels sprouts, plum pudding, and shortbread. Everyone wore a paper hat from his or her cracker. Everyone helped do the dishes, except the Turtle, who went to her room for a nap.

After the meal, Polly and Tarka went over to Biddy's and looked at her Mickey Mouse doll and the rest of her presents; then Biddy and Luke and Bramble walked back to examine Polly's. She was embarrassed that she and Maud had received so many more. They played Parcheesi until Biddy and Luke went home for supper.

Polly had thought after dinner that she could never eat another thing, but she managed to sip some of the clam chowder that Aunt Jean brought over. Then they sat in the living room, lit the candles on the tree again, and played games: Charades and Twenty Questions and Consequences. Alec and Cynthia arrived, and they and Gregor went out to visit some friends.

Polly fell asleep while Uncle Rand was reading aloud from *A Christmas Carol*. She woke up when she felt herself being carried up the stairs. Her heart leapt: Daddy? Then she realized it was Uncle Rand who was carrying her. She kept her eyes closed so she could at least *pretend* it was Daddy.

CHAPTER NINE

THE TURTLE TELLS

On Boxing Day, Aunt Jean and Uncle Rand arrived for lunch with a pheasant pot pie. It was so delicious Polly decided that, except for venison, she couldn't be a vegetarian yet. Anyway, if she didn't eat meat, what *would* she eat? She didn't like vegetables, and it probably wasn't healthy to just eat potatoes and dessert. She would be a vegetarian when she was a grown-up.

After lunch they sprawled in the living room, Polly and Maud and Noni with new books and Uncle Rand with the newspaper. Aunt Jean sat at the card table laying out a game of Patience, and Mrs. Tuttle snored in a chair. Outside, the wind made the waves crash onto the shore. But inside, the fire rustled peacefully.

Polly knelt on the window seat. She put down her book

and drew pictures on the steamy panes with her finger. Tarka was a tight ball in his basket by the fire.

Snort! The Turtle woke herself up. She yawned noisily, then looked around the room as if she were counting everyone.

"Where's Gregor?" she asked.

"Off with his friends," said Aunt Jean.

"He's probably gone to see that Cynthia. Are we going to hear wedding bells soon, Jean?"

"If we are, it will be for Cynthia and Alec, not Cynthia and Gregor," said Jean calmly.

"*Really!* Well, that will be nice for the Cunninghams. Cynthia Scott comes from a very good family—I knew her grandmother. Don't worry, Jean, I'm sure Gregor will find himself a nice girl one day. Is he in a good crowd at varsity?"

"I'm not worried at *all*, Lydia," said Aunt Jean, "and I have no idea about whom Gregor knows. I believe in mothers minding their own business," she added pointedly.

This was so untrue that Polly and Maud exchanged a smile. Aunt Jean was constantly grilling Gregor on who his friends were.

"How are your books, girls?" asked Noni. "Mine is very interesting."

The Turtle was not to be deterred from her subject. "It's a risky time for young people, choosing whom they'll marry. We were so lucky that Blanche found Walker. He's such a decent man, and so hard-working. He's going to be vice president of his company, did I tell you that? Best of all, he's *honest*. You must have been horrified, Clara, when Daniel turned out to be a thief."

"*Lydia!*" Noni's voice rang out like a shot.

"Oh!" The Turtle covered up her mouth. "I'm so sorry! I forgot that Polly doesn't know!"

Noni stood up. Her voice was like steel. "Maud and Polly, come with me."

A *thief!* The word zoomed around Polly's head like an angry wasp.

"My dear girls, I'm so very sorry that Lydia brought this up," said Noni. Her voice shook.

"Is it true?" croaked Polly.

Noni put her arm around Polly's shoulder. "Yes, hen, I'm afraid it's true."

Polly shook off Noni's arm. "Did *you* know this?" she asked Maud.

Maud nodded, her face white. "I'm sorry, Polly. I wanted to tell you, but they all said *not* to!"

"It was for the best, Polly," said Noni. "You were too young—you still are. We knew you would find out one day how wrong Daniel was, but we wanted you to have an unclouded picture of your father while you were still a wee bairn."

Polly started to cry. "Daddy *isn't* wrong! He's good! He would *never* steal anything!"

Maud fixed her eyes on Polly. "What a silly, talking about Daddy as if he were still alive! Sometimes she forgets," she said to Noni.

"Of course she does, poor wean," said Noni. "Polly, I understand that you want to defend your father. Maud has told me also that she believes in his innocence. I admire your loyalty, but you both have to face the fact that your father *was* a thief. He was desperate, I suppose, but that doesn't excuse the fact that he stole. Do you want me to tell you more about it?"

Polly sat on the edge of the bed. She didn't want to hear, but she had no choice.

"Your father stole a large sum of money from a safe in the office of his last job," said Noni, spitting out the words. "They found the money in Daniel's pocket. They locked him up, but he escaped and . . . well, you know the rest. He drowned himself in the river."

Once Polly had been outside in a storm of hailstones so large that they'd battered her head. Noni's stinging words felt exactly like that. Her sobs increased and Noni took her in her lap, holding her tight and stroking her hair.

"Daddy didn't do it!" sobbed Polly. "He couldn't have!"

"But he did, hen," said Noni. "Whisht, now. It's a shame you know this about your father, but he's gone. Try to remember all the good things about him, not this."

Maud stood up. "Noni, I'm going to take Polly to our room."

Noni looked exhausted. "That's a good idea, Maud. The two of you probably want to talk by yourselves, and I need to lie down. Thank goodness that woman is leaving on the afternoon boat. I don't want to see her again."

Polly ran over to the wash basin and threw up her lunch. Maud wiped her face and led her to her bed.

"Oh, Maud, why didn't you *tell* me?" wailed Polly. "It can't be true!"

"I wanted to, Doodle. I wanted to tell you so much, but Daddy said not to. I'll tell you now, though."

They squatted on each end of Polly's bed. She reached back and clutched the bed rail, afraid of the intensity in Maud's eyes.

"First of all," said Maud fiercely, "Daddy *didn't* do it."

Relief flooded Polly. "I knew it! But how do *you* know?"

"Because Daddy told me in the letter he sent. But he said not to tell *you* until you were older. And all the adults— the social worker and the police—also made me keep it from you. I had to hide the newspapers in case you saw them."

"Why did they *think* he stole the money?"

"It was just like Noni said. Mr. Rayburn, the boss, noticed the money was missing from the safe. They accused Daddy because he'd been alone in the building during the lunch hour, reading—all the other workers were sitting outside in the sun. They searched him and found the money in his coat pocket."

"What happened next?" Polly's heart thumped. This was like hearing about someone in story or a movie, not her own father!

"They locked Daddy in a basement room and phoned the police. But the police were busy with a bank robbery, so they said to hold Daddy there until the end of the day. Daddy found some paper and a pencil in the room. He wrote a note saying he was going to take his own life and left the note on a table. Then he climbed onto a cabinet and got out through a window. He ran to the river, got into an old boat, and drifted away."

"Then what?" breathed Polly.

"You *know* the rest, Doodle," said Maud wearily. "When Daddy was far enough away, he abandoned the boat and slept in a barn. The next day he walked to the nearest town and ate at a soup kitchen. They gave him some paper and a stamp and envelope and he wrote me the letter explaining everything. Then he hopped on a train and went east."

"Maud, where *is* Daddy?" whispered Polly.

"I don't know, Doodle. All he said was that he was going to Ontario to look for work."

Polly shivered. "But if he was accused of stealing, won't he be caught? Maybe he'll be sent to jail!"

"He won't be caught. Remember, everyone thinks he drowned. And he said he was going to change his name."

"Maud, I'm so confused! Why was the stolen money in Daddy's pocket?"

"Daddy thinks Mr. Spicer put it there. He was the guy in charge of the payroll, so he had access to the safe. Mr. Spicer had a grudge against him because one day Daddy imitated his lisp to the other men."

"How do you know?"

"Because that's what Daddy said in his letter."

Polly glared at her. "Maud, are you *sure* you don't have that letter any more?"

"Polly, I told you! I burned it, just like Daddy asked me to!"

"So you don't know where Daddy is? Are you still keeping secrets from me?"

"I honestly don't know where he is. I promise that you know the whole truth now—cross my heart and hope to die."

"But why can't Daddy write to us?"

"Of course he can't write—he's supposed to be dead! That's why we have to forget about him and carry on as if he *is* dead. You almost gave it away to Noni just now, Poll—you have to be more careful! Just remember that we *will* see him again, when we're grown up. That's what he said."

Polly crawled under the covers. "Grown up!" she wailed. "That's forever! I want to see Daddy *now!* Oh, Maud, I miss him so much!"

"I need to go outside," Maud muttered. "I'll take Tarka for a walk on the beach. Will you be all right for a little while?"

All right? How could she *ever* be all right? But Polly nodded. She knew that Maud needed to be alone so she could cry. After Maud had left, she pulled the covers over her head and let herself remember.

———

The night before her life changed forever, Polly had wakened and heard someone downstairs. She'd crept down to find Daddy in the dim living room, the spark of his cigarette end glowing.

"What are you doing?" she asked sleepily, crawling into his lap.

Daddy was holding a framed photograph of Polly's mother. He put it down and butted his cigarette. "Just thinking, Doodle. You should be asleep."

"Thinking about what?" Polly asked, but she already knew what he was worried about. His boss had just told him there was no more work for him; tomorrow would be his last day.

"Things that are too complicated for little girls to know about," he answered.

Polly shivered at how sad and shaky his voice sounded— as if he were trying not to cry. Daddy was *never* sad! He was always cheerful, no matter how many jobs he lost.

"Don't worry about losing your job, Daddy," she said.

"We can go on the dole again, and you'll find other work—you always do."

"Yes, but it never amounts to anything, does it? Oh, Doodle, I'm so ashamed of how we live! You girls deserve the best, not terrible food, and handouts from the government. I'm going to have to use all of my last pay for the rent. And now Maud isn't going back to school. What a waste for such a smart kid! I'm a bad father to you girls—that's all there is to it."

Polly couldn't bear this. "You're *not* a bad father!" she cried. "You're the best father anyone could ever have! It's not your fault you can't get work. Lots of my friends' fathers can't either. It's all the fault of the e—emon*omy*, right?"

She had pronounced the word wrong on purpose. To her relief, Daddy chuckled as he said, "The econ*omy*, Doodle. Canada is having a depression, just like the rest of the world. You're right that it's not my fault, but it's still bloody frustrating when a man who's willing to do damn near anything for a buck can't take care of his girls!"

Daddy *never* swore! He had to be really upset. Polly couldn't think of any words to comfort him. She pressed against his warm chest, breathing in the leathery smell of the carbolic soap he scrubbed himself with every evening. Daddy hated getting dirty. Before the depression he had worked as a clerk in an insurance firm, but now he could only find manual labour jobs that left his skin embedded with grime.

They sat without moving, while the little house creaked around them. Finally Daddy sighed, kissed Polly's forehead, and made her go back to bed. Polly couldn't sleep until she heard him come upstairs.

———

The next morning, however, Daddy was his normal self, singing "Pack Up Your Troubles" as usual when he woke them up. As Polly got dressed, she could hear Daddy in the kitchen, making Maud laugh with his gangster imitation while he braided her hair. "Get a wiggle on, Doodle," he called up the stairs. Polly banished the night's sad conversation from her mind.

As usual on the days when Daddy had work, Maud walked Polly to her best friend Audrey's house. Then she continued to the babysitting job she'd had all summer.

When Maud picked her up at the end of the day, Polly waved goodbye to Audrey, not knowing that this would be the last time she would ever see her.

"We sort of got into trouble," said Polly on the way home.

Maud sighed. "Oh, Doodle . . . what did you do?"

Polly giggled. "It's so hot that we took an egg out of the icebox and tried to fry it on the sidewalk! It didn't work, though—it just made a mess. And Mrs. Makowitz was really mad at us because we wasted an egg."

"So she should have been! Poll, you have to be good when you go there or she won't look after you! I'll give you some money to pay for the egg."

Polly wished she hadn't told her. Maud used to be a lot more fun, but in the past year she had become as serious as a grown-up. "Race you down the block!" Polly shouted, but Maud lagged behind, wiping perspiration from her face.

They arrived at the shabby brown house they had lived in all their lives. It was only rented, but Polly always pretended it was really theirs. Grannie had died almost two years ago, but Polly still expected to see her thatch of white hair in the window, as she sat bent over her sewing.

Maud let them in with her key and began cooking oxtail soup for supper. Polly helped her peel potatoes and cut up cabbage and carrots, frowning at the vegetables they ate almost every day.

"Only two more weeks of summer left," said Maud sadly. "Then I'll have to start work. Oh, Polly, I wish I didn't have to leave school!"

"Daddy doesn't *want* you to leave!"

"I know he doesn't, but I have to. Mrs. Colledge has offered me a good job as a maid—I'd be crazy to turn it down. It will be much steadier work than anything Daddy can get."

"Maybe *Daddy* will get a good job one day and you can go back to school again," said Polly.

"Maybe. But I'd be so far behind."

The soup was done. It simmered on the stove while they waited for Daddy, making the small room much too hot. Maud started mending Polly's torn blouse. Polly got out her crayons and drew pictures of puppies.

"If I ever have a dog, his name will be Bingo," she said.

"You'll never have a dog, so there's no point in wishing for one, Poll," said Maud. "We barely have enough to eat for the three of us."

"*Maybe* I will," said Polly stubbornly. "When I'm grown up. I'll have lots! A lab and a spaniel and a poodle and a terrier . . ."

Maud ignored her. She put down her sewing. "Where's Daddy? He's so late!"

Polly looked out the window, but she couldn't spot him. Usually Daddy opened the door with his special whistle, two long high notes and a short one. Then he would call, "Where's the Boss? Where's my Polly-Wolly-Doodle?"

"Here we are!" Polly would cry, running to him. She'd crawl up his legs and he'd flip her backwards. Then he'd hold on to her hands and whirl her in a dizzying circle. He'd hug Maud and then they'd have supper, each girl competing to tell Daddy about her day.

An hour later Daddy still hadn't come home. Maud had let the stove go out, but now she lit it again, reheated the soup, and handed a bowlful to Polly with a piece of bread.

Polly couldn't eat. "Where *is* he? Oh, Maud, what if he's been hit by a car, like our mother was?"

Maud drew in her breath sharply. Then she said firmly, "Don't say things like that, Doodle! Nothing's happened to Daddy—he's just late. Maybe he met some friends or went looking for work." She tried to smile, and Polly tried to smile back. Then there was a knock at the door.

Two people stood there: a policeman and an anxious-looking woman in a shapeless brown coat and hat. They made the girls sit down on the sofa beside them.

"We have tragic news for you," the woman said, putting her arm around Polly. "You're going to have to be very brave. I'm sorry to have to tell you that your father has drowned."

Polly felt drowned herself as the impossible words drenched her. But Maud stood up and became her most "Maudish"—dignified, fierce, and cold.

"How do you know?" she asked them.

"Keep calm, little lady," said the policeman.

"Sit down, dear," said the woman, but Maud remained standing.

"Your father left a note on a branch by the river," said the policeman, speaking gently. "It said he was so discouraged about losing another job and not being able to support you that he decided—well, he decided to drown himself. I'm sorry, girls. I know this is hard to take in, but it's a fact."

"Show me the note," demanded Maud.

"I'm afraid I can't do that," said the policeman.

Polly was vaguely aware that the woman's arm was still across her shoulders, but she couldn't feel it. She couldn't move or speak or she would disappear. She waited for Maud to save her.

"This doesn't make sense," said Maud slowly. "If my father drowned himself—and I don't believe for one minute that he did—how would you have found out? What were you doing by the river?"

The policeman looked uncomfortable. But adults were often unsettled by Maud. "Well, little lady, that's a good question," he said slowly. "I can see you're a smart one, but I'll try to explain. Your dad's boss, Mr. Rayburn, phoned us about five. He said that even though he'd told him yesterday that he'd be let go, your father didn't take it well at all. He yelled that he had two daughters, and how could Mr. Rayburn do this to him? Then he stormed out of the room. Mr. Rayburn is a good fellow. He was real concerned that your dad might do harm to himself. Believe me, we see plenty of sad souls like him these days. Something breaks in them and they just can't take it any more. So Mr. Rayburn phoned us and we came over with one of our dogs to see if we could track your daddy—just in case, you see. The dog followed his trail to the river, and that's where we found the note."

"You're lying," said Maud. "My father would *never* drown himself."

Her strong words revived Polly. She shrugged off the woman's arm. Maud was right, of course. Daddy would never leave them alone in the world.

"Now, girls, I know it's impossible to believe, but I'm afraid it's true," said the policeman. "This is Miss Reilly. She's a social worker and she's going to stay in the house with you tonight. Tomorrow you'll go to a foster home until we can get hold of your grandmother."

"Our *grandmother*?" asked Maud. "She's dead!"

"I'm talking about your mother's mother—Mrs. Whitfield, isn't it? Your father said in his note that he wanted you to live with her."

Now Maud couldn't speak either. The policeman left, after telling them again how sorry he was.

Miss Reilly put Polly to bed. Polly let her undress her and wash her. Miss Reilly kissed her good-night and Polly lay on her back staring into the darkness. She clutched her doll and turned over to go to sleep.

It was all a huge mistake. She would wake up in the morning and Daddy would be there as usual, poking his head in the door and singing "Pack Up Your Troubles."

Then Maud was in bed beside her. She pulled Polly close and whispered, "He can't be dead, Doodle. I just can't believe he'd take his own life. We'll just wait. Daddy will get in touch with us—I'm sure." Her words sounded more confident than her shaking voice.

"But where *is* he?" mumbled Polly.

"I don't know, but I'm sure we'll find out soon. Go to sleep now."

Polly slept late. She ran downstairs and found Maud standing by the window, so deep in thought that she didn't even respond when Polly took her hand.

Miss Reilly was cooking bacon and eggs—she must have brought them with her. Polly was relieved to see a blanket and pillow on the sofa. At least Miss Reilly hadn't slept in Daddy's room.

Maud gobbled up her breakfast, but Polly could only manage to eat a bit of egg. Miss Reilly tried to talk to them, but Maud answered in curt sentences and Polly just stared.

After breakfast Miss Reilly helped them pack all their clothes and books and toys. Then she drove them to a house on the other side of the city to stay with a couple called Mr. and Mrs. Marchant. Luckily they hardly spoke to them.

Polly and Maud stayed in their room as much as possible. Sometimes they read, but mostly they dozed on their beds without speaking. Whenever Polly tried to bring up Daddy, Maud would shush her. "All we can do is wait," she said firmly. "Maybe Daddy will write to us."

"But how will we get the letter?"

"I'll figure that out, Doodle. Stop worrying about it."

Polly moved through the day as if the air were molasses and her brain were mush. Whenever she tried to think, she could only remember how sad Daddy had sounded that night. Had he been sad enough to drown himself? *No!*

The next morning at breakfast Maud told the Marchants she was going to visit a friend and would be back for lunch. A few hours later she came into the room and closed the door. "Poll, Daddy is *alive!* He sent a letter!"

Polly gasped. "Let me see it! Where did you get it?"

"I went to our house on the streetcar and climbed in that back window that doesn't lock. Daddy's letter was on the hall carpet! I can't show it to you because I burned it in the stove. He asked me to do that the moment I'd read it. But listen carefully, and I'll tell you everything he said."

Maud took a deep breath. "Daddy's gone away, Doodle." Polly gasped again, but Maud shushed her and continued. "He's gone to Ontario to try to get a job. He wants us to live with Grandmother on Kingfisher Island. She can afford to look after us. Daddy said he's wanted to send us there for a long time, but he promised our mother he never would. So he's *pretended* he's drowned! That way he won't be breaking his promise, because now we have nowhere else to go. He left a note and got into a rickety boat on the riverbank. After he'd drifted for a while, he rowed to the other shore and went to a town and then he wrote me."

"*Gone?* Daddy's gone? But why didn't he say goodbye? Why couldn't we go with him? I don't understand!"

Maud pulled the counterpane up over both of them and held Polly tight. "I don't either. But it's what Daddy wants. He says we'll see him one day, after we're grown up and educated."

Polly began to cry. Daddy loved them! He would never

just leave them and not want to see them until they were grown up!

Then she remembered how Daddy had been staring at their mother's photograph when she came downstairs. He must have already made his plan that night. That meant that he *knew*, when he kissed Polly good-night, and when he kissed her goodbye the next morning, that he was leaving them. He knew he was leaving, yet he didn't say anything! Polly tried desperately to remember his last hug. She hadn't been paying attention—she'd been trying to tie her broken shoelace.

Polly's insides felt raw. She clutched Maud and sobbed until her eyes burned. Maud held her, but she didn't cry; she looked as if she were thinking hard.

That night, after they were supposed to be asleep, Maud made Polly solemnly promise never to tell anyone that Daddy was still alive. They sealed their pact with blood from their fingers, which Maud pricked with a needle. Polly didn't even feel it. The pain in her finger was nothing compared with the pain in her heart.

_____

The rest of those two weeks was a terrible time of adults hovering over them and making whispered plans. Grandmother telephoned, but she only talked to Maud.

"She's very glad to have us come and live with her," said Maud. "Her friend Mrs. Tuttle is going to take us west on the train, but we have to wait until she's finished her visit here. And guess what, Doodle. I'm going to a boarding school in Victoria! It's called St. Winifred's. They've agreed to accept me without writing the entrance exam, and Grandmother's asked them to send me their brochure."

Polly couldn't bear how much more cheerful Maud was after that. The brochure arrived and she spent every minute poring over it.

The social worker came to visit and told them that Daddy's jacket had been found washed up a few miles downstream. Even though his body had not shown up, there would be a memorial service for him before the girls left Winnipeg. They had to wear the cheap black dresses Mrs. Marchant made. After the service, Polly stood stiffly beside Maud. Mrs. Tuttle came up and introduced herself. Daddy's friends told them how sorry they were. All the adults looked sad, but they also looked embarrassed. That was because they thought Daddy was a thief, Polly realized now.

"Poll?" Maud was sitting on her bed and Tarka was licking her face. "Are you awake? It's almost six o'clock."

Polly sat up. She hadn't been asleep, but she'd been

so far away that for a few seconds she wondered where she was. Then all of the horrible day rushed back. "Oh, Maud . . . what's going to happen now?"

"Nothing's going to happen. We're going to carry on exactly as we have been. The same rules apply, Poll. We won't talk about Daddy, even between ourselves, and we won't think about him. He's still dead."

"But he isn't *really* dead, and he didn't steal anything," said Polly firmly.

"Right."

"Maud . . . can we talk just a *little* more? I'm still confused."

Maud sighed. "What are you confused about?"

"You said that Daddy was locked in a room and then he escaped. But the policeman told us that he got mad at his boss and left!"

"The policeman made up that stupid story to protect us—so we wouldn't know about the stealing."

"But how did *you* find out?"

"I went out early the next morning—I pretended we needed milk. I found a newspaper and read all about it. So I confronted Miss Reilly before you got up. Then they all knew I knew. I had to promise not to tell you. And then, of course, Daddy told me later."

"Did Daddy really leave a note on a tree?"

"No—he left it in the room where they locked him up.

But he knew the police dogs would track him to the river. He left a lot of footprints in the mud and threw his jacket into the water. He knew they'd *want* to believe he'd drowned."

"It's like a movie!" said Polly.

"Yes, it is. But you know Daddy, Doodle—he always did like acting."

They sat in silence, while Tarka rolled on the bed, whining because no one was rubbing his tummy.

"Come to dinner now," said Maud finally. "Noni sent me up to get you."

Polly laced up her shoes. Then her heart lifted a little. Daddy *hadn't* neglected to say a proper goodbye that morning! He hadn't known he'd be accused of stealing, so of course he hadn't known it was the last time he'd see Polly.

"Has Mrs. Tuttle gone?" asked Polly on the way downstairs.

"Yes. I hid behind the bushes and watched Aunt Jean and Uncle Rand walk her to the wharf."

None of the grown-ups would meet Polly's eyes at the dinner table. "Thank you for coping with Lydia, Jean," said Noni. She took a sip of water. "The girls and I have talked about Daniel. I had to explain to Polly what happened, of course. Now we will simply carry on. No one is to ever know what Daniel did—do you understand, girls? But of course you wouldn't want to tell anyone."

The three adults looked so ashamed—ashamed of

Daddy, her good father who would never do anything wrong! Polly wanted to shout, *He didn't do it! And he's still alive!*

But she couldn't. She had to "carry on," as Noni said. Her secret was so heavy she didn't know how she could carry it at all.

The next day Maud left for Duncan to spend the rest of the holidays with Sadie. She would go back to school from there.

"But you won't be here for your birthday!" said Polly.

"I know, Poll. I wish I could, but Sadie's having a New Year's party and she wants me to be there."

Polly sighed. "When will you come home again?"

"I'll be here for Easter in April."

"April!"

Maud looked guilty. "I'll write to you every week, Doodle. Will you promise to write back?"

Polly nodded. She was so drained from the day before that she had no energy left to argue.

PART TWO

"DEAR DADDY"

CHAPTER TEN

VALENTINES AND LAMBS

December 27, 1932

Dear Daddy,

Oh, Daddy, I know all about the stealing! There was a stupid woman here and she told us, so it's not Maud's fault. I know you didn't do it, Daddy! I'm so angry that all the grown-ups think you did. Even Noni does! They all act so ashamed of you. I want to persuade them that you are not a thief, but we're not allowed to talk about it. And I wish so much I could tell them that you're still alive. It's such a big secret to keep.

Daddy, why did you say in the letter to Maud not to tell me that you were accused of stealing the money? She says you didn't want to upset me, but I was more upset when I thought you had left us because we were poor. Now I know that you had another reason too.

Daddy, I want to be with you! I don't know how I can wait until I'm grown up to see you again. I pray every night that it will be sooner.

Your loving Doodle

January 10, 1933

Dear Daddy,

I still feel angry, but everyone in the family is acting so normally that I have to as well. I wish I could talk to Noni about how you are innocent, but I know she won't let me. If she knew you better, she would know that you would never steal anything.

We celebrated New Year's the way Noni and Aunt Jean used to in Scotland. They call it Hogmanay. I wore Gregor's old kilt that Aunt Jean made over—it's red and green and white, which is the MacGregor tartan. I was allowed to stay up until midnight, and I even had a sip of wine!

Gregor was the First Footer. That means if the first person to come through the door in the New Year is a dark-haired man, it's good luck. Gregor has dark brown hair, so he waited outside the door and came in one minute after midnight, carrying coal and shortbread

*for the house. Then we all linked arms and sang "Old
Lang Sign." (I can't spell it, but that's what it sounded
like.) Aunt Jean was crying, and I felt like it too, but I
didn't cry until I went to bed, and then I cried for you.*

*The next day I really missed Maud because it was
her birthday. We had a cake for her anyway and we
toasted her health, but it seemed so wrong that she
wasn't here. I can't believe she's sixteen!*

*Now Gregor has left and I've gone back to school.
Biddy and I are studying the local flora. That means
all the plants that grow on the island. Miss Hunter lets
us work on our own. We've made a mural that goes
all around the classroom. We're doing it with poster
paints. Biddy did a blue-and-green background and
I painted all the trees and flowers. I liked painting the
arbutus tree the best. Chester told me how realistic it
looked and I felt proud. He is the oldest pupil in the
school and he's always nice to me.*

*Yesterday Alice made Miss Hunter cry. She called
her a "stupid bitch"! I know I shouldn't say bad words
like that, but I'm just telling you what Alice said. Luke
thinks we should tell the grown-ups how awful Alice
is. But then her mother might whip her again and
she'll be even meaner to us and Miss Hunter.*

*Tarka rolled in otter doo again after school and I
had to bathe him. He hates that. I keep telling him that*

if he didn't roll in it, he wouldn't have to have a bath,
but he doesn't listen. He also stole a piece of venison pie
from the larder. Later he threw up on the living room rug.

Daddy, do you think it's right to eat animals?
Gregor shot some grouse and we had them for New
Year's dinner. They were so good, but then I saw some
running in the ditch the next day and I felt bad that
I'd eaten their relatives.

Much love,
Your Doodle

January 26, 1933
Dear Daddy,

Last night we celebrated Robbie Burns Day. A lot
of adults came for dinner. Some of them are Scotch,
like Noni and Aunt Jean. I wore my kilt and passed
things around. Mrs. Hooper made the most dis-
gusting dinner—a kind of pudding cooked inside a
sheep's stomach! It's called haggis and I didn't eat
any of it. Everyone made a big fuss over the haggis
and Captain Hay even made a toast to it. Then he
recited some of Robbie Burns's poems, but I didn't
understand them.

One of the guests was Mrs. Mackenzie, Alice's
mother. I see her in church every week, but this was
the first chance I've had to look at her close up. She's

stern-looking with slitty eyes. She asked me how I was
and I only said "Fine." Even though I don't like Alice,
I feel sorry for her having such a mean mother. I don't
know how Noni can be friends with someone who
whips children, but I'm sure she doesn't know that
Alice gets beaten. Maybe I'll tell her one day.

Daddy, do you have a job in Ontario? Do you
have friends? How I wish I could really talk to you!

Lots of love,

Polly

———

Polly and Biddy were making valentines in Biddy's room.
They had bought red paper and gold paper and doilies at the
store.

"Would you draw me another heart, Polly?" asked
Biddy. "You're so good at them."

Polly drew many hearts. She and Biddy cut and glued
industriously until they had a pile of eighteen valentines,
one from each of them for every girl in the class—except
for Alice, of course. Polly's were neat and intricate. Biddy's
were sloppy, with smears of glue in the wrong places. On the
back of each one they had written "Be My Valentine" with a
large question mark.

"Polly . . ."

"What? Why are you laughing?"

"Well . . . I'm going to make one more valentine—for a boy!"

"Who?" asked Polly, because she knew Biddy wanted her to.

"George."

"*George?*" George was so dull. He rarely spoke, and everything about him was slow, from his plodding gait to his earnest way of cleaning the blackboard.

"I've always liked him," said Biddy. "He has such long eyelashes! Draw me a really big heart, Polly. Make two—you could give a valentine to a boy too!"

"I don't want to," said Polly. She didn't like it when Biddy was silly like this.

"Why not? They'll never know who they're from."

"I just don't, that's all."

She helped Biddy decorate an especially large heart. If she *did* want to, Polly thought, she'd make a valentine for Chester. He was the kindest boy she had ever met. Last week, when Polly had been late for school on her day to sweep the classroom floor, Chester had already done it for her so she wouldn't get scolded.

After they finished the valentines, Biddy took Polly to her meadow to see the new lambs. It was so warm for February that they didn't need to wear jackets. They leaned on the fence as the tiny lambs chased each other as if they were playing tag. They had long tails like puppies.

Polly had never seen lambs before. "Oh, Biddy! Look at that one!" she kept saying as the lambs leapt straight up into the air.

As Polly walked home, she decided that she'd once again try to be a vegetarian.

Polly and Biddy sat on the grass after school and compared their valentines. Polly had got ten. She smiled when she recognized Biddy's messy heart. Biddy had received only nine. Who could Polly's tenth one be from?

It couldn't be from Alice. Like the boys, she scoffed at valentines.

"Counting your stupid valentines, Goldilocks?" she said, coming out of the school. Alice often called Polly that, since she was the only girl in the school who didn't have a bob.

As usual, Polly ignored Alice's question. If you answered, she'd say something worse. To her relief, Alice walked away.

"Did you see George's face when he saw his valentine?" giggled Biddy. "All the other boys teased him!"

Polly was still wondering about her tenth valentine. It stood out from the rest because it was bought from a store: a stiff, shiny heart with fancy lace all around it. On the back it said, "From a secret admirerer."

"Whoever sent this isn't a very good speller!" said Polly.

"I know who sent it," Biddy told her. "Chester!"

"Chester? How do you know?"

"Because that's how he makes his *s*'s! You watch, the next time he writes on the board."

"It couldn't be Chester. Why would he send *me* a valentine?"

"Because he's sweet on you, of course! Polly has a sweetheart, Polly has a sweetheart!"

"Biddy, stop! I'm only ten! I'm much too young to have a sweetheart. Let's not talk about it."

Biddy shrugged, but she kept chuckling as they gathered up their valentines and walked over to their bikes.

Polly watched Chester carefully the next day in school. He was as friendly as ever, but he didn't act embarrassed. Had he really sent it? Maybe he had! Maybe he felt so safe in his anonymity that he didn't act any differently.

After a few weeks Polly burned all her valentines in the stove—except the one that was maybe from Chester. She hid that one with her letters to Daddy.

———

March 5, 1933

Dear Daddy,

A terrible thing happened—an eagle snatched up one of Biddy's father's lambs! He saw it happen. I think that's so sad.

I'm not doing very well in arithmetic, Daddy. I used to be good at it, but I just don't understand long division. This is the first time I've ever not done well in school! One evening I started crying when I couldn't do the extra homework Miss Hunter gave me. Then Noni asked Uncle Rand to help me. Now I go to his study in the rectory every day before supper and he tutors me.

I like Uncle Rand. He told me stories about when he was in France during the Great War. He didn't have to fight, but he was a chaplain and comforted the men. I'm so glad you were too young to be in the war, Daddy. Uncle Rand says there will never be another one. I hope he is right.

Daddy, you would be amazed to be here in the winter. There's no snow! I miss it. I keep telling Biddy about tobogganing and making snowmen and snow forts and she's envious. She said there was some snow last year, but it only lasted a few days. The snowdrops and crocuses are already up. I wish you could see them.

Much love,
Polly Wolly Doodle

March 25, 1933
Dear Daddy,
There's a lot to do here in the spring! Aunt Jean and I have planted seeds for radishes, beans, peas,

and lettuce in the rectory garden. I helped Noni prune her roses. She paid Biddy and Luke and me a nickel for each starfish we collected at low tide. Noni cuts them up and digs them around the roses for fertilizer. Her roses grow so big that they win prizes at the fall fair.

Last week there was a loud thumping in the woods behind the house. I asked Noni what it was and she said it was grouse! In the spring the boy grouse thumps his wings to attract the girl grouse—isn't that strange? I hear them every day.

Aunt Jean is having a feud with Mrs. Cunningham because she said Aunt Jean cheated at Whist. Now they won't speak to each other. Noni told me they have always had feuds, even when they were both girls on the island. Biddy and I will never argue like that.

Love,

Doodle

April 4, 1933

Dear Daddy,

Noni ordered me a whole lot of spring clothes from the Eaton's catalogue because I've outgrown all my other ones. I'm getting two dresses (one blue and one yellow), several blouses, two skirts, black shoes and brown sandals, a blue tweed coat, and a straw hat with flowers to wear for Easter. I'll feel like a princess!

Maud is coming home for Easter. She's bringing her friend Sadie with her because Sadie's parents are in Vancouver looking after Sadie's sick grandfather.

I wish Sadie wasn't coming! They're going to sleep in our room and I have to sleep in the box room down the hall. Noni had to move her trunks and hat boxes up to the attic to make room for my cot. Biddy is going to visit her cousins in Comox for the holidays and I won't have anyone to play with.

Much love,
Polly

CHAPTER ELEVEN

NEW SECRETS

"And thank you for bringing our Maud and her friend Sadie home to us to share our Easter celebration," said Uncle Rand as he finished grace.

Sadie winked at Polly, and Polly winked back. Sadie was turning out to be a pleasant surprise. She joked as much as Gregor and she called Polly "Pollywog" just the way he did. Polly was enjoying showing Sadie the island. Yesterday she and Maud had taken her fishing off the wharf. They'd caught so many cod that Mrs. Hooper couldn't cook them all. They put the extra fish in a basket and took them to a poor family near the lighthouse.

Polly hadn't meant to eat any of the cod, but she'd tried a bit and it was so good that she couldn't resist it. Now she stared at the roast lamb Aunt Jean was putting on the table. She tried to think of the little lambs playing in the meadow. Before she could refuse any, a plate of lamb was passed to her. Polly nibbled at a bit of it. It was so delicious she had to eat more.

Everyone at the table was so jolly that it was hard to feel guilty. Gregor's and Sadie's voices rose in a crescendo as they teased each other. It was so obvious that they liked each other. Sadie managed to be wherever Gregor was, and he kept gazing adoringly at her. Aunt Jean seemed to have just as great a crush on Sadie as Gregor did. She had long conversations with her about her family and approved of everything Sadie said.

Sadie had already told Maud and Polly how much she liked Gregor.

"But he's so goofy!" Maud said.

"That's why I like him. He's goofy, but inside he's as principled as his father. I'm going to marry him one day."

"Marry him!" Maud looked stunned. "Sadie, how can you know that? You're only sixteen!"

"I just know," said Sadie quietly. "You wait and see. Now, who is this creature shadowing me?"

Tarka started whining. Sadie had taught him how to dance in a circle for a cookie.

After Easter dinner Polly went upstairs to change out of her new yellow dress. Maud came into the box room. "There's something I want to talk to you about, Poll," she said.

Polly shivered. Had Maud heard from Daddy? She had been unusually silent these holidays.

It wasn't Daddy. Maud sat down on the bed and announced that she had become a Christian.

"But you already are one!" said Polly.

"Now I'm really a Christian—I've been saved." Maud had a queer look in her eyes, as if she were staring at something in the air. "I've received Jesus in my heart, Doodle. It's incredible—I've never felt so certain about anything in my life!"

Maud told her how Miss Guppy had taken her and four other girls in her special group to her church in Victoria one Saturday afternoon. The minister had asked people to repent of their sins and come up and receive Jesus.

"I felt as if I was *pulled* up there, Poll. I was crying so much I could hardly walk. Everyone else was crying too."

"You were crying?" Maud never cried! "I thought you were an *Anglican* now," added Polly.

"I was, but that's not enough for me. It's not enough for Miss Guppy either. She has to pretend she's an ordinary Anglican in the school. Polly, you have to promise me to keep this a secret from Noni. Miss Guppy might get into trouble if someone found out."

"Okay, I promise. Why would I tell *anyone*? It sounds so strange, Maud! I don't think you should have anything to do with it!"

Maud gave her a most un-Maudish, sickening smile. "Dear Polly—I know it's hard for you to understand. This is all very new for you—for me too!—but you'll get used to it. I truly hope, Doodle, that one day you'll be converted as well. I'm going to send you a book to read. If you could accept Jesus like I have, I'd be so happy!"

Polly stood up. "I already accept Jesus! I go to church every Sunday and I say my prayers every night! I think this new religion sounds weird, Maud. Daddy wouldn't like it."

"Daddy has nothing to do with it," said Maud. "And we're not supposed to talk about him, remember? I knew you'd be like this, Poll, but Jesus is already working on you—I can tell."

"He is *not* working on me! You're crazy, Maud!" Polly flounced out of the room.

She found Sadie in the kitchen holding a wire mesh strainer to the wall. "Oh, Polly, you're just in time—I've trapped a hummingbird! It must have come in through the window. Help me put this cardboard under it."

They carefully slid a piece of cardboard under the strainer. For a few minutes they examined the tiny bird. It had a bib like dazzling orangey-red jewels.

Sadie pressed the cardboard to the strainer as she carried it into the yard. "Keep calm, sweetheart—we'll soon have you free." When she released the hummingbird, it zoomed straight up into the sky.

"Gosh . . . wasn't that nifty, Pollywog?"

Sadie was so kind and warm that Polly decided to ask her about Maud.

"So she told you." Sadie sighed. "That's a hard one, kiddo. When Maud first came to school, I'd sometimes hear her get up at night. She'd sit by the window for hours. I guess she was missing your dad. But now she seems so happy, and so certain that this religion is for her. *I* think she and the rest of the Guppy's group are nuts! But when I tell her that, Maud just smiles like a saint and says she hopes I'll be converted someday too."

"That's what she said to me!"

"Never mind. I'm sure she'll get over it. Last year Ann was part of the same group and now she won't have anything to do with them. Maud is still your sister and she still loves you—just hang on to that."

"I'll try," said Polly. But it was hard to be hopeful about Maud. First Polly had lost her to St. Winifred's. Now, it seemed, she had lost her to Jesus.

———

May 25, 1933

Dear Daddy,

> *We had a very nice Easter holiday, but Maud told me she has joined a strange new religion. I wish you were here so you could talk her out of it.*

Daddy, do you think I'm a wicked person for eating meat and fish? But Uncle Rand eats meat, and he's a rector. During Lent he gave a sermon about living up to your principles. I'm not very good at that, Daddy. I really think it's wrong to eat animals, but then I can't resist. It's so confusing.

Yesterday was Empire Day and it was so much fun! Kingfisher Island had a huge celebration and lots of people came in boats from other islands. There was a parade and lots of races. I went in the sack race and Biddy and I went in the three-legged race, but we didn't win. Biddy's mother won first prize in the egg-and-spoon race. There was a men's softball game between Kingfisher and Valencia. Kingfisher won! In the evening there was a dance and I stayed until after midnight! We had strawberry ice cream. Aunt Jean danced so much that she hurt her back.

Love,

Polly

June 22, 1933

Dear Daddy,

I feel so bad! Last night I left the deer gate open by mistake and this morning almost all of Noni's flowers had been nibbled to the ground. She scolded me very sharply—it's the first time she ever has. I couldn't stop crying. Noni loves her garden so much and now she has to start all over again. At least her roses were saved—they are enclosed in a separate garden.

Oh, Daddy, how could I do such a stupid thing! I'm usually so careful about shutting the gate, but while I was weeding I heard Tarka bark and I thought he was chasing a deer so I ran out. Tarka was greeting Biddy and Bramble and I was so glad to see them that I forgot to go back and shut the gate.

Noni isn't angry any more, but I can tell she's still upset. She keeps saying "What's done is done" and that I should stop feeling guilty, but I can't.

I'll tell you everything I've been doing and maybe that will help me feel better. Biddy and I have taught Tarka and Bramble to ride in the baskets of our bikes. Biddy had to tie Bramble in at first, but Tarka was good right from the start. He stays very still, even when he barks at other dogs we pass. He really likes zooming down hills—he puts his head up and his ears blow back. I used to hate leaving him at home when I went off on my bike, but now I can take him all over the island! He's such a smart boy.

I've been helping Biddy and Luke herd sheep. We run behind them and shout at them. Biddy's father and his helper sheared the sheep—it comes off their skins like a coat. We stuffed the wool into gunny sacks and my hands got slippery from the oil in it.

We went to Victoria for four days and stayed in the

*Empress Hotel again. Aunt Jean taught me how to swim
at the Crystal Pool. The water was lovely and warm and
it wasn't hard to learn. The adults were all so proud of
me. The trouble is, Daddy, that I'm still afraid to swim
in the sea, but I couldn't tell them that. At the end of
our stay we brought Maud home for the summer. St.
Winifred's gets out earlier than our school.*

   *I don't feel any better, Daddy, so I'm going to stop
now.*

   Much love,
   Polly

After Polly had hidden her letter to Daddy she began
weeping again. Maud came into the bedroom. "Doodle,
what's the matter? Are you still upset about leaving the gate
open?"

Polly nodded, sniffing up her tears.

Maud gave her a handkerchief and a hug. "Don't worry,
Poll. Noni isn't mad any more. She forgives you—so does God!"

Polly sighed. She had hoped Maud had changed since
Easter, but she was even stranger than before.

"Did you read the book I sent you?" Maud asked. "It
would help you right now."

The book was called *Jesus Is Calling You*. Polly hadn't
even opened it.

"No, I haven't," Polly told her. "I've already told you,
Maud—I'm not interested in your weird religion."

Maud just put on one of her holy looks. "You're just not ready yet, but you will be."

Was Maud going to be this impossible all summer?

—————

On the evening of Polly's last day of school there was a graduation ceremony at the community hall for Alice, Milly, Hana, and Chester. Almost everyone on the island came. Milly gave the valedictory address, and the school choir sang. Polly's eyes stung when Alice sang Daddy's favourite song, "There's a Long Long Trail A-Winding." Alice's voice soared like a lark and her expression was serene, not nasty.

"She's going to your school this fall," Polly told Maud at the reception. "You'd better watch out, because she's a terrible bully!"

"She won't get away with that at St. Winnie's," said Maud.

Polly went up to Milly and Hana, chatting in a corner. "What are you going to do now that you've finished school?" she asked them.

"I'm going to work in the hotel and Hana's going to work on her family's farm," said Milly.

"What's Chester doing?" asked Polly casually, as if this weren't what she really wanted to know.

"He's going to St. Cuthbert's in Victoria," said Hana.

That meant she'd only see Chester in the holidays, thought Polly. And he lived on Fowler Bay on the other side of the island, so she probably wouldn't see him much even then.

Oh, well . . . why did it seem so important? Chester was only a boy, after all.

Polly left the hall to go to the privy. When she came out, there was Chester! He was sitting on the stairs of the hall.

"Hi, Polly," he said. "It's so hot in there, I had to come outside."

"Hi, Chester." She tried to think of something to say. "Umm . . . congratulations on graduating."

"Thanks. It'll seem really odd not to go to school on the island any more. I've been there for seven years!"

"Are you—are you looking forward to going to school in Victoria?"

"Sort of. I'm hoping to get on the football team. But I'm glad it's not until the end of the summer. Isn't it great? Two whole months of freedom!"

Polly nodded. In school she'd always been able to talk easily to Chester; why did she feel so tongue-tied? She didn't know whether to go in again or to stay outside. Finally she sat down beside him.

Neither of them spoke. A frog chirruped from the ditch and the noisy din inside seemed far away. Chester leaned forward, pecked Polly's cheek, and ran away down the road.

　　Polly sat on the stairs for a long time, touching her cheek every now and then. *My first kiss!* she thought.

　　But that was the sort of silly thing Biddy would think. It was just a friendly kiss. Still, as Polly walked back into the crowd, she felt as if she were floating. The kiss was a secret between her and Chester—a thrilling new secret that made her other secrets easier to bear.

———

July 4, 1933

Dear Daddy,

　　It's swell to be out of school! I got almost all A's, and a B in arithmetic because of Uncle Rand helping me with it. He gave me a whole dollar for working so hard! Last week when I was driving around with Uncle Rand I told him that I didn't understand any of his sermons. He asked me why, and I said it was because he used such big words and long sentences. He thanked me for telling him and said he would try to make his sermons simpler and write them as if he was preaching only to me.

　　Much love,

　　Polly

July 9, 1933

Dear Daddy,

Today I saw whales! A whole lot of them, racing and leaping by the lighthouse. Noni and I were there walking Tarka. They were black and white and enormous. I have never seen anything so amazing in all my life.

Oh, Daddy, I wish you could have been there with me to see them!

Love,

Polly

———

July 13, 1933

Dear Daddy,

Yesterday Biddy and Luke and I climbed to the top of Vulture Ridge. It's the first time I've been up there. We could see all the little islands around us and Vancouver Island in the distance. We had to keep Tarka and Bramble on their leashes so they wouldn't fall off the steep cliff. We sat and ate our sandwiches while turkey vultures floated up from the valley. They have tiny red heads.

When I got home, I tried to paint the different blues of the sea and the hills with the vultures flying

above. I didn't think it worked, but Noni said it was
the best painting I have ever done. She said it was
because I really looked when I was up there.

I think I want to be a painter when I grow up,
Daddy.

Much love,
Polly

September 4, 1933

Dear Daddy,

I feel so bad that I didn't write to you for the rest
of the summer! I promise I haven't forgotten you, but
it was so warm and dry that I was hardly ever inside.
Maud was home for the whole time, except for one
week when she went to stay with Sadie.

Sadie's parents think she's too serious about
Gregor, so they wouldn't let her visit the island. But
then Gregor went to see her in Duncan, and her par-
ents liked him so much that they let him stay with
them for a week!

Now Gregor calls Sadie his sweetheart. Aunt Jean
is so pleased, because she likes Sadie and because Mrs.
Cunningham is always boasting about Alec and Cyn-
thia being a couple.

Maud was so strange this summer, Daddy. She
read her Bible all the time when we were in our room,
and the only time she talked to me was when she was

trying to convert me. I told her if she didn't stop, I'd tell Noni. But she knows I won't, because I promised not to.

Maud and I both helped a lot with the garden and the cooking. We picked cherries and plums and dug clams and fished, but we still had lots of time to play. Biddy and Luke and I rode our bikes to Shell Bay and made rafts out of driftwood. The sand there is white because it's made out of crumbled shells. The water is warmer than by our house and I went swimming! I was still afraid, but I tried not to let on and I don't think they guessed. Tarka also learned to swim! He just copied his mother. He loves fetching sticks. We found an old dugout canoe and the dogs came out with us in it.

It only rained a few days, and then Biddy and Luke and I played in the empty schoolhouse. No one cares if we go into it. Guess what we played—school! Biddy was the strict teacher and Luke and I were the naughty pupils.

In July, Noni gave watercolour lessons to children and Biddy and I were part of the class. Some of the girls were staying with relatives on Kingfisher for the summer and we felt proud that we live here all year round. I did a lot of paintings besides what I did in the classes and Noni has framed some of them.

A few nights it was so hot that Maud and I slept

on the porch. We could hear the otters squealing across the road.

We went on lots of picnics with the family—to the lighthouse or to Walker Island, or to a tiny island called the Boot.

The best part of the summer was the fall fair—they call it that even though it's in August. I entered three paintings—one of a hummingbird, one of whales, and one of turkey vultures—and they won first-, second-, and third-prize ribbons! Noni won first prize for roses like she always does, and Aunt Jean got second prize for her chocolate cake. Biddy won for the best carrots in the children's category. She and I and Luke dressed up as the Three Musketeers for the parade.

The only thing I didn't like about the summer was in July, when Aunt Jean and Uncle Rand had paying guests. Maud and I had to help make beds and clean and cook for them, and they always wanted to use the rowboat.

I am very brown and I've grown two inches! Uncle Rand measured me on the kitchen door. My arms and legs are strong from doing so many chores.

Last week Noni told Aunt Jean she was pleased that Uncle Rand's sermons were easier to understand. He doesn't use big words or long sentences any more, and sometimes he even makes jokes! He looks straight at me when he tells them. I didn't tell Noni that he changed because of me, but I felt warm inside.

I talked to Uncle Rand about Maud (she only made me promise not to tell Noni). He said he was glad Maud had found a way to God that suited her, but that he hoped she would learn to be tolerant of other ways. He agreed with me that I already have Jesus in my heart.

Tomorrow I start school again. I'm looking forward to it because Alice won't be there!

I've been living on Kingfisher Island for a whole year now! It seems more like a hundred years. So much has happened that I can hardly remember my life in Winnipeg.

But I still remember you, Daddy. I still miss you so much, and even though I often forget to write to you, I pray for you every night before I go to sleep. Are you all right? How I wish you could come to see me!

All my love,
Polly

CHAPTER TWELVE

VIVIEN

"School this term is going to be much easier without Alice," said Biddy as they got off their bikes and crossed the field.

It will seem lonely without Chester, though, Polly thought. She had run into Chester a few times during the summer, but their secret embarrassed them so much that they couldn't speak.

"Look, Polly—a new girl!" whispered Biddy as they entered the classroom.

Polly followed Biddy's gaze. A skinny girl with dark hair and bright blue eyes stared boldly back.

"Biddy and Polly, this is Vivien," Miss Hunter told them. "She's in grade six, like you. Vivien, you can sit with Dorothy. I want all three of you to help Vivien feel comfortable."

Miss Hunter turned to cope with the little ones who were at school for the first time. Vivien continued to stare, until Biddy finally said, "Hi," and the others followed.

Vivien didn't answer; she just gave a little grunt and sat down beside Dorothy. Dorothy, who was very shy, couldn't even look at her.

At recess Vivien answered their questions curtly. They found out she was an only child and had moved with her parents to a fruit farm near Fowler Bay. "We used to live in Sidney," she told them, "but my father lost his job. Now he's starting over again on the island. His brother owns the farm, and he asked us to come and live with him. Biddy— that's your name, right?—did you know you have something between your front teeth?"

Biddy giggled nervously. "Oh, that must be bacon from breakfast!"

For the rest of the first day of school Polly and Biddy tried to make Vivien feel comfortable, as Miss Hunter had asked them to. But Vivien didn't have to be made to feel comfortable. She was so confident it was as if they were the new girls and she had been at the school for years. Even though her clothes were shabby and ill-fitting, she wore them as though they were brand new. She told Polly a better way to tie her shoes and ordered Dorothy to clean up their shared desk. And she asked a lot of snoopy questions.

Polly listened to her quiz Biddy and dreaded her turn.

Sure enough, after school Vivien turned to her and asked what her parents did.

"My mother died a long time ago, and my father drowned last year," Polly muttered. How she hated saying that!

"How did he drown?" Vivien asked.

"Polly doesn't like to talk about it," explained Biddy.

"Why not?" asked Vivien.

Polly just shrugged. Was Vivien going to be as bad as Alice?

Vivien came home with Polly and Biddy almost every day. She didn't have a bike, so she rode on the back of one of theirs. She stayed with them until suppertime, then her father picked her up in his truck.

Vivien always wanted to be the boss. She told them they were too old to play with dolls. She told Polly she should train Tarka not to bark so much and Biddy not to bite her nails. Every day they tried to think of a reason not to have her over, but Vivien assumed she could come, so she did.

After Noni met her parents in church she gave them Polly's outgrown clothes, because Vivien was a smaller size. Polly thought she wouldn't like wearing someone else's clothes, but Vivien held her head high as if she didn't care, just as Maud had when she'd had to wear second-hand clothes in Winnipeg.

"Are you going to invite Vivien to your birthday

party?" Noni asked Polly. Polly didn't want to, but Vivien had already found out when her birthday was. Polly had no choice but to include her.

The party was so much fun that Polly didn't mind Vivien being there. Maud was home for the weekend, and she didn't once talk about religion. Polly liked all her presents, but her favourite was a new box of paints from Noni. As she blew out her eleven candles, she made the usual wish to see Daddy again. This year it didn't seem quite as desperate. Even though she tried to write to Daddy, it was getting harder and harder to remember to.

I must do better! she told herself. If—*when*—Daddy came back, he could read the letters and know all about her life on the island.

—————

October 20, 1933

Dear Daddy,

We're getting on better with Vivien. She's still bossy, but she's not mean like Alice. She's so smart that she helps me with my arithmetic. And she has good ideas. Last week when we were walking Tarka and Bramble, we went deep into the woods behind the church. We came to a clearing with a rundown shack in it. Vivien said we should fix it up and it could be our secret house! We ran back to Biddy's room and started making lists of all we would need: lumber, hammers, nails, and many other things.

Since then it has rained every day so we can't start work. But planning is so much fun! Even in school, when we're supposed to be studying together, we make lists and drawings and whisper about our house. We're going to call it Oz because The Wizard of Oz is our favourite book. Now we'll have our own hideout!

Love,
Polly

November 4, 1933

Dear Daddy,

This has been a Melancholy day. (I saw that word in a book.) This morning Noni had a toothache so Aunt Jean and Uncle Rand took her to the dentist's in Vancouver. I have to stay here alone for two whole days with Mrs. Hooper looking after me.

It was so wet and windy that I couldn't ride my bike, and Biddy and I got soaked walking home from school. Mrs. Hooper left me a note that she'd gone to visit her daughter. So Tarka and I went over to Biddy's, but she was helping her mother do the ironing and I was just in the way so I went home.

The house felt so empty! Sometimes Noni leaves me alone in the evenings when she goes out to a musical evening or to play Whist, but the house is always nice and warm and I just go to sleep. Today it was freezing and the wind made the windows rattle. I sat in the window seat with a blanket around me and waited for Mrs. Hooper to come back and light the stove and cook supper.

I felt so sad. I thought about you and how much I missed you and how hard it is not to tell anyone that you're still alive. If only I could just tell Biddy! I'm sure she'd keep it a secret. But you wouldn't want me to and Maud would be so angry.

I thought of everything that has happened and I wondered if I would ever see you again. Oh, Daddy, where are you? Sometimes it seems as if you are dead.

Your loving Doodle

Polly and Biddy were in Biddy's kitchen, tying ribbons around jars of preserves for the church bazaar on Saturday. Biddy's mother was at the parish hall with Noni and Aunt Jean and the other members of the Women's Auxiliary, setting up the tables. She'd taken little Shirley with her, but Biddy and Polly were supposed to be looking after the twins.

Tying the slippery ribbons around the rims of the jars was tricky. Fanny kept grabbing the finished ones and yanking off the ribbons. William was playing in the wood-box, throwing pieces of wood around the kitchen for Bramble and Tarka and getting filthy. He ignored Biddy when she told him not to.

"It's not fair!" complained Biddy. "Luke doesn't have to help with the bazaar, and he never has to babysit. Fanny, stop that!" She slapped Fanny's hand and the little girl screamed. Biddy looked close to tears herself.

Polly got up and found two huge carrots. She handed one to each twin. Fanny's mouth closed on the carrot and William came out of the woodbox and sat on the floor with his.

"Thanks, Polly," said Biddy. "I shouldn't have slapped her, but sometimes the twins drive me crazy!" She and Polly carried on tying ribbons and cutting them. The only sound was the twins' steady munching. Then it stopped.

"Look," whispered Polly. The twins had fallen asleep on top of each other. The dogs lay beside them, finishing the half-nibbled carrots.

"Whew! It's okay—we can talk normally. Nothing wakes them once they're asleep." Biddy looked hesitant. "Polly . . . there's something I think I should tell you."

"What?"

"It's about your grandmother. My mum is really upset with her."

How could anyone be upset with *Noni?* But Polly made herself listen.

"You know Mrs. Osaka, Seiji's mother?"

Polly nodded.

"Well, she and Mum are good friends, and she asked Mum if she could join the Women's Auxiliary. Mum asked your grandmother and she said she couldn't—because she's Japanese! Mum didn't say anything more because she's so much in awe of Mrs. Whitfield. But she doesn't think it's right, and neither do I."

Polly reddened. "I'm sure my grandmother must have a good reason," she said stiffly. "She's a good person. She wouldn't say no just because Mrs. Osaka is Japanese."

"Well, she did," said Biddy calmly. "I'm sorry to tell you, Polly, but maybe she's not as good as you think."

Polly jumped up. "I think I'll go now. Come on, Tarka."

She ran all the way home and waited for Noni. When her grandmother entered the house, Polly said in a rush, "Noni, did you tell Biddy's mother that Mrs. Osaka couldn't join the Women's Auxiliary because she's Japanese? Biddy told me you did."

"Oh, hen . . ." Noni sat down at the kitchen table. "Let me explain. These things are too hard for children to understand. Mrs. Osaka is a very nice woman and I have nothing against her. But she's not the same as us. She would feel out of place and uncomfortable in our group—that's why I said no."

"But she *wanted* to join!"

Noni's mouth was set. "Yes, she did, but her request was inappropriate. I decided what was best for everyone. I don't want to talk about this any more, Polly, and I don't want you and Biddy discussing it further. I wish her mother hadn't told her. Do you understand?" She smiled. "Now, tell me how you got on with the preserves. Did you finish them?"

Polly nodded, unable to speak. "I have to walk Tarka," she muttered, and left the room.

She marched along the beach, wiping tears from her eyes. Her kind Noni had done something wrong! Polly couldn't bear feeling so disappointed in her.

It was too confusing to think about. Maybe Noni was right; maybe Polly was simply too young to understand.

CHAPTER THIRTEEN

"I MISS YOU TERRIBLY"

January 1, 1934

Dear Daddy,

It's hard to believe that a whole year has gone by! Last Christmas Mrs. Tuttle was here and I found out you were accused of stealing. That was awful, but then things got better.

I'm happy here, Daddy. I have a wonderful dog and two good friends and a loving family. I miss you terribly and I miss Maud, but I see her in the holidays and I know I will see you one day.

We had a very nice Christmas and I got lots of presents. I gave everyone a painting and they said they liked them. The concert and the pageant went very well. We had a delicious roast goose for dinner, just like last year.

I still feel guilty about eating meat, but I don't think I have the will power to be a vegetarian. I won't eat venison, though, because I see deer every day. I see chickens every day too, but chickens don't seem as real. I wish I was stronger, but maybe when I'm older I'll be able to stand by my principles.

Maud acted as if she wasn't really here and kept looking at us all in a superior way, but Noni said she's just being normal for her age. I am never going to be like that.

Daddy, I hope that wherever you are you had a good Christmas as well.

Much love,
Polly

February 22, 1934

Dear Daddy,

This month is so cold that I have to take a hot water bottle to bed. Tarka tries to lie over it. There was a layer of ice in my water pitcher this morning. It's not usually this cold in B.C. The road is too slippery to ride bikes, so Biddy and I have to walk. We wear scarves over our faces just like I used to have to do in Winnipeg.

The boys at school have made an ice slide! They poured water down the hill at the back of the playground and every day at lunch we slide down it on

pieces of cardboard. I pretend my cardboard is my old
toboggan.

Your Polly

March 10, 1934

Dear Daddy,

Our house (Oz) is finished! I wish so much you
could see it. We've swept out all the dirt and scrubbed
every inch of the walls and floor. We tapped away the
old glass in the windows and nailed canvas cloth over
them. There are three stumps for chairs, and a table
made out of boxes. In another box we keep cups and
cookies and a bottle of water and sometimes we have
meals there. There's an old green rug on the floor. Every
day we pick leaves and flowers and put them in a jug
on the table. As soon as we go in, we pin back the cloth
in the windows and it's nice and bright. We're hoping
that when it's warmer, we can sleep there.

Love,

Polly

———

In late spring Polly, Biddy, and Vivien got permission to
sleep overnight in Oz. Uncle Rand had inspected the house
to make sure it was stable. He told them it used to belong

to a hermit. "His name was Gus. He built this house a long time ago. We were terrified of him when we were kids. He'd come out of the woods and stumble along the road to the store, his beard almost down to his knees!" He smiled at them. "You've done an excellent job of fixing it up—and all by yourselves too! I'm proud of you."

After they'd eaten the supper they had packed, the three girls and two dogs all piled together on the old mattress Uncle Rand had helped them drag over from the rectory. They huddled under a thick quilt, squished and cozy.

"The dogs shouldn't be allowed on the bed," complained Vivien. "Make them sleep on a blanket in the corner."

"We want them here," said Biddy calmly. They were used to Vivien now, and had discovered that if they ignored her commands, she usually gave up.

"Has your dad left yet?" Polly asked her.

"He's going in a week," said Vivien sadly. Vivien's father had to leave the island for the whole summer to log on Vancouver Island so he could make some extra money.

"Never mind, the summer will go so fast he'll be back before you notice," said Biddy.

At least he'd be back, thought Polly with a pang. She liked both of her friends' fathers. Biddy's was easygoing and Vivien's was tense and quiet, but kind.

If only they could meet *her* father! Polly's friends had

always liked his joking and his good ideas. One time, when Audrey and another friend had been over, Daddy had shown them how to make an orchestra by filling glasses with water and rubbing wet fingers along the edges. What a commotion they had made, and how they had laughed!

Polly turned over and buried her face in Tarka's side. Why was she suddenly thinking of Daddy, instead of enjoying this overnight adventure?

"Let's tell one another secrets!" said Vivien.

"Okay," said Biddy. "What do you want to be when you grow up? I want to be a vet."

"An artist," said Polly.

"An actress," said Vivien, "but we already know all that. I meant a secret we've never told one another."

Biddy and Polly were silent.

"I'll start," said Vivien. "When I was born, I almost died!"

"You did?"

"Oh, Vivien, really?"

"Yup. I wasn't breathing properly and it was touch and go for a few minutes, but then I took a deep breath and yelled, my mum said! Okay, Biddy, your turn."

"I can't think of anything."

"Think harder."

"I once . . ." Biddy's voice became very small. "I once made Luke eat a slug."

"That's so tame! Can't you think of something that's more interesting?"

"I'm sorry, but that's the only secret I have."

"Oh, well. Polly?"

Polly could imagine how impressed the others would be if she told her secret. What if she just said casually, "My father didn't drown. He's alive!" They would be so shocked— and so glad for her. She longed to release what had throbbed inside her for so long.

But of course she couldn't. What other secret could she tell them? Not about Chester's kiss! They would tease her, and it was so long ago it seemed unreal. "My secret is pretty boring," she said. "I wish I could stop eating meat because it seems so cruel to eat animals, but I don't have the will power."

"Oh, brother, you two are *both* boring!" said Vivien. She yawned. "Let's go to sleep now."

Biddy was already breathing heavily and the dogs had been still for ages. But Polly couldn't sleep. She lay awake and listened to an owl. It was such a lonely sound. She missed Daddy more than she had for a long time.

———

September 22, 1934

Dear Daddy,

I haven't written to you for so long! That doesn't

mean I've forgotten you, but it's so hard to write when I know you can't answer.

Today is my twelfth birthday! That means Tarka is two, because I got him when I turned ten. He's a much better behaved dog than he used to be, although he still barks too much and he steals food whenever he can.

It's Saturday, so I don't have to go to school. At breakfast Noni gave me this new fountain pen and some ink, so I'm trying them out for the first time.

This afternoon the whole family is going for a birthday picnic on the Boot. Biddy and Vivien are coming too. Some of us will go in the gasboat and some of us will row. I hope it's warm enough to swim.

This will be my last year at school on the island. Next year I'll have to go to St. Winifred's. Oh, Daddy, I don't want to go! Especially since Biddy and Vivien will be staying here. I've begged and begged Noni to let me stay too and have a governess, but she says I'll get a better education at St. Winifred's. She also told me not to worry about it but to just enjoy this year, so I'm trying to do that.

When we went back to school, we found out that Miss Hunter got married! Now she is Mrs. Oliver. None of us can remember to call her that, but she says we'll gradually get used to it and that she keeps forgetting her new name herself!

I wish women didn't have to change their last names when they get married—I never want to be anyone but Polly Brown. I told Noni that, and she said that if I became an artist and got married, I could still use my maiden name as my artist's name.

Maud got her hair bobbed! Her face looks more relaxed without her tight braids pulling back her skin, but I told her she shouldn't have cut her hair, because you liked it long. She could have just worn it loose like I do. She said Maudishly that she was seventeen and could do what she liked. I promise you I'll never get my hair bobbed, Daddy! Noni trims it sometimes, but it's still below my shoulders.

Maud doesn't try to convert me any more. She says that when I get to St. Winifred's, the Guppy will instead. That made me so mad! I yelled that of course she wouldn't, but Maud just smiled with that dumb holy look on her face.

Maud is in the upper sixth form now (that's what they call grade twelve at St. Winnie's) and she's head girl! Now she wears an ugly mustard-coloured blazer instead of an ugly maroon one. Noni said Maud was born to be a head girl. Gregor pretends to act scared and keeps asking her if she'll give him an order mark.

Sadie's parents let her stay with us almost all summer. Now she and Gregor are engaged! They will get married next summer, after Sadie graduates and after Gregor is finished theology school. Maud and I will be bridesmaids! Aunt Jean is over the moon because she likes Sadie so much. Noni worries that they are too young to get married, but Aunt Jean says that sometimes you find the right person early in life and that's that. Aunt Jean spent a lot of time with Sadie showing her how to take care of the church—she says she'll be a perfect minister's wife.

Alec and Cynthia are still a couple, although they are not engaged yet (Aunt Jean gloats about that). The two of them and Gregor and Sadie spent a lot of time together, and Maud was left out. I asked her if she'd like to have a boyfriend too. She told me there are no boys on the island who interest her, and that if she had a boyfriend he'd have to be the kind of Christian she is. I told her she'd never find anyone if she was that fussy, and she got all Maudish and wouldn't speak to me for the rest of the day.

Maud has changed so much, Daddy. Sometimes she doesn't seem like my sister any more. She didn't even come home for my birthday, because she was so busy at school.

There was a terrible accident this summer—it was so sad. Two men tried to row to Walker Island and got caught in the current and one of them drowned.

They were summer guests and they didn't know how to check the tides.

I know all about the tides and I can run the gas-boat on my own and I can swim really well! I'm not afraid of the sea any more.

Have you heard of the Quintuplets? They are five little babies exactly alike who were born in Ontario in May. When Noni and Aunt Jean were talking about them, all I could think of was whether they were born near where you are.

Daddy, I miss you so much. I wish I didn't have to wait until I was grown up to see you again.

Much love from your Polly Wolly Doodle

PART THREE

NOW THAT SHE
WAS TWELVE

PART THREE

NOW THAT SHE

WAS TWELVE

a WISH COME TRUE

Now that she was twelve, thought Polly, perhaps it was time to admit that she no longer enjoyed writing to Daddy.

She wiped her new pen on a rag and replaced its cap. Then she sealed the letter in an envelope, wrote "Mr. Daniel Brown" on the front, and placed the letter with the others in the chest.

Tarka was snoozing on her bed in the sunshine. He didn't stir as Polly dragged his warm body into her lap. She leaned back against her pillow, stroking his wiry fur.

Daddy didn't seem real. She'd written that she still remembered him, but she could hardly conjure up his face or hear his voice. It was almost as if she'd stopped believing in him—just as she'd stopped believing in Santa Claus!

At first the letters had helped soothe Polly's terrible longing. But she was happy now. She had a loving family and friends—and the best dog in the world! The last sentence in the letter had been a lie. She didn't miss Daddy any more. Her life with him seemed like something she had read in a story; living on the island was her real life.

I miss missing him, thought Polly. Her eyes prickled and she wondered if she would cry, but her tears retreated.

Polly looked around the attic room—all hers now. The last time Maud had been home, she'd been so disgusted by the clutter she had moved to the box room.

The floor was strewn with clothes and dog toys, and a long table was piled with art projects. On the walls were tacked Polly's paintings and pictures of art cut out of Noni's magazines. Her neglected dolls sat in a dusty row on the windowsill.

Polly sighed when she thought of Maud. Her sister was becoming more and more like a stranger. Maud's entire life consisted of her school and her religion. This summer Maud kept saying that Polly was spoiled, that her life on the island was too soft. "The family treats you like a princess," she told her. "It's a good thing you're coming to St. Winnie's—it will toughen you up."

Polly didn't think she was spoiled. She was just well loved—what was wrong with that? And she was already tough, much tougher than when she'd first come here. She could carry a whole sling of wood and a whole basket of apples, she could chop kindling, and she knew how to row and fish and swim and garden.

I'm tough inside too, thought Polly. *I've kept the secret about Daddy all this time.*

But when she thought about St. Winifred's, Polly didn't feel tough at all. If only she didn't have to go there! If only everything could stay exactly as it was!

Then Polly jumped up, startling Tarka awake. What was she doing brooding inside on such a sunny morning? It was Saturday and it was her birthday!

"Dance, Tarka!" she said, pulling a dog biscuit out of her pocket. Tarka stood on his hind legs and hopped in a circle until she gave him the biscuit.

Polly clattered downstairs. She grabbed an apple from the empty kitchen and stuffed it into her pocket. Noni was at Aunt Jean's, helping her make sandwiches for the picnic, and Mrs. Hooper had the day off.

Polly called Tarka and ran across the road and onto the beach. She was going to look for interesting pieces of driftwood to add to the display she'd started in the front garden.

It was a dazzling day. The sun broke up the waves into shiny discs—Aunt Jean called them "sun pennies." A light breeze scattered leaves and curls of arbutus bark. The air smelled briny. Polly crunched along the beach, hopping over logs and scolding Tarka when he nibbled at barnacles, trying to rip them off the rocks. She picked up possible branches of driftwood, then dropped some as she found better pieces. Tarka darted after the ones she dropped and brought them back to her.

Polly sat down on a log to sort out the best pieces and to eat her apple. Tarka flopped beside her. He liked to bake in the sunshine until he was gasping, as if he were a brown bun in an oven.

A row of dusky cormorants perched on a floating log, drying their spread wings. Gulls and crows argued, and a lone boat putted around the point. The neighbouring islands were soft rounded outlines against the sky. A king-fisher perched on a nearby tree.

Polly studied the kingfisher as it swooped towards the water, its rusty warble announcing that it had spotted a fish. How could she capture how it shot like a blue arrow into the sea? Perhaps she could paint it on wet paper, so its outline was blurred . . .

Then Polly heard a faint whistle, like a bird song. She tossed Tarka her apple core, listening hard.

It wasn't a bird. It was someone whistling the same notes again and again: two long high notes and a short one. Her heart turned over as the whistle turned into a song.

"'Oh, I went down south for to see my Sal, singing Polly Wolly Doodle all the day,'" sang a man's voice softly.

Polly stood up and looked around frantically.

"'My Sal she is a spunky gal, singing Polly Wolly Doodle all the day,'" the voice sang louder.

Someone stepped out from behind the trees between the beach and the road: a tall man in a suit and hat with a small rucksack on his back. Tarka trotted up to him, wagging his tail.

Polly flew. She crashed into the man's chest, and cried over and over, "Oh, *Daddy*—oh, Daddy—oh, my Daddy!"

She couldn't stop crying. Daddy took her hand and pulled her back into the trees. Then he sat on a log and held her, stroking her hair and kissing her forehead. "Happy Birthday, Polly Wolly Doodle! Happy Birthday, my dear little girl!" he whispered, his voice breaking. His hat fell off and Tarka ran off with it.

Polly sobbed into his shirt front. She tried to wipe her eyes on her blouse, but Daddy handed her a grubby handkerchief. Then he took it back to wipe his own eyes. He held her away from him, studied her, and said, "But you're not a little girl any more, Doodle! You're a young lady!"

Daddy had changed too. He was still handsome, with his long, dignified nose, jutting chin, and brown eyes, but his thick brown hair had receded, making his forehead look bigger. Fine lines extended from the corners of his eyes and purplish circles were under them, as if he hadn't slept for days. Black stubble, which had scratched Polly when he kissed her, covered his chin and upper lip. His face, which used to shine with exuberance, looked tense and sad and exhausted, as if . . . as if he were *broken*. His suit was grimy and his shirt sleeves were frayed. Most unsettling of all, he had dirt under his fingernails—*Daddy*, who used to be so meticulous!

Tears coated Polly's cheeks and she hiccuped out the end of her sobs. How could she have forgotten Daddy or thought she didn't miss him? "How did you *get* here?" she managed to ask as she cuddled in his lap.

"I came on yesterday's steamer from Vancouver. I slept on the beach, and this morning I've been waiting for you to come out of the house. Finally you did! I wanted to surprise you on your birthday." He reached into his pocket. "Here, I've brought you a present."

"*You* are my present!" laughed Polly. The first shock of seeing Daddy was wearing off. How could she ever have thought he wasn't real? He was *here*, as real as he ever was!

She opened up the twisted wad of tissue paper he handed her. Inside was a necklace: a small silver heart on a chain. Polly bounced sunlight off its surface. "It's beautiful!" she breathed.

He helped her fasten the necklace. "Not as beautiful as my girl! You look so much like your mother. And you're so tall! I know I should have expected that, but all this time I've imagined you and Maud as you were when I left. She must have changed too."

"She has! She bobbed her hair! Oh, Daddy, Maud will be so glad to see you!"

"And I can't wait to see *her!* Could you run up and get her?"

"But, Daddy, Maud's not here! She goes to boarding school in Victoria!" Polly felt dizzy when she realized he didn't know that.

"She does? I'm so glad for her—she always wanted to go to boarding school and she'll be getting a good education. You'll have to tell me how to get to her school. I could try to get to Victoria tonight and see her tomorrow."

"Tonight? But you would come right back here again, wouldn't you?"

"Let's not talk about that yet. I shouldn't have come at all, but I missed you both so much." Daddy sounded as if he were going to cry again.

Polly was bursting with so many questions she didn't know where to begin. "How—where do you live?" she asked.

"In the Okanagan."

"Where's that?"

"About two hundred miles from Vancouver."

"But I thought you went to Ontario!"

"I did at first. But jobs weren't any easier to get there than they were in Winnipeg. I heard you could earn money picking fruit in B.C., so last summer I rode the rails west and ended up in a place outside of Kelowna. I picked cherries and apples for a farmer and he let me and three other fellows live in his cabin for free all winter. We helped him build a fence."

Polly was stunned. All this time Daddy had been living in the same province she did!

"Maud said you changed your name," she whispered.

"I didn't really change it," said Daddy, "I just call myself by Michael, my middle name. Now I'm 'Mike Brown.' That's such a common name no one is going to recognize it."

"I know why you have to do that," Polly told him. "You were accused of stealing some money, and that's why you had to go away and pretend that you drowned! That's so unfair! You're innocent!"

Daddy wiped his hand over his face. "Oh, Doodle, I was hoping you wouldn't find out about all that until you were much older!" He looked away. "I'm glad you believe I'm innocent, but if you don't mind I'd rather not talk about it—it's all water under the bridge now."

"Okay." Polly shivered. "Let's move into the sun," she suggested.

Daddy shook his head. "It's too risky. Someone might spot us and wonder why you're talking to a stranger." He took off his jacket and wrapped it around Polly. "Let me just hold you close for a moment. I can't stay much longer, Doodle."

Polly jumped up. "You can't go, Daddy—you just came!"

"I have to, Polly. No one here will recognize me, but I can't be seen hanging around a young girl—it wouldn't be proper. I'll try to find a boat ride to Victoria this evening. I'll visit Maud and then I'll go back to the Okanagan. Apple picking has already begun—I don't want to miss it. All I wanted was to see you both and make sure you're all right."

"Couldn't you get a job in Vancouver or Victoria? Then at least you could come and see us again!"

"There's no work in the cities, Doodle. At least where I'm living I have guaranteed work every summer and a few odd jobs in the winter. And surely this depression will end one day and I can get a proper job. After you and Maud are grown up we can see each other freely."

"But that's such a long time away! I want to be with you *now!*"

Daddy hugged her. "I know you do, Doodle. Enough about me, now. I want to hear all about *you!* Are you happy living with your grandmother? And who's this crazy pooch?" Tarka was trying to bury Daddy's hat in the sand.

"He's Tarka!" It finally sank in that Daddy didn't know anything about her life or Maud's during the last two years. She began to explain about Tarka.

They sat on the beach for an hour. In a rush of giddy words Polly told Daddy everything she could think of about her life on the island and Maud's life at school. Every once in a while Daddy would ask a question or make a comment, but mostly he just listened, gazing at her as hungrily as she gazed at him.

"I haven't seen any of your mother's family since her funeral," he said, "and only your grandmother and aunt came to that. I met Rand and Gregor at the wedding. Gregor was just a little guy and a scamp—he ran his finger through the icing of the wedding cake, I remember."

"What wedding?"

"Your mother's and mine, of course. Rand married us in the church here."

"But then you had a fight with Noni," remembered Polly.

"How do you know that?"

"Noni told me."

"Yes, we had a terrible argument," said Daddy sadly. "At least, your mother did."

"What was it about?"

"You're too young to know yet, Doodle. I'll tell you one day. But after that, Una refused to have anything to do with her family. Before she died she made me promise not to either. That wasn't a hard promise to keep, because I knew they didn't approve of me. But I'm grateful that your grandmother didn't lose touch with you girls and that she took you in. I don't know what would have happened to you if she hadn't."

"We didn't want to come!" said Polly.

"I don't imagine you did, and it must have been very hard at first, Doodle. But from what you've told me, it sounds as if you and Maud are very happy here." He looked wistful.

"We are," said Polly slowly. "But I'd rather be with you! Oh, Daddy, why can't you just take us with you? We could all be together again, the way we used to be!"

"Nothing will ever be the way it used to be, Doodle. I'm so sorry. I wish we could be together again too—I wish it with all my heart. But it's just not possible, don't you see? I can't provide you with what your grandmother is giving you. In fact, I'm almost glad this all happened, since it got you here. When I lost that job, I was on the verge of breaking my promise to Una and sending you here anyway."

"You were?"

Daddy nodded. "That's why I couldn't sleep that last night. I had decided it wasn't fair to subject you both to poverty when your grandmother was so well off. The next morning, however, I knew I couldn't bear to let you go. But when . . . well, anyway, after all that happened that day I didn't have a choice. Perhaps it was meant to be."

Polly flinched at the anguish in his eyes. "It *wasn't* meant to be!" she cried. "We're your *daughters!* We're supposed to live with *you!*"

Daddy passed his hand over his face again, as if he were trying to erase it. "Dearest Polly . . . I'm going to say goodbye to you now. Give me the directions to Maud's school and go off to your grandmother. I'll see if I can find someone with a boat to take me off the island."

Polly started to cry. Daddy held her for a long time. She mumbled the address of Maud's school and he said he could ask how to get there when he reached Victoria.

"Oh, my dear, dear little girl," said Daddy. "How could I have been out of touch with you for so long? I wish we could write to each other."

"But Daddy, I've written to *you!*" Polly jumped up. "I've been writing letters to you for two years! I'll give you all of them. Can you wait here a little longer?"

Daddy nodded. Polly ordered Tarka to stay with him and pelted up to the house, relieved that Noni was still out. She emptied the letters into a paper bag. She added the Christmas present she'd made for him her first year on the island—a painted cardboard bookmark. Then she dashed back, running so fast that she tripped on a root and almost fell. What if Daddy wasn't there?

But he was, holding Tarka on his lap and tickling his tummy.

"Here!" she puffed, handing him the bag. "There's something I made for you in here too."

"I'll be honoured to read your letters and delighted to see your present," said Daddy. "Now, Doodle, I'm afraid I really have to go."

Nothing about Daddy indicated that he wanted to. He looked as if he yearned to curl up on the ground and go to sleep.

Running so hard had cleared Polly's mind. "Daddy, you *can't* go! You'll never be able to see Maud—that school's like a jail! But if you stay here I'll ask her to come home next weekend and you can see her then!"

Daddy sighed. He looked like a lost little boy. "You're right, Polly. I can't skulk around a girls school—I'm sure to be caught. But how can I stay here? I can't afford the hotel and it was terribly cold sleeping on the beach."

"You can hide out in our cabin!" said Polly.

"Your cabin?"

"Yes! Biddy and Vivien and I have an old log cabin in the woods! We've fixed it up and it's really comfortable. It isn't heated, but I can give you lots of blankets."

Daddy looked doubtful, but finally, as if he were too exhausted to object, he let Polly take him by the hand.

They went along the beach and through the trees to the edge of the road. Polly picked up Tarka and looked up and down. Noni and Aunt Jean would still be in the rectory kitchen—luckily its windows faced the other way. She couldn't spot any people or horses or cars. She signalled to Daddy and he followed her up the hill and into the thick woods behind the church.

"Here it is!" Polly said proudly, pushing through the

branches. "We call it Oz. Didn't we do a good job of fixing it up? Here's a mattress for your bed," she said, after Daddy had ducked his head to enter the low doorway. "I'll bring you some more blankets and a pillow. And food and drinking water. You can wash in water from the rain barrel—look, here's a bowl you can use. I'll bring you some soap and a towel . . ." Frantically Polly tried to keep track of a growing list in her head.

Why wasn't Daddy saying anything? "Do you think it's all right?" Polly asked anxiously. "I'm sorry it's so dark, but we haven't got any glass."

Daddy looked around at the chinks in the walls that they had stuffed with rags, the worn rug on the floor, and the chairs they had fashioned out of stumps. "It's a grand cabin, Doodle, but what if you get caught bringing me things?"

"I won't," said Polly firmly. "Anyway, I'm always bringing stuff out here. No one cares. And maybe Noni will let me stay the night—sometimes I do. We're going on a picnic for my birthday, but I'll ask her if I can sleep out here after it."

Daddy looked at his watch. "It's two o'clock. What time is your picnic?"

"Three," said Polly. "I'll go and get you some food right away!"

She ran back to the house—still no Noni, thank goodness. Ransacking the pantry, she found a piece of chicken pie and part of a cake, some carrots and some apples. She added soap and toilet paper and a towel. Then she filled a bottle with water. She wrapped everything in Maud's blankets and put Maud's pillow under her arm.

Polly's face was bright red and sweat was dripping into her eyes by the time she'd pushed through the trees. She paused at the door. Would Daddy still be there? Maybe this was all a dream and the cabin would be empty.

But there he was, sound asleep on the mattress. Polly draped another blanket over him and carefully set the food and water on the table. She studied her father's sleeping face: it looked much more peaceful than when he was awake. All Polly wanted to do was curl up beside him, but she had to get ready for the picnic. Polly longed to telephone Maud and tell her what had happened, but there was no time to before they set out in the boats.

The next hours went by in a daze. Polly smiled and talked and waded as if someone else were doing these things. She wouldn't swim, claiming the water was too cold; she was afraid that if she took off her shorts she would lose the necklace she had hidden in her pocket.

Luckily everyone was so noisy and busy that they didn't notice how distracted she was. Vivien and Biddy kept tumbling off a huge log they were trying to ride. Aunt Jean stretched out on her back in the sun and shrieked when Gregor splashed her. Uncle Rand and Noni fashioned a table out of driftwood and stones.

Before the picnic, Gregor and Biddy had a swimming race around the tiny island. Tarka's and Bramble's barks joined the noisy cheering. Biddy was an excellent swimmer and she almost beat Gregor.

"Next year!" she told him as Aunt Jean wrapped her in a towel.

They sat around the low table and stuffed themselves with food. Every once in a while Polly fingered the necklace in her pocket. She couldn't believe the others couldn't *see* her enormous secret, as if she had turned purple.

"You're awfully dreamy, chickie," said Aunt Jean. "Something on your mind?"

"She's thinking about being twelve!" said Gregor. "Pretty soon you'll have boys chasing after you, Pollywog!"

Polly swatted him with the end of her napkin, while Aunt Jean scolded. "Don't be silly, Gregor. Polly's far too young to be interested in boys! You certainly are getting to be bonnie, though," she added.

"She looks more and more like her mother," said Noni sadly. "How proud she would be of you, Polly!" She tried to light the candles on Polly's cake, but the breeze kept blowing them out. "Never mind," said Noni. "Just make a wish anyway."

For two years Polly's birthday wish had been that Daddy would come back. Now her wish had come true! She smiled at her family and friends gazing at her with so much affection. If only she could tell them!

I wish that Daddy could stay here always, she thought.

After it was dark, Gregor built a small bonfire and they sat around it singing songs, and lying on their backs looking at the stars. Usually this was Polly's favourite part of being on the Boot, but all she could think about was getting back to the cabin and Daddy.

Finally they lit the lanterns on the boats, loaded them, and made their way back. Uncle Rand drove Biddy and Vivien home.

"Noni, can I sleep in the cabin tonight?" Polly asked.

"All by yourself? But Polly, why would you want to do that?"

"It's—it's such a beautiful night. And I wouldn't be alone—I'd have Tarka."

"No, hen," said Noni firmly. "The nights are too cold and dark and you have school tomorrow. No more sleeping in the cabin until the spring, and then only if your friends are with you."

Polly sighed; she should have realized Noni would say no. She kissed her good-night and went to bed.

Noni came up a few minutes later. Polly lay there stiffly, wondering if she could sneak out. But the stairs were so creaky Noni would hear her for sure. Polly could call that she was going to the privy, but that wouldn't give her enough time to get to the cabin. There was no hope of seeing Daddy tonight; she would just have to wait until the morning.

Polly tossed for hours. Was Daddy warm enough? She

kept seeing his tense and troubled face. Maybe he would leave after all.

It was thrilling to have him here, but now everything was incredibly complicated. What if Daddy was seen? How was she going to keep Biddy and Vivien away from the cabin? How was she going to persuade Maud to come home?

Polly clutched Tarka, feeling six instead of twelve. She yearned for Maud, for advice and comfort.

Most of all she yearned for Daddy to be the way he used to be, for him to be cheerful and confident and to take care of her the way he always had. Now it was as if Daddy was the child and she was in charge. She should have made her wishes more specific; she should have wished for Daddy not to have changed.

CHAPTER FIFTEEN

THe LONG WEEK

That was the longest and most difficult week of Polly's life. It was even harder than after Daddy had left them. Then she'd been like a limp doll, passed from her house to the foster home to Mrs. Tuttle to Noni.

Now Polly had to think clearly every moment, to plan and connive and steal and lie. She sat in church on Sunday and recited with the rest of the congregation that she had "done those things that we ought not to have done." Polly had no idea then how many of those things there would be.

She had stolen and lied even before church began. While Noni was getting dressed, Polly had taken the leftover bacon from breakfast and put it with some bread and plums in a bag. She'd made tea and filled a Thermos with it. Then she'd stuffed it all into her rucksack.

"I'm just taking Tarka for a walk," she called up to Noni.

"A walk? He's already been out, hasn't he? I don't think there's enough time before church, hen."

"He acts like he's going to throw up," said Polly.

"Then you'd better take him! If you're not back, I'll go ahead and you can meet me there."

Polly called Tarka and dashed through the trees to the cabin. Daddy was sitting outside it, shaving. He'd filled the wash bowl with rainwater and was frowning at his face in a small mirror. He must have had the razor and mirror in his rucksack.

When he saw Polly, his frown changed to a wide smile. "It's my Doodle!" Polly flew into his arms almost as quickly as she had the day before. "I can't stay," she puffed, handing him the food. "I have to go to church and then we have Sunday dinner, so I won't be able to come back until this afternoon. There's hot tea in here."

"Hot tea! You're an angel. Go back now, Doodle. I don't want you to get into trouble."

Polly kissed him, ran back to the house to deposit Tarka and fetch her hat, and caught up with Noni at the church door.

Her next lie to Noni was when she asked her after dinner if she could phone Maud.

"But you know telephone calls are only for emergencies, hen," said Noni. "Can't you write to her?"

"I need to ask her to come home next weekend and a letter might not reach her in time," said Polly.

"Come home? Maud won't want to do that. You know how involved she is with school, especially now that she's head girl."

Polly made her voice sound weepy. "But I really *miss* Maud! She couldn't be here for my birthday and I was hoping she could come this weekend instead."

Noni looked surprised. "Why Polly, I thought you were used to Maud being away! Is there anything bothering you?"

Polly shook her head.

"Are you sure?" Noni flushed. "You haven't—you haven't started to grow up, have you?"

Polly shook her head again, her cheeks as pink as Noni's. Maud had already informed her in a very practical way about getting her monthlies, but Noni had never brought up the subject.

"No, it's not . . . that." Oh, help—what could she say? Perhaps part of the truth . . . "I just—I just need to talk to Maud about our father." Her quivering voice disgusted her—she sounded eight, not twelve.

Noni pressed her lips together. "Your father? All right, then, hen—you may phone Maud. But don't be too disappointed if she can't come."

"Thanks, Noni." Polly walked away quickly so Noni wouldn't see her guilty face.

"Come home? That's impossible. I've already told you, I can't come until Thanksgiving. I have too many responsibilities."

"It's *really* important, Maud. It's the most important thing that's ever happened!"

"But what is it?"

"I can't tell you on the phone. You just have to come!"

"It can't be *that* important. Can't you write me about it?"

"No! Oh, Maud, just come!" Polly's voice broke. *"Please . . .* believe me that you have to."

"Settle down, Poll. Are you in trouble?"

That wasn't exactly the right word, but it would do. "Yes, I'm in real trouble and so are you if you don't come!"

"Is it something to do with—?"

"Yes!"

There was a short silence, then Maud sighed. "All right, Doodle, I'll come. I really wish you could say more, though. Have you heard from—?"

"Maud, just *come* and you'll find out everything. Come on Friday night. The longer you can stay, the better."

"Okay. See you on Friday, then."

Whew! Polly had to sit down to recover. At least Maud suspected it had something to do with Daddy. How amazed she would be that he was here!

Polly had the rest of the afternoon to spend with Daddy. First she found some leftover pork and a few of the bottles of beer that Noni kept in the house for Uncle Rand. Thinking a moment about what Daddy liked, she added some books and the chess set from the living room.

"I'm going to our cabin, Noni," she called. At least she didn't have to lie about that! Polly rushed out before Noni noticed her rucksack full of stolen goods.

Daddy was still sitting outside in the sunshine, rolling a cigarette. After he hugged Polly and thanked her for the food, he looked serious.

"Doodle, I really appreciate everything you're doing for me, but it's not right for me to be here. I think I should just go to Victoria and try to see Maud. I could telephone her and maybe we could meet somewhere."

"But Daddy, Maud's coming on Friday! It would be much easier for you to see her here, and you'd have more time."

"Friday is a long way off. It's too much for you. I hate the thought of you having to keep me a secret. And I'm sure you're having to steal all this food, aren't you? That's not right, Doodle."

"It's not really stealing," said Polly. "We have lots of food, and they would feed you if they knew you were here.

And I spend a lot of time at Oz anyway. Please, Daddy, you *have* to stay!"

As he had yesterday, Daddy looked too exhausted to object. "All right, Polly . . . I feel very uncomfortable about this, but I'll stay until a week tomorrow. But if it's too difficult to hide me, we'll think of something else."

She showed Daddy the books she had brought and he examined them greedily. "These look perfect! And chess! Shall we have a game?"

Daddy had taught Polly how to play chess when she was six. They pulled the table and another stump chair out into the sun. Tarka dozed beside them, keeping an eye out for squirrels.

"Thank you so much for the beautiful bookmark, Doodle," said Daddy. "I'll treasure it always. And I've read all your letters. I'm so touched that you wrote so many."

"I tried to, but sometimes I'd forget for a long time," said Polly.

"That's entirely understandable. What touches me the most, Polly, is how happy you are here. You seem to be thriving on the island. You have a loving family and friends, you've become strong and capable, and you have opportunities I would never have been able to give you, like art lessons and piano lessons and the chance to go away to a good school."

"I'd rather have been with you, though," Polly whispered.

"I know, Doodle. And I know how much anguish I caused you. Things turned out for the best, though, didn't they?"

Polly wanted to scream *No!* She couldn't deny anything Daddy had said, however: she *was* thriving here.

"What moves can the bishop make?" she asked, trying to still the confusion inside her.

———

The next days settled into a routine. For the past year Mrs. Hooper had not been arriving until after Polly had gone to school. Polly would make toast and tea, take them up to Noni in bed, and eat breakfast with her. Then she'd walk Tarka.

There was lots of time, therefore, to pack the rucksack with Daddy's food for the day and take it to him. She would talk to him for a few minutes, then give him a hug and kiss, run back to the house, go upstairs as usual to say goodbye to Noni, and wait with her bike in front until Biddy stopped for her.

Polly sat in school plotting and worrying. "You're daydreaming this week!" Mrs. Oliver told her, when Polly didn't answer a question. Polly was usually such an attentive pupil, however, that Mrs. Oliver didn't scold her.

Biddy and Vivien were not as tolerant of Polly's vagueness. "Polly, it's your turn!" said Vivien when they were playing hopscotch in the squares they had scratched in the schoolyard.

"Sorry," muttered Polly.

Biddy looked puzzled and hurt when Polly didn't laugh at her description of how the twins had cut each other's hair.

At least the weather was sunny and dry, so Daddy was warm enough at night. He and Polly sat outside the cabin and talked and talked, catching up on two years.

Polly wanted to hear about all his adventures. "Tell me about escaping and finding the boat!"

But Daddy didn't want to talk about that—he said it was too painful. Instead he told her how he had hopped onto a train heading east. He'd had to run along the side of a freight car and jump for the ladder, then lie flat on the top. "At first it was a thrill, lying there with the breeze in my hair and the blue sky above, but then it rained and I was miserable," he said. As he talked, his voice regained some of the spark it used to have when he told her stories.

In Toronto, Daddy ate from soup kitchens and slept with a group of other men who lived outside—he called it a "jungle." They cooked stew over a fire and someone always had a harmonica. "I liked those fellows," said Daddy. "We had a real camaraderie. Sometimes I'd recite for them—they called me the Thespian."

Polly grinned. Daddy knew all of Robert Service's poetry by heart and he could make the rhythmic words come alive.

"When I decided to return west, I was lucky enough to find an empty boxcar," he told Polly. "I climbed into a gunny sack and I was snug as a bug!"

Polly was sad to see Daddy's tattered clothes. Even when he'd been unemployed he had always worn a clean shirt and creased pants. "Daddy, do you have enough money?" she asked.

He flushed. "I have some. Enough for the boat rides. When I get back to Vancouver, I'll hitch a ride to Kelowna— that's what I did on the way here."

"I bet Gregor has some old clothes that would fit you," Polly said. "Uncle Rand's would be too short. I could sneak up to Gregor's room in the rectory and get them."

Daddy laughed ruefully. "Oh, Polly Wolly Doodle, I'm turning you into a thief! No, don't you try to steal me clothes. It's bad enough that you're stealing food. I'm fine the way I am—I have one change of underwear and I've washed out some in the rainwater."

Polly had noticed his underwear hanging on a branch. "It wouldn't be stealing—it would be borrowing!" she said. "I'm sure Gregor wouldn't mind if he knew."

"He'd mind, believe me! They all would, especially your grandmother. I can just imagine how furious she'd be to find me here."

"Daddy, I still don't understand . . . why was Noni so mad at my mother and you?"

"She didn't like me," said Daddy. "None of them did."
He looked embarrassed. "I can't tell you all the reasons yet,
Doodle. But I'll tell you some of them. I didn't have much
education and my job as a clerk was leading nowhere. They
thought I was far too young to be marrying their daughter—I
was only eighteen. And they didn't approve of my parents.
My father had been dead for years, but when they ques-
tioned me about him—it was more like grilling—they found
out he'd been a bricklayer. When I told them my mother—
your grannie—was Ukrainian, that really clinched their disapproval. I was glad that Mother was ill and couldn't come to
the wedding—who knows how they would have treated her?"

"But I don't understand," said Polly. "What's wrong
with being a bricklayer or a Ukrainian?"

"Nothing, of course," said Daddy. "But sometimes
people decide that one group is not as good as another.
That's called prejudice. I don't mean to put down your
grandmother and aunt and uncle, Polly. They're basically
good folks, but they can also be narrow-minded and snob-
bish."

Polly flinched, remembering how Noni had behaved
towards Mrs. Osaka.

"I bet my *mother* didn't care who your parents were," she
told him.

"Of course she didn't," said Daddy softly. "Your mother
loved me for myself."

He looked so sad that Polly changed the subject. She began to tell Daddy how much she dreaded going to St. Winifred's next year.

"You'll just have to be brave, Doodle," he told her, "and you may like it more than you think. I'm pleased that you're getting such a good education. I wish I'd had that opportunity." He sighed. "If I had, I would have been in a better position when the crash came. I'm so sorry you had to go through such hard times, Doodle, especially after your grannie died. I felt so bad that I couldn't feed or clothe you properly and that Maud was going to have to quit school. At least you were spared all that."

"But it was fine!" said Polly. "I never felt hungry and I didn't care about what I wore! We were happy!"

"Yes, we were happy," said Daddy. "But I'm still glad you ended up here."

If only he would stop saying that!

—

Polly's biggest worry was that Biddy and Vivien would want her to play with them as usual after school, and that they would go to the cabin. On Monday she said she didn't feel well, and on Tuesday she told them she had to help Aunt Jean polish the church silver. To her relief, on both days they decided to pick blackberries.

On Wednesday, however, Vivien said, "We haven't been to Oz all week! Let's take Biddy's new movie magazine there."

What could Polly say? All she could try was a version of the truth. "We can't go to the cabin right now," she told them. "And I can't do things with you after school, and I can't say why. If I promise to tell you later, will you promise me not to go there?"

Biddy, as usual, was compliant. "Okay." She shrugged. "It sounds very mysterious, but whatever you want, Polly."

Vivien, of course, was much more difficult. "But *why* can't we go?" she asked.

"Please, Viv, it's a secret!" begged Polly.

Finally Vivien agreed, but she was so sulky about it that Polly worried she'd go anyway. And what was Polly going to tell them later? She would just have to deal with that, as with everything else, when the time came.

———

As Daddy became more rested, he lost some of his anxiety. He tried to tame a raven by imitating its croak and holding out a bit of bread. "I'd forgotten how beautiful and peaceful this island is," he said.

He told Polly about his own cabin, which was in an orchard. It didn't have running water, but it was near a stream. The cabin was heated by a fireplace.

"It's very snug—in fact, it gets too hot. We don't spend much time there. During the day we're outside working, and we go into town almost every evening."

Daddy shared the cabin with two men called Jim and Perry. "They're both single fellows, younger than me," said Daddy. "We get along well—they call me the Geezer!"

"Do you ever tell them about Maud and me?" asked Polly.

"No, Doodle," said Daddy gently. "Remember, I'm supposed to be dead. My old self doesn't exist, so you don't either."

Polly gasped and Daddy looked guilty. "Sorry, Doodle, that came out wrong. You girls certainly exist to *me*. Even though I didn't talk about you, I thought about you every minute!"

"Look, there's the raven," said Polly, glad of a diversion. She couldn't bear to discuss Daddy's life away from her for too long. What was going to happen after he left? When would she see him again? Should she try to persuade him to take her with him?

Most worrying of all . . . did she want to go?

On Thursday afternoon Daddy went into the cabin to get the chessboard. There was a rustle in the bushes, then a giggle. Vivien and Biddy! Polly jumped up and saw them dash away.

Daddy came out, but luckily he hadn't noticed. They had *promised!* thought Polly angrily. And they must have seen Daddy. What was she going to tell them?

The next day before school Polly confronted her friends. Biddy looked guilty and Vivien defiant.

"I'm so sorry, Polly!" cried Biddy. "I didn't want to spy on you, but Vivien made me!"

"I'm sorry too," muttered Vivien, but she didn't sound it.

"You promised not to!" said Polly tightly.

"I know. But we thought maybe you were in some kind of trouble and we should find out so we could help you," said Vivien.

Biddy looked worried. "*Are* you in trouble, Polly? Who was that man? He looked like a tramp!"

"He could be dangerous!" said Vivien.

"He's *not* a tramp, and he's not dangerous at all! I'll tell you all about it next week." Suddenly that seemed like an enormous relief. "Will you promise to leave me alone until then? And promise to keep it a secret?"

Reluctantly they crossed their hearts and hoped to die. Polly's only choice was to trust them.

At least Maud was coming tonight and Polly would no longer be the only one responsible for taking care of Daddy. Maud was the strong one. Maud would take care of everything.

Maud turned as pale as milk. "*Daddy's here? Polly, are you sure?*"

"Of course I'm sure! He's hiding in our cabin and he can hardly wait to see you!"

Polly hadn't wanted to tell her right away. Her plan had been to lead Maud to the cabin and surprise her with Daddy, like a present. But Daddy said that would be too much of a shock. "You'll have to prepare her," he'd told her.

"You surprised *me*," Polly pointed out.

"Well, I had no choice. I tried to warn you by singing our song, but there was nothing else I could do."

Now Maud was pacing up and down Polly's room. With her short mop of hair and generous figure, she looked so much like a grown woman that Polly wondered if Daddy would recognize her.

"I just can't *believe* it!" she kept saying. "When did Daddy come? How long is he staying?"

It was so rare that Polly knew more than her sister that she couldn't help gloating a little. She took Maud by the hand. "No more questions. Let's just go and see him!"

The rest of the family were in the living room, having their usual game of cards after dinner. Polly and Maud slipped out the back door. "We're taking Tarka for a walk," called Polly. Tarka's frequent need of walks had certainly been handy this week.

She kept hold of Maud's hand all the way and was surprised

to find that it was shaking. By the time they reached the cabin, Polly's strong and intrepid older sister was trembling all over.

"Is it the Boss?" called Daddy as they entered the cabin.

Maud froze. She and Daddy stared at each other.

"My Maudie is all grown up," said Daddy gently.

Then Maud started to cry, huge wracking sobs that almost choked her. Daddy came over and held her tight. "It's all right, dear old girl. This has been so hard for you, but I'm here now."

Daddy led Maud to the mattress and sat her down. Polly sat down on the other side of Daddy, leaning against his side. Maud pulled out her hankie and dried her tears as her sobs subsided. She kept saying, "I can't believe it! It's really *you!*"

"It really is," said Daddy, "even though I'm rather dishevelled at the moment. And it's really you, Boss, although you've changed even more than Polly has. Your beautiful braids have gone! But I like your bob. And what a handsome girl you are. I'm so proud to be your father."

Daddy handed Maud a necklace like Polly's. "It's a very late birthday present," he told her. Maud examined it silently. Then they sat around the table. Polly had brought some left-over cake from dinner and a bottle of Aunt Jean's huckleberry wine. Daddy opened it and poured them each some.

"A toast to us being together again!" he said. His eyes sparkled and his voice was as vibrant as it used to be.

Polly tried to pretend everything was just like before,

as if the three of them were sitting together in their little house in Winnipeg. "To us!" she cried. Maud clinked her glass with theirs but seemed unable to speak.

"Now you can ask Daddy all about the last two years," Polly prompted. But Maud was still silent.

"Leave her be, Doodle," said Daddy. "She's still in shock. Maud, let me explain why I'm here."

He told her everything he'd told Polly: how he couldn't bear to go any longer without seeing them, and how he'd travelled from Toronto to the Okanagan after "I staged my own death."

This roused Maud to words. "It was in the paper," she muttered. "All about the robbery." Why did Maud sound so suspicious?

Daddy had noticed too. "What do you think about that, Maudie?" he asked quietly.

Maud averted her head. "I'd rather not discuss it."

Daddy looked relieved. "That's the best idea, I think. Tell me all about your school. I hear you're head girl!"

Maud recited her duties, but her voice was cold and detached. "How long are you staying?" she asked suddenly.

"I really should go tomorrow," said Daddy. "It's not fair to ask you to hide me out here any longer—what if you get caught?"

"Tomorrow!" cried Polly. "Oh, Daddy, please stay at least until Monday, after Maud goes back to school!"

Maud was silent—why wasn't she supporting Polly? Daddy looked from one to the other.

"I'll stay until Sunday afternoon," he said finally. "Now, let's not think about that yet, Doodle," he added as Polly started to protest. "Let's just enjoy this precious time together. You'd better get back to the house now, before the others wonder where you are."

"We'll come early in the morning with your breakfast!" called Polly, after they had kissed him good-night.

———

Polly couldn't stop talking. She sat on Maud's bed in the box room and released the burden of this tense week in rapid sentences—all about how difficult it had been to sneak out and lie and plan.

"And Biddy and Vivien saw him!" Polly moaned. "What if they tell someone, Maud? I trust Biddy, but I'm not sure about Vivien."

"Is there anything bad you know that you could threaten her with?" asked Maud. Her voice was detached, as if she didn't really care.

"Well, a while ago she broke her mother's best tea-cup. Biddy and I were there. She buried it in her yard. Her mother hasn't noticed yet that it's gone."

"Talk to her on Monday—say you'll tell her mother if

she tells anyone about Daddy," said Maud, in the same dull voice.

"Okay," said Polly reluctantly. She never liked confronting Vivien, but this was so important she would have to.

Maud was pulling her nightgown over her head. Polly took a deep breath. "Why were you so rude to Daddy, Maud? You hardly talked to him!"

"He shouldn't have come," mumbled Maud.

"*What?*"

"You heard me, Poll. Daddy shouldn't have come! He's spoiled everything. You and I were both contented. We'd put him out of our lives, and that was a good thing. Now everything that happened that summer has come up again. And he's made you lie and steal for him."

"That was *my* choice," said Polly. She stood up, her heart pounding. "I can't believe you're saying these things, Maud. He's our father! He loves us! He came all this way just to visit us! And you seemed glad when you first saw him."

Maud's voice quivered. "I couldn't help it. You're right, Poll, he *is* our father, and he loves us and I—well, I love him too, of course. But we have to get him out of here as soon as possible. Then everything will be *safe* again, the way it was before." She sighed. "I'm sorry to be this way, Doodle. I'll try to be nicer to Daddy tomorrow. It's really hard, though."

"Hard to be nice to *Daddy*?"

Maud got into bed and faced the wall. "I don't want to talk about it, Poll. Seeing Daddy is such a shock, I need to be alone to absorb it. Wake me up when you're ready to take him his breakfast."

Polly ran to her room. She lay awake, while Tarka twitched and yelped in his sleep. He was probably dreaming of chasing squirrels. Polly wished her own life were as easy.

———

"Why are you two being so secretive?" Aunt Jean asked. She had bustled into the kitchen after lunch, just as Maud and Polly were about to leave. "You keep going off on your own and I've scarcely had a chance to catch up with Maud!"

"Leave them be, Jean," said Noni. "Polly wanted to have Maud to herself this weekend. They have things to discuss."

"What things?"

"That's their own business, Jean."

"But where are you girls going? You've already been out all morning!"

"Jean, will you stop being such a Nosy Parker! You know Polly has a cabin in the woods. That's probably where you're spending your time, isn't it?"

Polly nodded. "Noni, can we take some cookies and tea there?"

"Take whatever you like. Dinner's not until six, so you can stay until then."

"But Clara, I wanted to show Maud the new altar cloth I embroidered!"

"She can see it this evening. Run along, hens, we'll see you later."

Polly couldn't believe Noni was making it so easy. She shovelled food into her rucksack, grateful that for once she didn't have to steal it.

They had already spent all morning with Daddy, playing so much chess that Polly's brain was woolly. Maud had asked Daddy a few stiff questions about his life in Kelowna, but soon she'd stopped talking. Every time Daddy asked her something she responded so coldly that he gave up.

Polly couldn't bear the hurt look in his eyes. She tried to keep up a nervous chatter, but most of the time the three of them sat silently around the chessboard. The happy reunion they had enjoyed yesterday had dwindled into awkwardness.

"We've brought you tea and oatmeal cookies!" Polly called now. Daddy was outside as usual.

He looked up from his book. "You spoil me." His smile was so sad. "Shall we have another game?" he said quickly.

Too quickly, thought Polly. As long as they were playing chess they didn't have to talk to one another.

"No chess," said Maud bluntly. "Daddy, I have something I want to say to you."

"Uh-oh," said Daddy. "I'm in trouble with the Boss!"

Maud refused to smile. "Daddy, are you *sure* you didn't

steal that money? I've read all the papers and it certainly looks as if you did."

"Maud!" cried Polly.

"Hush, Doodle, let her be. Maud, sweetheart, I hate it that you think I'm a thief."

"But if you were innocent, why did you run away as if you were guilty?"

"I've told you, Maud. The money was found in my possession. If I'd stayed, I would have been convicted and gone to jail for years. You would have had to live with that disgrace."

"We already do!" said Maud. "We do in the family, anyway. Everyone thinks you did it and they're all ashamed."

"I'm sorry about that, but your mother's family never did like me. I hope *you're* not ashamed, Maud."

"Of course she isn't!"

Maud frowned at Polly. "Let me finish!" Her voice became more and more Maudish. "I'm sorry, Daddy, but I *am* ashamed. I think you *did* take the money. I understand why—you wanted to support us and you were tired of never getting good jobs. And you were upset about me leaving school. I understand, but it was still wrong. It's a *sin* to steal. It's against God's commandment. You should have stayed and taken the consequences."

Now Maud was standing, her cheeks flaming. Daddy tried to touch her, but she shrugged him off.

"I'm really sorry, Daddy, but I don't believe you. I'm glad we don't live with you and I wish you'd never come!" Choking on a sob, Maud ran away.

Polly gasped. She crept onto Daddy's lap. "I can't believe Maud said that! What's *wrong* with her?"

Daddy took out his handkerchief and wiped his eyes. "You know our Maud," he said, his voice strained. "She's always seen things in black and white. It's easier for her to believe I was wrong and to dismiss me. Then she can stay in her secure world and not have to think about me."

"I *hate* Maud!" said Polly. "She's so different from the way she used to be! How can she not believe you?"

"Don't hate her, Doodle," said Daddy. "I don't blame her, really. Perhaps I *would* have stolen the money, if I'd been really desperate. You never know the depths you might go to to save your family."

"But you didn't," said Polly firmly.

Daddy wiped his hand over his face. "I'm glad you believe that, Doodle."

They sat in the sun for a while, then Daddy said gently, "I think you should go back to your grandmother now, Polly. Give me a kiss."

Polly stumbled to her feet. "I'm going to tell Maud to apologize! And I'll bring you some dinner. We're having venison and apple pie."

"I've really appreciated how well you've been feeding

me, Doodle," said Daddy. He hugged her so tightly her chest felt crushed. Polly hugged him back, called Tarka, and walked away, forcing her voice to sound cheerful as she called over her shoulder, "See you later!"

———

Polly marched straight to Maud's room and opened her door, but Maud snarled, "Go away!" Polly slammed the door as hard as she could and stomped downstairs. At dinnertime she fumed as Maud and Gregor discussed a book they'd both read. How could Maud talk so coolly, as if nothing had happened?

"You're not eating a thing, hen," said Noni. "Are you feeling all right?"

"Our Polly won't eat a dear deer," laughed Gregor, "but she'll eat dear little lambs and dear little chickens!"

"Leave her alone, Gregor!" said Noni sharply.

"Sorry, Pollywog," said Gregor. "How about you and me going fishing after dinner? Want to come, Maud?"

Maud nodded, but Polly refused. She had to take Daddy the leftovers from dinner.

As usual, she waited until the grown-ups were safely in the living room with their cards. She'd forgotten her rucksack at the cabin, so she packed the food into a paper bag. She was so exhausted that her arms could hardly lift it. How much longer was she going to have to do this? she wondered wearily.

"I'm back!" she called as she arrived at the cabin. Tarka ran ahead, barking a welcome. But the cabin was empty. Daddy's few possessions were gone. On the table was a piece of Polly's drawing paper with writing on it.

Daddy had left.

CHAPTER SIXTEEN

a FaMILY MEETING

Dear Maud and Polly,

I'm so sorry I didn't say goodbye, but I've decided that leaving is best for all of us. I shouldn't have come. I've put Polly into a deceitful and dishonest position all week and that's not right. I've renewed our relationship when you were both probably starting to forget about me.

The trouble is, I love the two of you so deeply that I had to come. Even though my being here stirred up so much turmoil, I'm grateful I saw my two best girls again and that they both seem so well and happy.

I don't think I should see you again until you are adults. It's too difficult when we have to be under-handed about it, and it's too painful when we can't be together all the time.

My dearest girls, I can't bear for us to be out of touch again. I'm going to write to your grandmother and tell her I'm alive. There's a risk that the family will tell the police, but I imagine that the publicity and scandal that would result will keep them from reporting me.

I'll also tell her I was here and that Polly is not to be scolded for hiding me. After my next stint of work I'll send her some money to pay for the food I ate.

I'm going to ask her if I can write to you. If she says yes, I'll give a post office box number in Kelowna and you can write to me there. But I don't want to send you my address until your grandmother gives her permission. She's your legal guardian now and I have to respect her wishes.

Dearest Maud, as the eldest, you have suffered the most through all of this and I don't blame you for wanting me out of your life. I fervently hope, however, that eventually you can bring yourself to write to me and that you'll remember that I'm exactly the same father you have always loved, and who loves you so deeply that I cannot express it.

Doodle, I am so heartened that you believe I am innocent. When the family finds out I'm alive, however, you're going to hear a great many things against me, so try to hold on to your trust in me, and try not to be angry with them.

I'm devastated that we can't be together for so long, but I was also glad to see how happy you both are. I want you to stay happy. I want Maud to be the best head girl that St. Winifred's ever had, and to graduate with distinction. I want Polly to savour her last year at her present school and to go to St. Winifred's bravely, with an open mind.

You are both such clever girls that I hope you will go to university; I'm sure your grandmother will be happy to pay for it. After you graduate you'll be adults at last, and we can see one another again.

Please accept my apologies for causing you so much trouble, and please remember every day how very much I love you. I look forward to hearing from you both.

Your ever loving Daddy

Polly skimmed the letter, then read it again more slowly. She started to sob as the words registered. Then she gasped. There was no steamer tonight, so Daddy must still be on the island!

Shoving the letter into her pocket, Polly dashed to the trees where she had first seen Daddy—only a week ago. She searched all along the beach but couldn't find him.

Gregor and Maud were bobbing in the rowboat by the point. The sea was so still that she could hear Maud laugh. How *could* she?

Then Polly spotted another boat: a crab boat slowly *put-putt*ing out into the pass between Kingfisher Island and Walker Island—heading towards Vancouver.

She dashed to the end of the wharf. A young man was crouched there, emptying crabs from a trap. Polly knew everyone on the island—he was David Hayes.

"Hi, there, kiddo," said David.

"Do you know who's in that boat?" Polly asked frantically.

"Yup. My brother Frank and a stranger. He waved to us as we were coming in with our traps and offered to pay us to take him to the mainland. It's such a calm evening that Frank said he would. Frank will have to spend the night in Steveston, but he can stay with our sister."

Polly wanted to scream at the boat to come back, but it was too far away. She waved uselessly as it disappeared from sight.

"Do you know who that fellow was?" asked David. "I've never seen him here before. He said he'd come to the island to find work, but of course he had no luck. I was surprised he had money he looked so hard up."

Polly couldn't answer. She trudged back to the house and up the stairs to Maud's room to wait for her.

"I won't write to him," said Maud, putting down the letter.

"But you have to, Maud! He'll be so hurt if you don't! He's your *father*!"

"He's not my father any longer. I'm . . . I'm disowning him."

"What does that mean?" whispered Polly.

"I'm not recognizing him as my father. You can, if you like. But what Daddy did was wrong. He's a thief and he's also a liar, because he won't admit he took the money. I can't forgive him for that and I don't want to have anything to do with him."

Polly glowered at her. "If you don't, then I'm going to disown *you*!"

"Calm down, Doodle. I know you're angry at me, but you're just going to have to accept that we disagree."

Maud was in control again, the calm and reasonable head girl. She smiled tightly at Polly. "At least Daddy's gone. It was so stressful having him here! Can't we still be friends?"

No! thought Polly, but she couldn't speak. She listened in disbelief as Maud said, "I'm going to make some new rules for us, Doodle." She got out a piece of paper and wrote silently for a few minutes.

Polly sank onto Maud's bed. She longed to leave the room, but her legs were rubber. *Daddy has gone, Daddy has gone*, she kept telling herself. Nothing else mattered.

"Okay!" said Maud. "Here are the rules. Number one:

You can write to Daddy as much as you like, but I won't. And tell him not to write to me."

Polly made her voice work. "Could you at least *read* his letters?"

"All right, if you want me to. Rule number two: You can talk to me about Daddy, but we're not going to discuss whether he stole the money. We're never going to agree, and arguing about it will only drive us further apart."

"But Maud, you *used* to believe Daddy was innocent! Why don't you now?"

"I only thought he was innocent because he told me he was. But I've been thinking about it for a long time and it just doesn't make sense that he is. I could give you lots of reasons, but what's the point? Let's go on to rule number three, which is the same as before: We can't tell anyone outside of the family that Daddy is alive, or that he was accused of stealing. And rule number four is that we're each going to carry on our lives as they were before Daddy came. That's the only way we'll be happy, Doodle. Do you agree to keep these rules?"

"No, I don't, and you can't make me. I don't care about your stupid rules!" Finally Polly had the strength to get up and leave. She turned at the door. "I think you're completely wrong to be against Daddy, Maud. I don't *like* you any more!"

———

Polly didn't speak to Maud for the rest of the weekend. After Sunday supper the family walked her to the wharf. Polly let Maud hug her goodbye because everyone would think it was strange if she didn't. She kept her body stiff, however, and avoided Maud's eyes.

As soon as Polly got back to the house, she went straight to bed. On Monday morning she told Noni she was sick. That was true—her head pounded and her stomach churned. She spent the whole day in bed, mostly sleeping. In the evening she came downstairs in her dressing gown and sipped some soup at the kitchen table, feeling as if she had emerged from a battle.

"Are you feeling better, hen?" asked Noni. "Maud's visit seems to have been a trying one. Did you discuss everything you wanted to? Is there anything you want to talk to *me* about?"

If only Noni knew! Well she would, as soon as she heard from Daddy. Polly longed to spill out everything, but she would wait for his letter.

———

Polly went back to school on Tuesday. She told Vivien and Biddy she wouldn't talk about anything until after school. Then Vivien cornered her.

"Well?" she asked. "Are you going to tell us who that man was?"

"Let's go to the cabin," said Polly. "Then I'll tell you."

Polly's heart twisted as they approached the cabin. She wanted so badly for Daddy to be sitting on his stump outside the door! But all that was left were some dirty dishes and the books and chess set. Biddy and Vivien stared at these things curiously and waited for Polly to speak.

She couldn't think of a lie and she was tired of secrets. "My father was here," she said bluntly.

"Your *father*?"

"But your father's dead!"

"He's not dead," said Polly. "He only pretended to be."

Slowly she told them the whole story—all except the stealing. She couldn't be sure that they would believe Daddy was innocent.

At the end Biddy looked stunned and Vivien suspicious.

"But Polly, you said your father had drowned! Didn't they find a body? Wasn't there a funeral? How do we know you aren't making this up?"

Polly tried to suppress her anger. "Of course they didn't find a body because he *didn't* drown! They believed he drowned because he left a note saying he was going to kill himself by walking into the river. And there was a funeral because everyone thought he was dead—but he wasn't! And why would I make it up? You *saw* him!"

"We saw a strange man," said Vivien slowly. "But he was so scruffy and ragged. He didn't look like anyone's father."

"He'd travelled all the way from the Okanagan. And he has no money for clothes. You can believe what you want, Vivien, but I'm telling the truth!"

Not the whole truth. But it was such a relief to tell most of the truth—that Daddy was alive and had been here.

"*I* believe you, Polly," said Biddy. "She's right, Vivien— why would Polly meet with a stranger? It *must* have been her father."

"Okay, I believe you too. But *why* did he pretend to drown?" asked Vivien. "It's such a weird thing to do!"

Polly was prepared for this. "He pretended he had drowned so we could come and live on the island. A long time ago my mother had an argument with my grand- mother. She made Daddy promise he'd never bring us here. But then, when we were so poor, Daddy was desperate. He staged his own death so we'd *have* to come and he wouldn't be breaking his promise."

"That's so noble!" cried Biddy. "He gave you and Maud up so you'd have a better life! It's just like a movie! He sounds like a wonderful man. Oh, Polly, you must have been so glad to see him after so long!"

"Gave you and Maud up": what terrible words. "He—he *is* a wonderful man," Polly stuttered. "I was really glad to see him. But my father's gone back to the Okanagan now and I won't see him again until I'm grown up."

"That's such a long time to wait," said Biddy.

Polly tried not to cry. "Listen, you two. You have to promise never to tell anyone this. If you do . . ." Oh, help. She couldn't say that if they did, Daddy might be put in jail.

Then Biddy rescued her. "Of course we won't tell! If we did, then maybe you'd be sent to live with your father *now*! I'd hate that!"

Polly looked at Vivien. "I wouldn't like that either," she admitted, giving Polly a small smile.

Could Polly trust her? She had no choice.

"Let's clean up the cabin!" said Biddy.

Polly picked up a broom, as if everything was just the same.

———

For the rest of that week Polly felt as if she were slowly waking up from a long, jangled dream. Everything on the surface was normal. She went to school, she played with Tarka and her friends, and she talked to her family.

But every night she lay in bed and tried to sort out her turmoil. What a lot had happened since she had turned twelve!

She missed Daddy terribly: she missed his face and voice and touch, she missed looking after him, she missed talking to him and listening to his stories and sitting in his lap and playing chess. But she didn't miss the tension and guilt of hiding him.

She hated to admit it, but part of her was even glad he had gone. Now she could resume her normal, secure life. She wanted to be with Daddy and she didn't want to wait for years until she could be; yet she was also glad she could stay here with Noni. The island seemed so much her real home now that she couldn't imagine living anywhere else.

At least she would be able to write to Daddy—surely Noni would let her. And surely Maud would come around and love and accept him again. Maybe Polly would even forgive Maud—but not yet.

On boat days Polly listened avidly for the whistle of the steamer. Then she ran to the wharf and joined the small crowd waiting for the mail. Finally, about ten days after Daddy had left, his letter came: an envelope addressed to Mrs. Gilbert Whitfield in his clear, round handwriting.

Polly handed it to Noni without a word. Then she went up to her room so Noni could read it undisturbed.

"Oh, *no!*" Polly heard Noni cry. Then she called Polly downstairs. "Is it true?" she whispered. Her hand trembled as she held the letter.

Polly nodded mutely.

"Your father is *alive*? You *saw* him?"

"Oh, Noni . . ." Polly stumbled out the story of that long, difficult week. "I'm so sorry I stole food and lied to you," she finished.

Noni's lips were trembling even more than her hands.

"It's all right, hen," she quavered. "What you did was wrong, but it's understandable under the circumstances." She stood up and took a deep breath. "Now, Polly, it's going to take me a while to absorb this. It's such a shock! Maud will have to come home again. Obviously we all have a lot to talk about, but that will have to wait until she's here. In the meantime we'll carry on normally. I don't want you to worry about this. You've already had more than enough to bear. Will you be all right by yourself while I tell Jean and Rand?"

Polly barely had time to nod. Noni seldom moved quickly, but now she actually ran to the rectory.

_____

Polly was handed the phone, even though she didn't want to talk to Maud.

"This is such a nuisance," Maud complained. "I'm supposed to read the lesson in church this week! Oh, well, I know I have to come, and it will be good to see you again, Doodle. After this it will be *settled*," she added firmly, as if she were packing all that had happened into a box. She didn't seem to notice that Polly didn't answer.

Several days that week Polly arrived home from school to find a note from Noni saying that she was over at the rectory. Polly knew they were all discussing Daddy. But every night at dinner no one said a word about him. They were gentle with Polly and kept giving her concerned looks. Some evenings Aunt Jean had puffy eyes, as if she'd been weeping. Noni had such deep circles under her own eyes that Polly knew she was barely sleeping. Were they happy that Daddy was alive? Polly wouldn't know until Maud came home.

For all of Polly's life her sister had been her ally, even though they had grown apart in the last few years. Now that was over. By betraying Daddy, Maud had betrayed Polly as well.

But could Polly really disown her? She still needed Maud. They were still sisters.

Maybe, now that Maud had had time to think about it, she had changed her mind. Maybe when she came she would help Polly stick up for Daddy. Then Polly would forgive her and they would be friends again.

———

As soon as Maud arrived home on Saturday afternoon, two meetings took place: one in Noni's bedroom and one with the whole family in the living room.

Noni asked them to sit on her bed, while she paced in front of them. "First of all, Maud, I want you to know that Polly and I have already talked about how wrong she was to lie and steal for her father. I understand why she needed to. I also understand how you couldn't tell us Daniel didn't drown. You made a promise to him."

Maud simply nodded. The skin on her face was as taut as if her braids were still pulling it back.

"I'm very glad for you, girls, that your father is alive," continued Noni. Her words sounded forced. "You must have been amazed to see him!"

Maud didn't answer, but Polly's eyes prickled as she remembered hearing the song on the beach.

"It's such an astounding thing he did, to pretend he had drowned," continued Noni, "and what a tremendous secret for you both to keep!"

"We did, though," said Maud. "We didn't tell anyone, did we, Poll?"

Polly refused to respond to Maud until she knew her position. "Every time you mentioned Daddy I *wanted* to tell," she said to Noni.

"Well, now the secret is out." Noni took Polly's hand. "We have a lot more to discuss, but let's include the rest of the family. Come downstairs now, girls."

Aunt Jean and Uncle Rand and Gregor were waiting in the living room. They stated in strained voices how glad they were that Daddy was alive. They didn't sound at all glad, but as serious and solemn as if they were saying that he had died.

"Daniel has asked me if he can write to you, hens," said Noni, "but I'm of two minds about it. It seems unkind to stop him, but it's against my better judgment."

Polly whirled around to stare at her. *Why?*

Then she found out. "Maud and Polly, we know how thrilled you must be that Daniel is alive," said Uncle Rand slowly, "but we feel we must tell you our position. Daniel is still a thief—that's a fact that hasn't changed."

"He didn't do it!" cried Polly.

"Hush, dear, and let me finish. It's very difficult for a child your age to imagine that your own father would do such a thing. I admire your loyalty, but all the evidence is against Daniel. The money was found in his possession."

"But someone put it there!" cried Polly.

Aunt Jean put her arm on Polly's shoulder, but Polly shrugged it off. "Listen, chickie," she said gently. "Why would anyone do that? It's very clear that your father stole the money. Why would he run away? And he said nothing in his letter about being innocent."

"He ran away because he knew no one would believe him! And he didn't need to say anything because he *is* innocent!"

"No, Polly," said Uncle Rand. "Your father ran away because he was *guilty*. You need to accept this, my dear. What he did was very wrong."

"He did it for you," said Noni, "but that's no excuse."

Waves of disappointment crashed over Polly. "Do *you* believe my father stole the money?" she asked Gregor.

Gregor looked as if he wished he were playing tennis. "I'm sorry, Pollywog, but I do."

"I never did trust Daniel after what he did to our Una!" said Aunt Jean.

Polly stared at her. What did she mean?

Noni said sharply, "Be quiet, Jean! Our personal feel-ings about Daniel have no place in this discussion." Then her voice softened. "Girls, we know how hard it is for you to hear these things about your father. We don't expect you to believe them yet, but you're going to have to one day. I don't doubt for one minute that your father loves you—that's why he stole the money. But just remember that he's capable of breaking the law."

Maud spoke for the first time. "Are you going to tell the police that our father is alive?" she asked them.

Hope fluttered in Polly. Was Maud going to defend Daddy?

"No, we are not," said Uncle Rand. "We've decided that it's not fair for the two of you to suffer the publicity that would follow from that. A man presumed drowned who is found alive is going to make a much bigger story than before. It might hit the B.C. papers, and then every-one on the island would be talking about it. We can't do that to you."

Or to yourselves! thought Polly. Daddy was right. None of them was going to risk the scandal.

"At least your father has promised not to try to see you again until you're adults," said Noni. "By then I think both of you will have realized how wrong he was."

"I already know that," said Maud. "I know our father is a thief."

The family all looked approving. "Oh, poor chickie," said Aunt Jean, giving her a hug. "What a cross to bear!"

"I hope you are praying for him, Maud," said Uncle Rand.

"I am," said Maud tightly, "but I've already decided I don't want to write to him."

"You don't have to, Maud," said Noni. "You're being very mature and sensible and I'm proud of you for that decision. What about you, Polly? Don't you think it would be better not to correspond with your father? All of this is simply too much for you right now. I'm sure he'd understand."

"That would be so much easier, chickie," said Aunt Jean. "If you and Daniel had no communication he could be out of our lives. It really would have been better if he *had* drowned," she added to Uncle Rand in a murmur, but Polly heard her.

Gregor smiled at Polly. "Let's just forget about your father and carry on with the good times we've had since you arrived."

"Nobody but us is aware that Daniel's alive," said Uncle Rand, "and I know that you girls will continue to keep that a secret. So nothing needs to change from before, Polly. Your happy life here can continue. But if you and your father start writing to each other, you're always going to be reminded of him and you won't be as happy. I don't think it's fair of him to ask you to write."

"Neither do I," said Noni. "Polly, you can cling to your belief that your father is innocent. In time I think you'll realize he isn't, but we're not going to try to change your mind. In fact, as Gregor says, after today we'll just carry on. We'll continue to keep Daniel a secret and we won't talk about him among ourselves. But Rand is right, hen. Writing to him will just upset you. Wouldn't you rather put all that misery behind you?"

Polly sat on the fender stool in front of the fireplace as her family's voices pelted her. She looked up at the circle of faces—the faces she had thought she loved. They had all betrayed her . . . even Maud and even Noni.

She stood up, swallowing hard—she would *not* cry. "Of course I want to write to Daddy," she said quietly. Then fury whipped her voice into a shout. "Of *course* I do! Daddy isn't wrong—*you* are! He's not a thief! He didn't steal the money and I will never believe he did! I hate all of you! I wish I could leave this place and live with Daddy!"

She fled.

Polly pressed her face into the mattress in the cabin, trying to catch a whiff of Daddy. She pulled the blanket tightly around her, but she couldn't stop trembling. Tarka curled into a ball at her feet.

"I hate them, I hate them!" she whispered, pounding her fist into the mattress.

Maybe she should run away. She could go and live with Daddy. She'd have to take the boat to Vancouver, but how would she get to Kelowna? She didn't know where Daddy lived. She had no money, and someone would be sure to stop a child travelling alone.

That was the whole problem. She was still a child, so the adults wouldn't listen to her. She had no power.

I hate *them!* thought Polly again. The word was like an icicle inside her. She wished she could cry, but her tears were frozen as well.

Tarka whined—he wanted his dinner. Polly hadn't touched her lunch. She was hungry too, but she couldn't bear to eat with any of the family.

She decided she would sneak back to the house, get food for both of them, and hide herself and Tarka out here the way she had hidden Daddy. They might *think* she had run away. They would worry and cry. *That* would teach them to listen to her! She'd return in the morning, but she would make them all miserable for a night.

What could she do with Tarka? If he came back with her, he might give her away, but if she tied him up, he would bark so shrilly that someone might hear him from the road. She would just have to keep hold of him and hope he'd be quiet.

The rucksack she had used for Daddy's food was still lying on the table. Polly picked it up and walked slowly back to the house, using her belt as a leash for Tarka so he wouldn't run ahead. When she reached the back door, she picked up Tarka and paused.

Luckily it was Mrs. Hooper's day off. Polly crept to the kitchen window and peeked in: no one was there. Maud and Noni must be in their rooms.

It was too difficult to hold Tarka and try to open cupboards. Polly put him on the floor. "Stay!" she whispered. Quickly she ransacked the pantry, stuffing cold chicken, Tarka's meat, carrots, and cookies into her rucksack.

When Tarka smelled his dinner, he rushed over and yapped at her to hurry up and feed him. "Shush!" said Polly, but it was too late.

"Is that you, hen?" Noni came into the kitchen. She looked at the stuffed rucksack sitting on the kitchen floor.

"Oh, my poor Polly, what were you doing?"

There was no point in lying. "I was going to spend the night in the cabin," muttered Polly, not looking at Noni. "I don't want to be with any of you."

Noni started towards her, then stopped. "I don't blame you, hen. We've all let you down, haven't we? I'm very sorry you're so disappointed in us. Will you listen to me for just a few minutes?"

Polly just stood there, gazing at the floor.

"Polly, you are simply too young to understand. I admire your loyalty to your father, but one day you'll have to realize he did something very wrong."

"You don't like him," said Polly. "You're pre—" What was that word Daddy had used? "You're *prejudiced.*"

"I don't know Daniel," said Noni. "I've only met him a few times. And yes, Polly, there are reasons I took against him, but those don't concern us right now. I'm far *more* concerned that he's a thief. However . . . he's still your father. I won't be able to stop him seeing you when you're grown up, and I've changed my mind about you writing to him in the meantime. I apologize for trying to persuade you not to, hen. I'll give you his address and you can write as much as you want."

"Good," muttered Polly. She couldn't say thank-you for something that Noni should have told her in the first place.

"Oh, my dearest Polly, all I want is for you to be happy! Enjoy your father's letters and enjoy being young while you can. Enjoy the island and your friends, enjoy your last year at school. You're going to like St. Winifred's too, despite what you think. You've become so contented, living here. I want you to keep on being happy and not worry so much about adult matters that you have no control over. All right?"

Part of Polly yearned to give in to that soothing, safe voice, but a new, stronger self didn't trust it any more.

Noni sighed. "I know you're still very angry at us, and

you can be angry for as long as you like. Just remember that
we love you very much and we're so grateful that you came
into our lives. Now, why don't you go up to your room and
tidy up for dinner? I'll feed Tarka."

"I won't eat with you," said Polly.

"Then I'll bring you up a tray. Off you go, now," said
Noni firmly.

Polly had no choice. She stumbled upstairs and closed
the door. Then finally, after this long, long day, she let herself cry.

———

For a week Polly spoke to her family as little as possible. She
spent as much time as she could with Biddy and Vivien, or
on long walks with Tarka. She was quiet with her friends, but
she knew they would think she was still worried about her
father. At home she ate quickly with her head down, then
slipped from her chair and went to her room. She began to
feel as if she were enclosed by glass walls.

Noni and Aunt Jean and Uncle Rand let her be angry,
although they gave her sorrowful looks. On the weekend,
Maud stayed at school as usual and Gregor didn't come
home. Vivien asked Biddy and Polly to a slumber party for
her birthday on Saturday. Noni told Polly she didn't have to
go to church.

The slumber party was a welcome escape from home. For the first time since Daddy had left, Polly felt light-hearted. They squatted on the floor in Vivien's attic room and wrote names of movie stars and colours and fortunes onto a folded paper square.

"Your turn, Polly," said Vivien.

Polly picked "Ginger Rogers."

Vivien rapidly opened and shut the flaps: "G-I-N-G-E-R-R-O-G-E-R-S."

Then Polly picked "Blue."

"B-L-U-E."

Under the "Blue" flap was a fortune in Vivien's printing: "You will marry someone with brown hair."

"Chester!" giggled Biddy.

"Mrs. Chester Simmons," pronounced Vivien.

Polly thumped her friends in protest, but she couldn't help laughing. The ice inside her began to melt.

When she arrived home late Sunday afternoon, the house smelled of roast beef and Yorkshire pudding. Tarka jumped into her arms and licked her face. Noni and Aunt Jean were turning over the pieces of a new jigsaw puzzle they had laid out on the card table. Uncle Rand was deep in his newspaper. They all looked up and smiled.

Try not to be angry with them, Daddy had written.

"I'm back," said Polly. She couldn't resist. The room was so warm and welcoming and she itched to get at the puzzle.

"We're so glad," said Noni. "Can you help us? This is a devilish one."

Polly pulled up a chair beside them and began looking for edge pieces.

CHAPTER SEVENTEEN

VALEDICTORY

Slowly Polly's life returned to normal. Nothing, of
course, could be the same as it was before Daddy's
visit. She acted friendly now to Maud and the rest of
her family, but it was a careful friendliness. She didn't hate
them any more, but she was still angry. Her anger gave her
an inner power. She *knew* she was right and they were wrong.

Now Polly felt free to wear her necklace. Its light weight
helped ease the ache of missing Daddy. At least now she
could write to him—letters that he answered, not letters that
she hid. Every Sunday afternoon Polly wouldn't let herself
do anything else until she had written out her week. She
ended each letter with the same sentence: "I can hardly
wait until the day we can be together again." Each time Noni
silently handed her an envelope from Kelowna, Polly would
rush up to her room to tear it open.

After apple picking had ended, Daddy had started a new job laying bricks. "I used to help my father sometimes, but I never thought I'd be doing it myself. I'm surprised at how satisfying a job it is," he wrote. Jim and Perry had left, and Daddy had found a room in a boarding house in town, with a widow and her daughter. He got a reduced rate for helping with repairs to the house. There were three other boarders, and Daddy seemed to get along with them well.

He always addressed his letters to both girls and constantly asked about Maud. Polly told him as much as she could, sometimes simply copying parts of Maud's letters from school—endless, boring details about prefects' meetings and the Guppy's teas and Maud's friends.

Polly forwarded all of Daddy's letters to Maud and quizzed her on them when she came home for Christmas: "Which person in the boarding house do you like the best? Do you think Daddy's right about his new boss?"

"You don't have to test me," Maud told her. "I've read every letter. I said I would, didn't I?"

"Oh, Maud, *why* don't you write back? Daddy would really like it if you did."

"I don't choose to," said Maud.

Polly sighed. She wanted to yell at Maud, but that wouldn't help. Instead she sat down to finish the painting she was sending to Daddy for Christmas.

———

While Polly was singing at the Christmas concert, she noticed Chester standing with his parents at the back of the hall. Ever since that long-ago kiss on the stairs, she and Chester had acted like polite strangers. But this evening Polly couldn't stop looking at him. He was taller than his parents now, and he looked so handsome in his grey suit. All during the last carol Polly tried to decide if she could just stroll up to him and casually wish him a Merry Christmas.

"'Joy to the World'!" she bellowed with the rest of the choir. The words gave her courage. As soon as the applause had ended, Polly made her move.

"Hi, Chester," she said quietly.

Chester smiled at her. But he couldn't seem to speak, and the blood rose in his face like a tide. Polly immediately regretted her decision.

"Why, Polly, how are you?" his mother said. "What a wonderful concert! You children get better every year."

Mr. Simmons chucked Polly under the chin. "What a pretty young lady you're getting to be! Don't you agree, son?"

That ruined everything. Chester stared at the floor; now even his ears were scarlet. Polly was trapped for agonizing moments while his mother asked her about her family. Finally she muttered, "I should go," and escaped.

He doesn't like me any more, Polly decided as she walked home under the stars. All the kindness he had shown her in school, his kiss and his shy greetings during the holidays—none of that meant a thing.

The encounter gave Christmas another tinge of sadness. Polly missed Daddy so sharply that the family's usual jovial festivities bounced off her, as if she were inside her glass walls again. Daddy had sent her a cheap ring with a fake emerald in it. Polly noticed Noni trying to suppress her disapproval. She wore her ring defiantly until it turned her finger black.

The Hogmanay celebration didn't feel like a fresh start to the year as it usually did. "Happy New Year!" everyone cried, but this was the year Polly had dreaded, when she would have to go away to school.

In March, Polly went to Victoria to write an entrance exam for St. Winifred's. She sat in a classroom at the school with four other girls, a stern-looking teacher presiding over them. The room was chillier than the air outside. Polly waited to start, rubbing her bare arms.

"You may begin," said the teacher. Everyone flipped over their papers.

The exam was in three parts: English, mathematics, and history. The questions were challenging, especially the math ones, but Uncle Rand's tutoring had been so helpful that Polly knew she could do most of them. But she put her pencil down for a few minutes as an idea came to her.

Why not *fail* the exam? Then she wouldn't have to come here! She could stay on the island and Noni would hire a governess. Biddy and Vivien could share her—it would be like having their own school!

Never in her life had Polly done something so deliberately wrong. Her pencil scribbled so fast she could hardly keep up with it, as if someone else were writing the exam. The math questions were the easiest to fake: Polly simply wrote down any numbers she could think of. It was also easy to choose the incorrect answers in the multiple choice sections for English and history, because, except for a few, she knew the right ones.

But then she had to write two short essays in ink. She put down her pencil and picked up her pen. The first essay was an analysis of a poem by William Wordsworth, the one that began, "My heart leaps up when I behold a rainbow in the sky." It was Noni's favourite poem; she knew it by heart and had recited it to Polly many times.

The good Polly longed to write out her own love for the poem. She knew how well she could do it. But the bad Polly dipped her pen into the inkwell and began the essay in her messiest writing, making large blots and misspelling as many words as she could.

"The first sentens in this pome means that Wordwooth likes rainbows. It is very hard to understand the rest. It dont make sens that a child is a father of a man. I think Wodwooth is a stupid poet."

Polly went on to write just as sloppily about the French Revolution, saying that she couldn't remember what it was about but that it had something to do with all the French people eating cake. Then she put down her pen.

Everyone else was still scribbling away. Polly hugged her cold arms and stared around the room, her cheeks flaming. The teacher at the front came down from her platform. "Is anything wrong, dear?" she whispered.

"I'm done," Polly whispered back.

"Already? But you still have half an hour!"

"I can't do any more—it's too hard for me."

The solemn teacher became kind. "Now, my dear, you're just nervous. Look over everything carefully and I'm sure you can add something."

She put her hand on Polly's shoulder, but Polly shook it off. She continued to sit with her arms folded for the rest of the exam period, looking haughtily at the other girls. The poor things. Some of them would have to come here, but she wouldn't!

Noni and Maud were waiting in the front hall of the school. Maud was allowed to go out for lunch with them. "How was it?" asked Noni.

Polly hung her head. "It was *really* hard. I don't think I did very well."

"Don't be silly, Poll. You're so smart you'll do fine," said Maud.

Polly could only nibble at her lunch. The person who had so skilfully mangled the exam had vanished. *What have I done?* thought Polly.

"If only I could still be at St. Winnie's when you start!" Maud told her. "But I have lots of friends who are going to look out for you. You'll have a really good time, I promise."

———

A week later Noni got a phone call from Miss Guppy. "She wants to interview you, hen," she said. "That must mean you passed the exam!"

I couldn't have! thought Polly. Probably the Guppy was going to tell her in person how disappointed she was that she couldn't admit Polly. Even though that was what Polly wanted, she squirmed to think of how stupid Miss Guppy must think she was.

A few days later she sat in the headmistress's study, unable to eat the cookies she was offered.

"Now, Polly!" barked Miss Guppy. "I simply cannot believe that you couldn't pass the entrance exam. You failed it deliberately, didn't you?"

No one could lie to those piercing eyes. "Yes, Miss Guppy," whispered Polly.

"That was very wrong of you. You have *cheated*. It was just as dishonest of you to cheat to fail as to cheat to pass—almost worse, because you cheated yourself as well. Do you understand that?"

Polly tried to shrink into her chair. "Yes, Miss Guppy."

Miss Guppy's voice became less harsh. "Did you do it because you don't want to come here?"

Polly nodded.

"Can you tell me why not?"

"Because I don't want to leave the island," muttered Polly. "I don't know anyone here and I'd be leaving my two best friends—and my dog."

"Well, all those reasons are understandable. It's frightening to leave your home and start a new school, and I know you'll miss your friends and family and your dog. But you must be brave, Polly. I promise you that you'll like it here after you get used to it. Let's make a bargain, you and I! Give it a try for a year. If you still don't like it after that, I'll suggest to your grandmother that she keep you at home. We don't have to tell her about our bargain, however. It will be a secret between you and me."

"But I failed the exam!" said Polly.

"Yes, you did—you failed it quite spectacularly. But I know from your school records that you're a bright girl, Polly, so I'm very happy to admit you. We're delighted to have Maud's sister here. Maud is a splendid young woman, the best head girl St. Winifred's has ever had. I hope you will end up being just as much a credit to the school as she has been. I won't tell your grandmother or your sister about your exam results—you wouldn't want them to know how you cheated. So, do we have a bargain? Will you give it a try?"

What choice did she have? Miss Guppy was a whirlwind that swept up everything in her path.

Then Polly thought of a whole long year away from the island—away from Tarka and Noni and her friends. She sat up straighter and forced herself to meet the Guppy's steely gaze. "I'll—I'll only come here if I can go home every weekend."

"Every weekend? But Polly, you'll miss so much! Maud must have told you what jolly times the boarders have."

Polly tried not to avert her eyes. "I don't care. If I can't go home every weekend, I won't come."

Anger flickered in the Guppy's face. *She doesn't like people to disagree with her*, realized Polly.

"You're a determined child, aren't you? Very well. I think you're making a big mistake, but if you're willing to give the school a try, that can be our compromise. So will you stick it out for a year?"

Miss Guppy offered her hand. Polly fingered her necklace. *Daddy* wanted her to come here. She nodded, and let her own hand be squeezed painfully.

"Good girl!" said the Guppy, in exactly the same tone that Polly used with Tarka.

The headmistress looked at her watch. It was an old-fashioned one, on a chain pinned to her dress. "Let's see . . . you have an hour before your grandmother picks you up. Your sister is playing basketball at another school this afternoon, so you won't be able to see her. I'll ask Alice Mackenzie to show you around. You know her from home, don't you?"

Alice? Polly quaked. She still saw Alice in the holidays, of course, but she avoided her. Maud had said how much Alice liked St. Winifred's, how she shone at music and sang solos at the school concerts. But at Christmas Alice had been as sullen and mean as usual.

Polly wanted to object, but Miss Guppy had already opened her door and asked a passing girl to fetch Alice.

"Hi, Polly," said Alice when she appeared.

Alice had changed! She looked calm and happy, chatting all the way to her dorm. "I'm so glad you're coming here! You'll really like it. The other girls are swell and there're lots of extra activities, like music and art. You're really good at art, aren't you?"

On and on she talked, while Polly listened in amazement. The other girls in her dorm seemed to really like Alice, and she was so kind to them, asking one girl if she had found her lost notebook.

After Alice showed her the rest of the school, they sat on the porch steps and waited for Noni to come back. "Your dorm is on the same floor as mine, so you'll be close to me, Polly," Alice told her. "It's too bad that Maud will have graduated when you come, but I'll take good care of you."

This was the same girl who had teased her so cruelly? The one who called her "Goldilocks" and pinched and twisted her arm? Polly finally got up the courage to ask, "Alice, why are you so . . . different?"

Alice looked ashamed. "I *am* different here. As soon as I'm back at school, I feel *good* somehow. I know I was really mean to you and the other kids, Polly. I'm sorry. But when I'm on the island, I get in a bad mood. It's because . . . well . . ."

"I know," said Polly quietly. It was because of her mother. She was a much worse bully than Alice was. No one ever talked about it, because mothers could do what they wanted to their children, even if they were cruel to them.

Alice flushed. "Well, so that's why. But at least I spend most of the year at school. And you know what, Polly? I'd like to be nice to you and your friends now, but I'm too embarrassed about how I was before. So when I come home for the summer, let's all do things together, okay? Tell Biddy and Vivien."

Alice might be nicer, but she was still just as bossy. Polly wasn't at all sure what Biddy and Vivien would think of this idea. Especially Vivien, because she liked to be the boss too.

"I'll have to ask them," said Polly warily. "But *I'll* do things with you at home, Alice."

She wasn't quite sure why she said this, but Alice beamed. "Swell! And then when you come to St. Winnie's, you'll have a friend!"

"Thanks," whispered Polly.

A strident bell sounded and girls clattered down the stairs for supper. Polly shrank from the noisy crowd. She still didn't want to come here, but having a friend might help.

The closer she got to graduation, the more Polly tried to slow down time. The island thrummed with spring. Each dawn she was wakened by a crescendo of birdsong. Grouse thumped their wings, otters slithered under rocks to feed their babies, and the firs were tufted with bright green caps. The meadow behind Biddy's barn was a golden veil of daffodils, just like in Wordsworth's poem. Later the hummingbirds came back and delicate, speckled fawns appeared on the road.

Polly and Biddy and Vivien started an absorbing new project. Polly drew a large blank map of Kingfisher Island, copying Uncle Rand's smaller one. On dry days they set out to explore and map all the land they could get to.

Each time they biked down a new road or climbed a hill or discovered a beach or followed a deer path, they marked it on the map. They drew in every house and labelled it. There were some areas that were too thick with trees and salal to penetrate, but by June they had covered most of the island. Polly painted the tiny houses and animals and trees they had pencilled in, and labelled everything in her best printing. They took the map to school; Mrs. Oliver was astonished to see it. She told them it would be the feature display at the graduation ceremony.

The five graduates—Polly, Biddy, Vivien, Wallace, and Fred—had assumed such importance in the classroom that Mrs. Oliver let them pull their desks into a corner and study on their own. They set one another quizzes and corrected one another's answers. When they weren't working, they helped coach the younger pupils. Even at lunchtime the five of them stuck together, settling disputes among the younger ones and discussing their plans for next year. Wallace and Fred were going to live with relatives in Sidney and Vancouver and go to high schools there. Biddy and Vivien were sharing the same governess that Dorothy already had. Vivien's family had planned to take her out of school, but Noni had called on them and persuaded them to let Vivien carry on studying.

"Oh, Polly, if only you could stay on the island!" Biddy kept saying.

"I'll be home every weekend, and it's only for a year," Polly reminded her. "Miss Guppy promised I won't have to come back if I don't like it."

"But maybe you *will* like it," said Biddy.

"I won't," said Polly firmly.

One day after school Mrs. Oliver asked Polly to stay behind. "I'd like you to be the class valedictorian at the graduation ceremony," she told her.

"Oh, but I couldn't!" said Polly. "Why don't you ask Vivien? She can speak much better than I can."

"She hasn't been in the school as long."

"How about Biddy, then? She's been here since grade one!"

"Biddy's marks aren't as good as yours, Polly. I really want you to do it. You've been such an asset to the school, and I know you'll have many interesting things to say."

It took Polly a long time to write her speech. She consulted Uncle Rand, who told her that a valedictory was a farewell. He suggested that she do it in three parts: things she remembered about the school, a thank-you to Mrs. Oliver and any other adults who had helped over the years, and something hopeful about the future.

As she scribbled down all the things about school she was saying goodbye to, Polly couldn't help remembering everything else that had happened in the almost three years she had lived on the island.

Her time here had been marked by three storms: the hurricane of coming to a new place, the thunder of the Turtle's announcement, and the lightning arrival and departure of Daddy. In between the storms, however, had been long, tranquil interludes when Polly had learned how to live in the country, laughed with her friends, and been healed by the love of her family.

She chewed the end of her pencil and stared out the window at the waves. Ahead loomed the worst storm of all: leaving the island to start a new school.

Right now, however, she had the whole summer to savour. She could paint, and play with Tarka, and ride her bike, and enjoy her friends.

Most exciting of all, Gregor and Sadie were getting married at the end of August! This summer was going to be a long, restful time full of treats; nothing unpleasant would happen until the fall.

On graduation day, Polly stood in front of the room of proud faces watching her; she knew every one. Her hands and legs trembled the whole time she was speaking. "And may the five of us carry into the future the proud principles we have learned at Kingfisher School," she ended. That had sounded grand when she wrote it, but now she worried it didn't make sense.

The room broke into loud applause and Polly grinned with relief. It was over! Now all she had to do was shake hands and bask in the attention of family and friends. Everyone kept praising her for her speech and telling her how much they admired the map.

"I can't believe we've really graduated!" said Biddy with awe. "Oh, Polly, I *wish* you didn't have to go away."

"Don't talk about it," pleaded Polly. "Tomorrow let's see if that old dugout is still at Shell Bay, okay? We haven't been there since last summer!"

Maud had also graduated; Noni and Aunt Jean had attended her ceremony. Polly couldn't bear facing Miss Guppy again, and she didn't want to go to the school before she had to. She pretended she had one of her upset stomachs and was allowed to stay home.

Maud arrived back on the island in triumph, loaded with cups and certificates and a report card full of marks of distinction. As head girl, she had also given her class valedictory. She let Polly read it. It was all about striving for Christian ideals and "playing the game." Polly thought her own speech was much more interesting.

All Maud could talk about was how excited she was to be going to university in Vancouver. She studied the calendar of courses at the University of British Columbia as avidly as she had once studied the prospectus for St. Winifred's. "I'm going to be a lawyer," she announced at dinner one night.

"A lawyer!" said Aunt Jean. "That's not very suitable for a lass, chickie."

"Of course it is," said Noni. "Young women are accomplishing more and more these days. Maud is so clever she can have whatever career she chooses."

Maud seemed more like her old self this summer. She rarely talked about her religion and she was interested in Polly again, the way she used to be.

Polly had been wondering if Alice would remember her suggestion of playing with her and Biddy and Vivien. She was both relieved and disappointed when Alice told her in a nasty voice after church that Polly's dress was too short. "You look like a baby," she said, "and everyone's going to tease you at St. Winnie's, Polly, if you don't bob your hair."

Polly turned her back. The nice Alice she'd met at the school had disappeared.

The summer felt like a condemned person's last meal. Frantically Polly tried to squeeze every drop of enjoyment she could out of the warm days. She walked and rowed and swam and picnicked and spent hours with her friends and Maud, soaking them up so she would have their affection to comfort her when she was away.

One late afternoon Polly decided to walk Tarka to the lighthouse. She sat on a log and watched the incoming tide foam around the rocks. Sometimes at this time of day a pod of whales would magically appear. She stared at the sea so closely that her eyes watered, but no black fins broke its surface.

"Hi, Polly," said a quiet voice.

Chester! Polly knew he was home; she had already seen him at a distance a few times. Here he was standing right beside her! Tarka jumped and whined for attention. Chester picked him up and sat down beside Polly.

All she could think of was how he wouldn't speak to her at Christmas. Now, however, he was talking rapidly. "I was just coming back from helping my uncle cut wood," he said. "I thought I'd see if the whales were passing. Have you spotted any?"

Polly shook her head. Chester went on chatting about all the work he was doing this summer, keeping his eyes on the sea. Polly kept glancing at him. His handsome face had a shadow of a moustache, and his arms were muscled and brown. His shirt smelled like a mixture of clean cotton and sweat.

"It's nice to see you, Polly. I'm . . . well, I've felt embarrassed to talk to you ever since that night outside the hall. I shouldn't have kissed you—you were just a kid!" He still didn't look at her.

"I didn't mind," murmured Polly.

They shared an awkward silence. Then Chester asked, "Are you looking forward to St. Winifred's?"

Polly shook her head. "I don't want to go. But at least I'm allowed to come home every weekend."

"St. Cuthbert's is pretty good. I like the other fellows,

and I got on the football team. Polly . . ." Chester cleared his throat, threw her a desperate look, then stared back at the sea.

Polly waited.

"After I graduate I'm planning to go to Victoria College. I know you're still too young right now, but when you're older . . . would you like to come to something with me? To a dance or something? Do you think your school would let you?"

Polly's heart lifted. Then she remembered. "But I won't be there! Miss Guppy said if I don't like St. Winifred's after the first year, I don't have to come back, and I know I won't like it so I won't."

Chester looked disappointed. "Oh, well."

"Thank you for asking," said Polly.

Finally they kept their eyes on each other and their words slowed down. "You're welcome," said Chester. "At least we can see each other here. But you know how hard it is. People start talking about you even if you just go for a walk or something!"

Polly thought of how the whole island had buzzed about Gregor and Sadie, and Alec and Cynthia. It would be so liberating to do something with Chester away from here. If only she could!

"Sometimes I go to Victoria with my grandmother and my aunt," she ventured. "They might let me see you there—when I'm old enough, of course."

"That would be swell!" Chester beamed at Polly so avidly she wondered if he would kiss her again.

Then he jumped up. "Look!"

A pod of whales surfaced in front of them, all in alignment, like a whale ballet. Their glistening fins sliced through the waves as their enormous black-and-white bodies bubbled and wheezed and leapt and slapped. They lingered in front of the lighthouse, then zoomed down the pass.

"That was swell!" said Chester. "Do you know why they slap the water with their fins?"

Polly shook her head, her eyes brimming.

"They're stunning the fish before they eat them. I never get tired of seeing whales."

He turned to Polly and enveloped her in a crushing hug. Then he smacked her forehead with a kiss, muttered that he had to be home for dinner, and hurried away.

Polly sat for so long on the log that she was late for dinner herself. She didn't know which was more thrilling: the whales or Chester's kiss.

CHAPTER EIGHTEEN

THE TRUTH

Gregor and Sadie's wedding preparations began to absorb the family like a giant sponge; there was nothing else to do or talk about. Despite her parents' objections, Sadie had insisted on getting married on the island. "It's such a beautiful little church, and I want your father to marry us there," she'd told Gregor.

Aunt Jean was thrilled, of course. Polly didn't think her aunt could ever be busier than she usually was, but now she whizzed around like a hummingbird, arranging food and flowers and wedding outfits, and cleaning the church until it sparkled.

"Jean, you're going to wear yourself out so much you won't be able to enjoy the wedding!" Noni told her.

"How about a game of Bezique?" Uncle Rand suggested each evening, but Aunt Jean and Noni had too many lists to make. He and Polly played Cribbage instead.

Sadie and her family and friends were coming to the island a few days before the wedding; they would all stay in the hotel. Gregor wanted to go and visit Sadie, but his mother wouldn't let him. "Let her have a last summer with her family," she told him.

Instead Gregor telephoned Sadie so often that his parents told him it was too expensive. Then he wrote daily letters. He constantly had a dazed grin on his face, as if he couldn't believe his good fortune.

———

At the end of July, Noni took Polly and Maud to Victoria to buy clothes: Maud for university and Polly for school.

How ugly her uniform was compared with the pretty skirts and blouses that Maud was trying on! The heavy wool tunic itched and the stiff white blouse rasped her skin.

"I can't move!" Polly complained, after the saleswoman had helped her into the thick blazer. She clomped around the dressing room in her heavy shoes, holding her arms out stiffly.

Noni laughed. "You'll get used to it, hen. And you look very nice."

Polly knew she didn't: she looked like a maroon-and-grey pudding. She was indifferent as Noni picked out the rest of the required clothing. What a waste it was, buying all these things when she'd be back on the island next year! But she couldn't tell Noni that; she didn't know about her bargain with Miss Guppy.

Polly cheered up as Noni took her and Maud to the dressmaker to pick up their wedding outfits; Polly was to be a bridesmaid and Maud the maid of honour. Noni had sent their measurements, but this was the first time they had tried on their dresses. They were shimmering blue silk, so long that they trailed behind with a satisfying swish. The dressmaker had made small silk hats to match. Polly had never had such grown-up clothes!

"I'm going to take your dresses straight over to the rectory to show Jean," said Noni as they walked to the house from the wharf. "You girls can go in and unpack."

Polly laughed as Tarka rushed out from the kitchen and leapt into her arms. Then she saw an envelope with Daddy's familiar writing lying on the hall table.

She hadn't had a letter from Daddy all summer. Usually he wrote just as regularly as she did, but the last time she had heard from him was in June. "I'm not going to be able to write to you for a while, Doodle," he had told her, after he'd congratulated her on graduating. "I have some business I have to take care of, but I promise I'll be back in touch as soon as I can."

What business? Polly had wondered. Then the summer had kept her so busy that she'd forgotten to worry.

She snatched up the letter—but it was addressed to Maud, not to her!

"Maud, here's a letter for you from Daddy," she said, trying to conceal her hurt.

"That's strange," said Maud, slowly taking the letter. "He knows I don't want him to write to me."

"Open it!"

"I'll read it in private. If it's addressed only to me, he must want only *me* to read it."

Maud took the letter to her room. Polly waited as long as she could bear, then went upstairs and hesitated outside Maud's closed door. She listened hard. Could Maud be *crying*?

"Maud?" Polly opened the door. "Are you all right? What did Daddy say?"

"Oh, Doodle . . ." Maud was a mess of tears, with a red, dripping nose. Polly got her a hankie from her drawer and sat down beside her.

"What's *wrong*, Maud?"

Maud mopped her face and blew her nose. "Poll, Daddy wants me to tell you something. You can read his letter, but he wants me to prepare you for it first."

Polly sat down, her legs turned to jelly. "What is it? Is Daddy all right? Is he sick?"

"He's fine. Now listen carefully, Doodle. This is going to be very hard for you." Maud took both of Polly's hands. "Daddy has confessed, Polly."

"What do you mean?"

"Exactly what I said. He's finally confessed that he stole the money."

"*No!* No, Maud, he couldn't have!"

"He did, Poll. Let me explain. As soon as Daddy got to work that morning, Mr. Spicer gave him his last pay because he had to go somewhere for the rest of the day. While Daddy was standing in his office, he noticed that Mr. Spicer only moved the dial a little bit when he closed the safe. Daddy always stayed inside at lunchtime to read. He slipped into the office, opened the safe, and took out all the money he could grab—about a hundred dollars, he says. He put it in his pocket and went back to his book. He didn't think anyone would notice until the next day, but Mr. Rayburn, the boss, opened the safe after lunch. You know the rest. They found the money in Daddy's pocket."

"No, no, no . . ." moaned Polly. "It can't be true!"

"Read the letter if you don't believe me," said Maud. She handed Polly the first page.

Polly's hands were shaking so much she could hardly hold the paper. "This is the hardest letter I have ever written, but I must now tell you the truth . . ." Daddy began. He talked about stealing the money just as Maud said, but went into much more detail. "I struggled with my conscience all morning, but all I could think of was how much I could do for my girls with all that money. I wasn't thinking clearly—it was as if someone else did it. I still can't believe I was so stupid and so wrong! Ever since I visited you I've tried to think of how I could make things right. Finally I resolved to tell you the truth, even though I hate you to know that your father is a thief. Then I—"

Maud was holding many more pages. "Maud, just tell me the rest," Polly said weakly.

Maud spoke fast. "Daddy says he hitchhiked to Winnipeg in June and went to the police station and confessed. They were so shocked to find out he was alive! He appeared before a judge, and because he pleaded guilty and because he stole the money to feed his family, the judge told him he would give him a suspended sentence."

"What does that mean?" whispered Polly.

"It means that Daddy should go to jail, but if he doesn't commit any crimes for six months, he won't and he'll be free. He has to stay in Winnipeg until the end of the year so they know where he is."

They sat together in silence. Polly felt as unreal as she had on the train coming to the island. "I still can't believe it," she said dully. "You did, though."

"I think I *always* suspected Daddy had taken the money. At first I didn't want to, but the more I thought about it, the more his story didn't make sense. How could Mr. Spicer have put the money in his pocket? He had already left before lunch. Daddy just told me that crazy story in desperation—he wasn't thinking. And he *was* desperate. He did it to help us. That doesn't make it right, but I understand why he did it."

"You're not being as hard on him as you were before," said Polly.

Maud flushed. "No . . . because he's finally told us the truth! I *hated* it that he lied. And he did it in such an underhanded way. After that first letter he wrote me, he never *said* he didn't take the money. He lied by omission, but that's just as much of a lie."

That was why Polly felt as if Daddy had slapped her. It was wrong that he had stolen something, but it seemed far more wrong that he had lied.

"Will you forgive him now?" she whispered.

"I'm happy to forgive him! I've been praying and praying that Daddy would come clean, and now he has! He's like the prodigal son. He committed a sin, but now he's repented. I'm really proud of him, Poll. It must have taken a lot of courage to go to that police station. He could have gone on like he had before, but he didn't. And he did it for us, remember. Oh, Doodle, I feel as if a huge weight has rolled off me, don't you?"

Polly shook her head. "I don't feel happy at all. I feel kind of . . . frozen."

Maud hugged her. "That's because you've been so loyal. It's going to take some time to get used to this, but I know you'll come round. And just think, Poll, after Daddy's allowed to leave Winnipeg he can come and see us again!"

"He can?"

"Of course! He'll be free! There's no way Noni can stop him, no matter what she thinks of him. He's given us his address in Winnipeg. I'm going to write to him right now and tell him how proud I am. You write too, Doodle."

Polly couldn't imagine what she would say. "Maud, are we going to tell Noni?"

"Sure we are! Daddy is afraid it's going to get into the papers—after all, it's not every day that someone who is presumed drowned walks into a police station! So we should tell the family before they hear about it."

Polly wanted to melt into a puddle. "You go and tell them, Maud. I'm going to lie down."

———

She retreated to her bed for the rest of the day. Tarka pressed into the crook of her knees, as if he was as miserable as she was. Maud kept checking on her and offering her food, but Polly couldn't eat.

That evening, Noni sat on her bed stroking her hair. "Poor wee bairn," she said. "Maud has told me everything. This must be a terrible shock to you, hen. You've been so loyal to your father, and now you've found out he was wrong after all."

Polly wanted to hide under the covers as if she were a little child. All she could do was keep her face turned away. How *stupid* she felt! How humiliated! The grown-ups had been right all along. Her father, whom she had always thought was good, was a thief and a liar.

"It was brave of Daniel to confess," said Noni, "and I'm glad for you both that he'll be a free man. He's very lucky the judge was so lenient—he could have gone to jail for a long time." Then she added awkwardly, "Maud has asked if your father can visit and I've given my permission. I don't know if Daniel and I will ever see eye to eye, but it's not fair of me to keep him from you."

Everything Noni was saying just made things worse. Polly didn't *want* to see Daddy! She wanted to disown him, just as Maud had once wanted to.

"You're too upset to talk, aren't you . . . would you like me to bring you some soup?" When Polly shook her head, Noni kissed her gently and left the room.

Polly's peaceful summer had exploded. She spent August trying to pretend she was as happy as Maud. To her relief, after the rest of the family had told her how glad they were that Daniel had confessed, the wedding plans again pre-occupied the household.

Polly received a long, loving letter from Daddy. She could hardly bear to read it. "I know you are probably upset with your old dad, Doodle, but I hope you will forgive him," he ended.

She wrote back a curt note saying that she was glad he had confessed and would be free. She couldn't ask Daddy the questions that buzzed in her head. Why did he *do* such a stupid thing? Why didn't he stay and confess instead of running away and abandoning them? He would have gone to jail, but at least they would have known where he was. He didn't need to act like someone in a movie and pretend he had drowned. He'd been thinking more about himself than his daughters!

Worst of all, Daddy had lied to them. Polly couldn't say in the letter that she had forgiven him. That would make *her* a liar.

She took off her heart necklace and put it in her drawer. It stabbed her to notice that Maud had now started wearing hers.

"Let's just hope the news stays in Manitoba," Noni kept saying.

A Vancouver paper picked up the story, however, and

then it reached the island. Everywhere Polly went, people either stared rudely or told her haltingly how glad they were that her father was alive.

"I can't go anywhere without someone commenting on it," complained Aunt Jean. "Mildred Cunningham kept me for half an hour in the store just now, pumping me for more information. I don't have time to deal with this—I have a wedding to plan!"

"Jean, it's not the girls' fault that the news became public," said Noni. "I'm so sorry this had to happen, hens. Never mind, it will soon die down like any other gossip. Just smile and try to change the subject."

No one who talked to Polly was brave enough to say anything about Daddy's crime—except for Vivien. "Why didn't you *tell* us he was accused of stealing?" she demanded.

"He didn't want us to," said Polly stiffly.

"Never mind, Polly," said Biddy. "Mother says he's paid his price by confessing and facing the music. *I* don't think it matters that he stole the money—he did it for *you*! Oh, Polly, I'm so glad we don't have to keep it a secret any more that your father is alive! It was really hard sometimes!"

"But we never told anyone," Vivien assured her. "We had a pact. Whenever one of us was tempted to say anything we'd tell each other first."

"Thank you for that," said Polly. "It was a lot to ask of you. Thank you for being so loyal."

"Polly!"

Polly turned around. She was sitting on the wharf with her paints, Tarka snoozing beside her in the sun. Painting was a good way to escape from everyone.

It was Alice. "I want to talk to you," she told Polly.

Polly finished applying a blue wash. Then she put down her brush and waited for one of Alice's nasty comments.

To her surprise, Alice looked uncomfortable. She sat down beside Polly. "I just wanted to tell you I heard about your father. I don't care about what he did, but I'm really glad for you that he's alive."

"Thanks," said Polly warily.

"I . . . well, I understand what you've been through, pretending all this time that your father is dead."

"You do?"

Alice nodded. "*My* father is alive too!" she blurted out. "Oh, Polly, what a relief it is to tell someone!"

Polly stared while Alice continued. She told Polly how her father had left her and her mother when Alice was six. "He just didn't come home one day. I'm sure it's because my mother drove him crazy. She was always nagging at him. He could never do anything right."

Mrs. Mackenzie had brought Alice to live on the island with *her* father. After he died, she'd continued to live in his house. "She told everyone that she was a widow," said Alice bitterly. "I had to promise to say that too. She kept saying Dad might as well *be* dead, because I'd never see him again."

"Have you?" asked Polly.

Tears slid down Alice's cheeks and her voice shook. "No, I never have. But you know what, Polly? When I'm a famous singer, I bet he'll hear about me and come to one of my concerts!"

"I bet he will," said Polly. "Do you remember him?"

"I remember him perfectly! He was so nice to me, much nicer than Mother. We used to sing together. He had a good voice—he was in a choir."

Alice wiped her cheeks with the back of her hand. "Polly, you are so lucky! When are you going to see your dad?"

"I don't know," mumbled Polly. "Maybe after Christmas."

"You must be so excited!"

Polly couldn't answer. How could she tell Alice, who might never see *her* father again, that she didn't want to see Daddy?

CHAPTER NINETEEN

THE WHOLE TRUTH

Polly took a sip of champagne, watching Sadie's radiant face as she and Gregor walked around arm in arm, passing out slices of wedding cake. *My heart is like a singing bird . . .* that was the first line of the love poem Noni had read to Polly this morning, in honour of Gregor and Sadie. Was that what Sadie felt like—a singing bird?

The wedding ceremony had "gone off without a hitch," as Aunt Jean said. It had happened so quickly that Polly wished they could do it all over again. Polly was the first of the bridesmaids to walk up the aisle. She clutched her bouquet of cornflowers and roses to stop her hands from trembling. After her came Virginia, who was Sadie's oldest friend from Duncan, then Sadie's cousin Marion, then Cynthia. Maud was the maid of honour, followed by Sadie's shy little niece, Christine, the flower girl. She kept her head down as she scattered rose petals from her basket.

Gregor waited eagerly at the front of the church. Aunt Jean had insisted he get a kilt made; he wore it with a black jacket that had shiny silver buttons. On one side stood Alec, his best man. Uncle Rand stood on the other side in his robes, his face filled with quiet pride. Aunt Jean sat in the front pew beside Noni, in her new pink suit and flower-strewn hat. She was already dabbing her eyes.

Everyone gasped as Sadie appeared at the back of the church, clinging to her father's arm. Mrs. Waddington boomed out "Here Comes the Bride" on the wheezy organ and Sadie walked up the aisle in her white organza dress. She couldn't stop grinning, especially when she reached Gregor.

It seemed only seconds later that the wedding party burst out of the church into the August sunlight to the accompaniment of Captain Hay playing the bagpipes. Aunt Jean had fretted endlessly about rain, but the weather was warm enough to have the reception on the church lawn.

Everyone on the island seemed to be there, eagerly crowded around the long tables of dainty sandwiches and fancy squares. Children dashed around the grown-ups' legs. The Carver brothers were playing a waltz on their fiddle and accordion, and some couples began dancing on the grass.

After the toasts were finished Polly took her glass of

champagne to a chair, so she could remove her pinchy shoes. She wriggled her freed toes and took another swallow of the sweet, fizzy drink. It made the inside of her nose tickle, but it was so delicious! And it seemed to loosen her thoughts, as if *they* were singing birds zooming around her head.

What would it be like, to love someone so much that you wanted to spend the rest of your life with him? Maybe that would happen to *her* one day! Biddy would be her maid of honour. Her bridesmaids would be Maud and Vivien. They would wear yellow, and Polly would carry Noni's yellow roses.

But who would the groom be? Polly remembered her fortune—would it be Chester? She glanced at him standing under a tree with his parents. Just before the toasts he had come up to her and said quietly, "Hi, Polly. You look swell!" He had scurried away before she could reply.

Maybe she would marry Chester, maybe not. One day she would find out. One day she and her new husband would walk around this same lawn and pass wedding cake to their guests.

If only she didn't have to go away to school next week! But she didn't have a choice. Still, it was only for a year. Somehow she would get through it.

Polly stretched out her long legs, sheathed in silk stockings for the first time. *I like being almost thirteen,* she decided. She was getting used to her changing body, to being a "young lady," as Aunt Jean called her. Even when she wasn't dressed up, adults kept saying how pretty she was.

When Polly looked in the mirror, she realized they were right. Maybe it was vain to think that, but it seemed to be true. And being pretty kept her from worrying about her looks as much as her friends had started to. Vivien moaned about her greasy hair and Biddy had decided she hated her freckles.

Polly took another sip of her sweet drink, observing the joyful scene in front of her as if she were painting it. Biddy and Vivien were playing tag with some of the younger kids, shrieking as loudly as if they were the same age. Alice and Milly were passing around sandwiches—their mothers must have told them to.

Mrs. Mackenzie and Mrs. Taylor were talking in strident voices to Mr. and Mrs. Oliver. Aunt Jean was standing near Polly, boasting to Mrs. Cunningham about Gregor's job. After their honeymoon in Seattle, Gregor and Sadie were moving to Chilliwack, where Gregor would be a curate. "He's so lucky to get a position in these hard times," said Aunt Jean, "but of course they recognized his skills in the interview. It's a very large parish, with lots of opportunities to move up."

More and more people were dancing, some in couples and some holding hands in a tromping circle. Mrs. Hooper and her grandson George were dancing the polka; Polly moved her foot in time with the beat.

Noni came up to her. "How do you like your first taste of champagne?" she asked.

"I *love* it!"

"Don't have any more," warned Noni. She smiled. "Isn't this a perfect wedding? I'm glad to see you happy again, hen."

Polly smiled back and Noni kissed her firmly on the forehead, as if she were sealing their affection for each other.

"Aunt Clara, come and meet Sadie's cousins!" called Gregor.

Her grandmother walked away, looking elegant in her cream-coloured satin suit. How could Polly have once thought that she hated Noni? Or busy Aunt Jean or solemn Uncle Rand or nutty Gregor or her principled but generous sister? She watched Maud's ample bottom jiggle as she joined the circle of dancers. *I love them* all! Polly thought.

But what about Daddy? The past few weeks had been so busy, Polly had managed not to think much about Daddy. Now she let her mind fill up with all that had happened.

Why couldn't she forgive him? She forgave him for stealing. She wished he hadn't done it, but she understood why he had. She could almost forgive him for abandoning them; he had simply been his usual impulsive, dramatic self. But why had he lied to her?

And then, finally, the answer came: To protect her.

Because he didn't want Polly to have a tarnished image of the father she adored. Because he loved her.

Surely that was all that was important. Now Polly wanted to cry. The truth—the whole truth, at last—was as deep as the sea around her. People were complicated. Daddy wasn't totally good, after all. Neither was Noni, neither was Maud. And Alice, it turned out, wasn't totally bad. She, Polly, was complicated too. That meant she could love Daddy even though he had disappointed her.

"Are you excited about seeing him?" Alice had asked.

Yes, she was! Polly realized. She could take him around the whole island without having to hide him. He could stay in Noni's house and eat meals with them.

What would that be like? Would they be nice to Daddy? There was still a secret she didn't know: why Noni and her parents had quarrelled. But she would probably find that out one day. Maybe her family here would never feel comfortable with Daddy, but she knew they'd be polite for her sake.

"You're so lucky!" Alice had also said.

She *was* lucky, thought Polly. Daddy was coming to see her in the new year and she could hardly wait. Tomorrow she would write and tell him that.

"Polly, why are you sitting there all by yourself?" called Maud. "Come and dance!"

ACKNOWLEDGEMENTS

Many thanks to Garry Anderson at the Canadian Museum of Rail Travel Archives in Cranbrook, B.C.; to Amy Black, Marie Campbell, Nora Clarke, Hadley Dyer, Peter Elliott, Christopher Grauer, Keith Hamilton, David Kilgour, Julie and Patrick Lawson, Logan McMenamie, Lynne Missen, Louise Oborne, Helen O'Brian, Doug Rhodes, the late Noel Richardson, and Brian Wallace. Special thanks to Poppy for allowing me to turn her into Tarka! And extra special thanks to my partner, Katherine Farris, for her steadfast encouragement and help.

Kingfisher Island is inspired by one of the Gulf Islands between Vancouver and Victoria, but it is a fictional creation. Although I have tried to be as historically accurate as possible, I have improved the boat schedule for the convenience of my plot and characters.